The Feng Shui Detective
Goes West

The Feng Shui Detective Goes West

Nury Vittachi

FELONY & MAYHEM PRESS • NEW YORK

All the characters and events portrayed in this work are fictitious.

THE FENG SHUI DETECTIVE GOES WEST

A Felony & Mayhem mystery

PRINTING HISTORY
First Australian edition (as *Mr Wong Goes West*)
(Allen & Unwin): 2008
Felony & Mayhem edition: 2011

ISBN: 978-1-934609-79-8

Manufactured in the United States of America

Printed on 100% recycled paper

Library of Congress Cataloging-in-Publication Data

Vittachi, Nury, 1958-
  [Mr. Wong goes west]
  The feng shui detective goes west / Nury Vittachi. -- 1st Felony & Mayhem ed.
     p. cm.
  Previously published as: Mr. Wong goes west.
  ISBN 978-1-934609-79-8 (alk. paper)
  1. Murder--Investigation--Fiction. 2. Chinese--England--Fiction.
  3. Feng shui--Fiction. 4. Buckingham Palace (London, England)--Fiction.
  5. Detectives--China--Hong Kong--Fiction. I. Title.
PR9450.9.V58M79 2011
823'.92--dc22
                        2011013172

AUTHOR'S NOTE

The feng shui lore and vaastu shastra principles in this book are all genuine. The text is interspersed with extracts from *Some Gleanings of Oriental Wisdom*, written by CF Wong and edited by Joyce McQuinnie. The Queen of England really exists but she doesn't have a sister named Marjorie. This book is dedicated to everyone who works to improve East–West relationships through good-humoured laughter.

The icon above says you're holding a copy of a book in the Felony & Mayhem "Foreign" category. These books may be offered in translation or may originally have been written in English, but always they will feature an intricately observed, richly atmospheric setting in a part of the world that is neither England nor the U.S.A. If you enjoy this book, you may well like other "Foreign" titles from Felony & Mayhem Press.

———•◆•———

For more about these books, and other Felony & Mayhem titles, or to place an order, please visit our website at:

www.FelonyAndMayhem.com

or contact us at:

Felony and Mayhem Press
156 Waverly Place
New York, NY 10014

Other "Foreign" titles from

FELONY&MAYHEM

The Feng Shui Detective Goes West

Chapter One

Tuesday

IN THE DAYS OF *the Yellow Emperor, there was a Minister of Laws who believed there was nothing perfect in this world, until the day he had a daughter. She was beautiful and intelligent and affectionate. There was not one hair on her head he would change.*

'For my perfect daughter, I need a perfect man,' he told the people. So he passed a new law: only a man who could draw a perfect circle could marry his daughter.

Many men tried. And every man failed.

Then came the day when there was only one man left who had not yet tried. He was in the dungeon, being punished for failing to show respect to the many laws of the country.

The man in the prison said: 'If you let me out, I will draw six perfect circles.'

His daughter was lonely for a husband so the Minister let him out.

'Take me to the edge of the Lake of Bottomless Calm in West Tianting,' he said.

The prisoner, the Minister of Laws and his daughter gathered at that place. The man dived from the edge of the cliff into the Lake of Bottomless Calm and disappeared.

At the point he entered the water, they saw six perfect circles radiating outwards.

Blade of Grass, we think of laws as things made by man. But who made the laws of nature?

From *Some Gleanings of Oriental Wisdom*
by CF Wong

Dappled, shifting, twice-reflected sunlight; the tenderest of trade winds lifting one's forelocks; blue sky and bluer water: the harbour was the most idyllic corner of God's universe.

Until a ship's foghorn farted so loudly it caused an entire flock of seabirds to defecate over an open-topped tourist boat. The curious acoustics of dockside water carried lively American curses the length and breadth of the harbour. The feng shui master watched over the scene, unperturbed. The momentary disturbance would pass, as all temporal things passed. But the life-enhancing combination of elements that made up this energising environment would remain. Perfection on a massive enough scale was not easily tainted.

'Ark,' shrieked a seabird.

'Shoot,' shrieked a tourist.

As he had aged, CF Wong had become increasingly aware that the most complex mental constructions were rooted in the simplest of truths. The entire art and science of environment optimisation lay in a single word: balance.

It was a simple concept to understand, but not an easy one to realise. He'd learned that the most powerful place was the point at which the most extreme opposites lay in exact, tense counterpoint. A man on a tightrope, if he was holding a long enough, heavy enough pole, was rooted firmly in place, at peace, safe, unshakeable, immoveable.

Wong took a long intake of breath, closing his eyes and lowering his shoulders, seeking out his own balance. He held the air in his lungs for a slow count of six and then gently released it. Then he opened his eyes and blinked happily at the little kingdom he had created, giving the space immediately around him one last look-over to make sure it was as perfect as the view.

The meeting about to take place was extraordinarily important for him. So he had arranged for it to happen at an ideal site: a luxuriously appointed floating terrace, the balcony of a first-class apartment-cabin on the sixth floor of the *Princess Starlight Charisma*, a cruise ship docked in Singapore harbour on a gloriously warm and bright winter's day.

Hanging terraces were the best possible places for achieving balance. A balcony was outdoors and indoors at the same time. Balconies gave you the feeling that you had come out of your protective shell and were part of the wider world, aware of the wind and the weather, in touch with the elements: you were connected to the pulsing, throbbing ecosystem; and yet, at the same time, they were enclosed and felt safe: you were in your own space, and intruders could not reach you; you controlled your environment, and no one could approach without your permission. It was the best place to be: on an open segment of God's earth, but a separated, lockable segment.

Having chosen a terrace as a place on which to meet, Wong had gone further and balanced the qualities of land and water by specifying that it should be on a ship. Boats were also marvellously balanced objects. A ship was a solid, strong, stable thing, like a building. Yet ships, however big they were, seemed to sit lightly on top of the water and could easily slide, move, spin and dance. They had a freedom of spirit that a land structure could not match.

On this particular occasion, the sense of balance stretched to the weather itself. This being Singapore, the air was hot. Yet the ship was positioned at such an angle it picked up a cooling breeze from the open sea. The balcony had no air-conditioner, but did not need one, with a westerly wind providing more than enough air to keep one's brow completely dry. The sea winds were full of salt, which widened the nostrils, expanded the lungs, and woke the spirit. This particular suite, not by chance, faced south when the ship was docked in its usual berth: the correct direction for a deal that would greatly advantage him on this day, a man born in the year of the tiger. A south–north energy line ran neatly through the terrace.

Happily, there was also balance in the light. The space was a bright suntrap, with glaring sunshine pouring in from the west. In this steaming city, just a few minutes in direct daylight was usually enough to raise a sweat; yet the canopy that covered the balcony meant the central part of it was in comfortable shadow at this time of the day. Wong had tried the different seats and ensured all of them were in the shade, and would remain so, even if the meeting dragged on for an hour or two—which it shouldn't. All he really had to do was to get the client to sign off on the deal and collect the money: a cashier's cheque, he hoped, that could be turned into fondlable, hoardable, gloatable-over cash straightaway.

Fortunately, the cruise ship's interior designer had good taste in furniture: the balcony was provided with a table and chairs in high-quality natural wood, and the colour scheme was tastefully muted in pale greens and earth tones. Wong had almost no additional actions to take other than making sure the area was not cluttered. He'd removed a couple of ornaments and several of the plants. Also, the life-belt, which he had furtively thrown overboard. Why leave a little subliminal reminder of danger and mortality in such a peaceful spot?

Then of course there was the sheer spectacle of the scene. Singapore was a striking city and no spot was more beautiful than its harbour. With its angular backdrop of clean-lined, multi-hued skyscrapers glinting in the sun over an expanse of calm, grey-blue water, there was clear visual enchantment. He was hopeful that a non-local would find the view so enrapturing she would feel moved to do something momentous—like completing the deal by handing over a large cheque.

Everything felt right. Borrowing the cabin from a rich client had been a masterstroke. And once he was sure of having a location at which major environmental factors were in balance, prosaic, smaller-scale matters, such as the furniture and space design, had been relatively easy to deal with. As he happily surveyed the balanced little kingdom he had created, he sighed with satisfaction—and then felt a slight creak under his feet.

It barely registered in his consciousness, until it was followed by a second, longer structural groan ten seconds later. What was that? Then, a slight unsteadiness crept up his body. He felt his weight shift involuntarily.

It could only mean one thing. The ship was moving.

How could this be? It was supposed to have docked for the entire day—for the next two days, in fact. Were the others even on board yet?

This must not happen: no, no, *no*.

Panicking, he raced out of the cabin and hared down a narrow corridor to the other side of the ship, to an open area where the liner abutted the dockside. Grabbing the railings, he leaned dangerously far over the edge, trying to find the mooring points. Men in kiddie-blue sailor suits could be seen unhooking thick cables of rope. And halfway down the length of the ship, the gangplank—a rather ornate covered walkway—was being wheeled away. He could hear the engines churning the water. The ship had already started to edge away from the land. Were his buyer and his contractor on board? They should have arrived several minutes ago. Or were they running late? Why was the damned-to-seventh-hell boat leaving? Would they have to wait until the boat docked again? What would happen to his all-important deal? This must not *be*!

Wong raced along the deck, half-ran, half-stumbled down a metal staircase and scrambled along narrow passages towards the sailors undoing the ropes. Luckily, he had a good sense of direction and had managed to navigate the corridors efficiently, reaching the men unhooking the mooring ropes before they had completed their jobs.

'No, wait, stop,' he shouted in English, and then repeated his words in Chinese.

The sailors, intent on their tasks, did not even glance at him.

'Stop,' Wong repeated, and then violently grabbed a cable, yanking it out of a sailor's hand.

The man was shocked. 'Hey! What? What do you want?'

'Must not go. Very important.'

Gathering all his strength, the feng shui master heaved a portion of the cable over the side, where it managed to hook back on to the black iron mooring pillar, more by luck than skill.

'You're crazy,' said the sailor. His comrades turned to stare.

Wong shook his head. 'Must stay. Very important.' Having hooked the mooring pillar, he pulled at the six-inch-thick cable in a bid to halt or reverse the ship's outward drift.

The sailor, a wrinkled, sun-roasted man of about fifty, moved in to retrieve the cable. Wong kicked out at him, trying to keep him back.

The sailor stepped back and grinned. 'Go on then. Go right ahead,' he said. 'Crazy idiot.'

More sailors turned to watch the spectacle, and several laughed out loud as Wong stuck his shoes against the railing to give himself purchase. He pulled with all his strength.

The cruiser continued to move away from the dockside.

'*Aiyeeaah*,' Wong squealed, as he felt the rope pull away from him. He repositioned himself so that one of his feet was on the top railing and he was leaning back at an almost horizontal angle.

The vessel continued to move away.

The sailors started to call out to comrades to come and watch. Passers-by joined the audience. Within seconds, a small crowd had gathered to watch the remarkable sight of a tiny, skeletal man weighing fifty-three kilogrammes doing battle with a ship that weighed forty-seven thousand, two hundred and sixty-five tons.

As Wong battled to keep the ship close to shore, his audience's faces betrayed shifting emotions: irritation gave way to amazement, and finally to admiration.

'He'll get dragged off the ship,' one of the sailors said.

'Hope so,' came the reply.

As Wong strained against the rope, a musical chord blasted itself through a public address system, and it was repeated twice more. It was followed by a silky voice, which echoed off the hard surfaces throughout the ship. 'Ladies and gentlemen, Princess Charisma Cruises welcomes you on board the *Princess Starlight Charisma*. The ship is slightly adjusting its position. It will re-dock again very shortly. You will not be able to disembark for the next twenty minutes. We apologise for any inconvenience caused.'

The engines roared more loudly, the water churned faster, and the ship picked up speed in its drift away from the dockside.

The rope started to move quickly and Wong was suddenly pitched over the railing—until he was grabbed by his trousers by two sailors and a passenger. Trying not to laugh, they placed the furious man on the deck where he angrily slapped their hands off.

'This is inconvenient,' he thundered. He looked at his hands, which were bright red and sore from rope burns.

'It's no problem, old man,' a young sailor said. 'We're not going anywhere. The ship is just going to another berth around the corner. Some bigwig on board is having a party for visiting delegates from some African country and wants a better view from his suite. So we're just moving for him. It'll dock again in a few minutes.'

'Where?'

'Over there.' He pointed to a part of the harbour that curved away from the open sea.

'Devils from the seventh layer of hell,' Wong cursed. The line of the harbour turned outward at that point. That would leave his balcony with a northwest energy line. This was disastrous. This was tragic. This was catastrophic.

'If you are worried about people missing the boat, you needn't be,' a staff member said, waving a clipboard. 'Almost everyone on the list is on board.'

Wong turned to face him. 'I have two guests coming. One is a rich *gwai poh* businesswoman.'

'Tall? Yellow hair? Designer clothes? She came on board just before we left,' the man said.

Aiyeeah. She was here already! Maybe waiting at his room door. Wondering where he was. Wong raced off without a word—back down the same corridors, up the same steps, through the same narrow passages, running to get back to the room before his client arrived and found it empty.

Seconds later, he arrived breathless at First Class Cabin 472 to see a tall European businesswoman with red-gold hair standing outside.

'Mr Wong! How nice to see you again,' she purred.

'Yes, yes, very nice,' he said and used the card key to let the two of them into the room. Although she gave him a large, toothpaste-advertisement smile, her eyes darted around the cabin, suggesting she was as nervous about the meeting as he was. 'Unusual place to meet, on a ship. What a lovely idea.'

She was abnormally tall and, in an apparent gesture to show she was quite content about having to view life from such a high elevation, was wearing high heels.

'Good feng shui,' the geomancer replied. 'Nice to see you, Ms Crumley. Very happy you can come on board before the ship start moving.'

'Yes. I wasn't expecting it to suddenly start drifting off like that.'

'Me also,' he growled.

'The staff told me that the ship was just adjusting its position and would dock again in a few minutes. Is Mr Daswani here? I hope he made it on board before they, er, rolled up the drawbridge, or whatever you call that bridge-stairs thing.'

'Coming, coming, very soon, already on board, I think, I hope, I think, yes, for sure, no doubt, maybe,' Wong said, wringing his hands together. 'Come, sit on the balcony please, very nice, very comfortable.'

He ushered her onto the terrace, where they both slipped into rattan seats. He poured her a glass of coconut water. Wong prayed for his contractor, Arun Asif Iqbal Daswani ('The Only

Known Indian Member of the Chinese Mafia'), to arrive soon, terrifyingly aware of his lack of skill in conducting small talk in English. The geomancer sat on the edge of the chair, smoothing down his suit—a grey mandarin-collared outfit made for him by his tailor, Mr Tommy of Wan Chai, when he had been six years younger and two kilogrammes lighter.

Ms Crumley, who was wearing a light grey, stretch-cotton, ruffle-trimmed, belted lightweight coat (purchased last week, $1,200 on sale at Prada), gazed over the balcony at the scene in front of her. Although the suite now faced towards the city instead of the estuary opening, it was still a dazzling sight.

'Well,' she said, waiting for her host to come out with some standard pleasantries.

'Well,' Wong replied nervously, unsure of how to proceed. 'Ha ha.'

The conversation showed signs of running out of steam at that point.

A buzzer sounded. Saved by the doorbell.

Wong stood, bowed, and raced for the door. Moments later, Daswani surged onto the balcony, his robes flapping around him damply. He was a large man given to wearing sheikh-like robes, into which he had had numerous pockets tailored.

'Sorry-sorry-sorry to keep you waiting. Comfortable you are, is it?'

The newcomer flopped down into his chair so heavily the rattan gave a moan and sank several centimetres lower, its legs spreading. He grabbed Wong's glass of coconut juice and swallowed it in a single draught.

'Wah! Never been so thirsty in all my life. Now, how are we, Miss Crum-bly?'

'That's Crumley. You can call me Cecily. It's actually Cecily-Mary—good Catholic girl, you know.'

Ah, interesting,' said Daswani. 'I am Sindhi.'

'Cindy?'

'Yes.' He looked at the surprised expression on her face and added: 'Do you know many Sindhis?'

'No. You don't look like a...Cindy.'

'Really,' said Daswani in a tone of surprise. 'What do Sindhis normally look like?'

'I don't know. I just...I used to have a Cindy doll when I was a child. Small blonde thing, skinny as a twig.'

Although Wong thought he could speak English, the logic of conversations in that language regularly foxed him. Where on earth had Ms Crumley encountered Sindhis who were small, blonde and skinny as twigs? There were none in Asia, that was certain. Would Arun Daswani be insulted at this? He'd better say something, to set things right.

'In this part of the world, Sindhis are big fat men, not many blondes,' he said. 'Like Mr Daswani. Very fat.'

'This fat is all muscle,' Daswani said, patting his pot belly. 'From all the digesting.'

Crumley chuckled at this, a tinkly, well-rehearsed laugh. But neither of the others did, so she stopped abruptly.

'Come,' said the Sindhi businessman. 'Let's get down to business, shall we?'

Wong swallowed hard. This was it. He suddenly felt hot, despite the cool breeze. This was a key moment in his life; this was the deal that was going to launch him on a new career. The fifty-seven-year-old geomancer, chief staff member of CF Wong and Associates, a feng shui consultancy, had set up a side business called Harmoney, the idea being to parlay his skill in creating harmonious places, with all elements in a positive balance, to setting up harmonious business deals. This was his first venture.

Ms Crumley was the buyer for a major European office supplies company. The group she represented, OffBox, was graduating from product distribution to own-label manufacturing. It had come to Singapore because the city-state boasted that it could produce goods with Western standards of quality at Asian prices. OffBox was launching a line of desk stationery, starting with highlighters that looked like small fruit.

She glanced behind Daswani, as if to see if he was somehow trailing the promised goods behind him. 'Where are the...er?'

He gave her an unctuous grin. 'The consignment is down-stairs, on the dockside, in a truck, parked nearby. It will be shipped to the provided address as soon as the final part of the required paperwork is done.'

Wong gulped again and a tremor of excitement raced through his body. He knew that 'paperwork' in this instance referred to the final part of the business jigsaw: payment.

'Cheque should be made out to Harmoney Private Limited,' the feng shui master put in. 'Harmoney with a "e". Like "Har" and "money".'

'Of course. Have you got samples? I need to check the quality one last time. Just a formality, of course, at this stage.'

'Of course,' said Daswani, producing a box from one of the folds of his robes. 'You can check as many times as you like.'

He placed on the table a white cardboard box emblazoned with the words: 'Highlighters: Banana'; and deftly tore it open. Lifting out a small plastic banana, he brandished it elegantly. 'This box contains twelve pieces of banana design. In total we have fifteen thousand packages, twelve units each, four different fruity designs, making one hundred and eighty thousand units in total. All at quality and prices unbeatable anywhere else on the planet.'

Cecily Crumley smiled, comforted by seeing the product. 'It looks fine,' she said. 'So I guess I just need to hand this over, then.' She started fishing in her expensive-looking, but politically correct, faux-leather briefcase for the plastic file containing the cheque.

Wong stood up and waved at Daswani to rise to his feet. He had been told by a businessman friend it was the right thing to do—to show respect when payment was being made and to acknowledge that the meeting had come to its climactic moment.

'Sit down, sit down,' she said. 'No need to stand on ceremony.' She handed Wong a white envelope, which he immediately started to tear open. He needed to make absolutely sure there was no chance of error.

She turned to Daswani. 'By the way, Cindy, how did you solve the ink problem?'

Wong paused, his finger deep inside the half-ripped envelope. He raised his eyebrows. 'Ink problem?'

Daswani, smiling just a little too much, said: 'I told Ms Crumley a couple of weeks ago we had temporary trouble sourcing fluorescent yellow ink.'

She nodded. 'So you did a different colour first?'

'Right. And we'll get the yellow ones to you before you know it.'

'So what colour ink is in this batch?'

'Hmm?' the contractor replied, as if he hadn't quite heard the question.

'What colour ink is this batch? Neon green?'

Daswani glanced nervously at her eyes and then looked away. 'We used a different colour for this batch. You'll have the yellow ink versions very soon.'

'But *which* colour? Pink? Blue?'

He picked up the highlighter. 'Er. Actually, we had trouble sourcing those colours too.'

The buyer froze. 'You had trouble sourcing those colours too? So what colour ink did you use?'

Daswani bit his lower lip. 'We used a very high quality ink obtained from a factory owned by a friend of my cousin. Highest quality, best possible flow, good value, special price for us, due to our connections. So please don't worry about the ink, Ms Crumley. It'll be fine. You have Mr Wong's personal guarantee.'

She was becoming impatient. 'But what colour is it?'

'Er, neutral,' he said, his voice betraying nervousness.

'Neutral. Meaning...?'

When the contractor didn't answer immediately, she reached for the plastic banana. He reached for it at the same time. Wong watched aghast, frozen to the spot.

She got to it first, pulled open the lid and with a violent sweep of her arm, slashed a mark across the table. All three of them stared at it—a jet black scar on the pale pine surface.

Ms Crumley spoke first. 'Black. You put *black* ink into the highlighters.'

'The very finest ink on the market today, Ms Crumley. None better.' Daswani wrung his hands and smiled unhappily.

'You can't put black ink into highlighters.'

'The ink was the finest quality, and flowed into the products' ink chambers very smoothly indeed. And it flows out equally smoothly. A pure, flowing, er, smooth line.'

'But...I mean...you can't have highlighters with black ink.' She looked at Wong and then at Daswani. 'Tell him. You just can't.'

'Some small problem?' Wong asked, now panicking inside.

Daswani slowly interlaced his fingers, trying to send 'keep calm' signals to her. 'May I remind you that when I phoned you two weeks ago and said we were having trouble finding yellow ink for the first batch, you said we could use other colours.'

'Yes, but I meant other *highlighter* colours. I meant neon green or baby pink or sky blue. Not *black*.'

'Be reasonable, Ms Crumley. You didn't specifically say we could not use black.'

For a moment, she couldn't speak. She took several deep breaths and then sat up straight, making herself considerably taller in her seat than the two Asians. 'Now let's get this absolutely straight. Are you telling me you've made me one hundred and eighty thousand fruit-shaped highlighters filled with black ink?'

Daswani did not reply.

Wong felt the world slipping away from him. 'Black very nice, very elegant colour,' he said desperately. 'Fashionable and good feng shui. Ha ha.'

Ms Crumley, her nostrils dilating, turned to the geomancer and spoke to him quietly through tight lips: 'If you think I am going to buy a single one of these, you are very much mistaken. Goodbye, Mr Wong. Goodbye, Mr Daswani.'

She neatly snatched the cheque out of Wong's hands and marched back into the cabin. They heard a door slam.

There was silence for two seconds and then they heard a door open again. Ms Crumley had accidentally marched into the bedroom.

'Door that way,' Wong called out helpfully.

'Thanks,' she muttered before storming through the correct door and slamming it behind her.

The two men on the balcony stared at each other.

'That did not go so well,' Wong said.

'She said we could use any other ink colour. She didn't say we couldn't use black colour,' Daswani said in a hurt tone.

Wong nodded. 'So what are you going to do with so many highlighters with black ink?'

The other man shook his head. 'Not my problem. You are the middle man. Deal is in the name of Harmoney Private Limited. I want my money. I want it now. Question is: What are *you* going to do with so many highlighters in black ink?'

❁ ❁ ❁

A travelling feng shui master entered a monastery in Guizhou.

'I have come to award a title,' he said. 'One of the monks here is to be called the Master of Humility.'

The monks went into an uproar. Which of them was the Master of Humility?

'I am the chief abbot. Surely the title must come to me?' said the chief abbot.

'I am the lowliest novice,' said the lowliest novice. 'Should it not come to me?'

'I am neither high nor low,' said a monk who was neither high nor low. 'Perhaps I deserve the title, having no other?'

'I deserve nothing,' said another monk. 'So you may choose to give it to me if you think it right.'

The debate raged for many hours. No agreement could be reached.

The feng shui master picked up his bag and started to leave.

'Which of us gets the title?' the monks asked.

'No one,' said the feng shui man. 'The Master of Humility is no longer here.'

Blade of Grass, sometimes giving is taking. Sometimes, taking is giving. The man who tries to catch a feather held by a breeze succeeds only in pushing it away, for some feathers cannot be caught.

From *Some Gleanings of Oriental Wisdom*
by CF Wong

Geomancer CF Wong walked morosely along the street, believing that nothing could worsen his mood, which was pitch-black and vivid crimson at the same time. His life had suddenly turned dark with horror and red with drama. Small and round-shouldered, he stooped even further than usual, his eyes fixed on the ground, a puny Atlas carrying an invisible planet on his shoulders. And the burden he was carrying might as well be as large as a world, given the impossibility of his finding any way to lift it from his back.

What had just happened was so nightmarish to be almost beyond his ken. He had just committed to spending a vast sum of money he did not have on the purchase of a large number of tiny, ugly, fruit-shaped pens he could not possibly use. He had experimented with the repulsive plastic bananas after Ms Crumley had left. They produced solid black lines that were too thick to write with and impossible to use for highlighting. Who would want them? They were useless. Harmoney Private Limited of Singapore was set to go bankrupt with its very first deal. Not exactly auspicious. If news of this got round to his rivals... It didn't bear thinking about. How could everything have gone so dramatically wrong? He blamed the unidentified Singapore bigwig who had ordered the ship be moved. But to whom could he complain? It was useless. Nothing could be done.

Arun Asif Iqbal Daswani had ended the meeting by saying he would give Wong ten days to make the payment. Daswani had handed him a fresh copy of his business card, pointedly calling attention to the line that described him as 'The World's Only Indian

Member of the Chinese Mafia.' He had then made some not very deeply veiled threats about getting his triad partners to 'take an interest' if the full sum was not delivered on time. He had become hard-eyed and stone-faced. It was the end of an ugly friendship.

Where could Wong get that kind of money at short notice? He kept very little money in the bank accounts he used, and his savings consisted of some tiny investment properties in Guangdong province, all of which were handled by a relative he talked to once a year. It would take weeks or months to arrange a sale. There were no liquid assets that could be cashed in to raise the sum Daswani was demanding.

The feng shui master wearily propelled his miserable bones to his run-down office on the cheaper bit of Telok Ayer Street, just off the main business district of central Singapore, and went up the stairs to the fourth floor—yes, he knew that number four meant bad luck, but it was the only one he could afford. He kicked open the office door, startling Winnie Lim, his office manager. She glared at him with naked hostility.

'*Aiyeeah*. You break the door, I no fix it,' she warned.

He returned her dagger-filled look, narrowing his eyes and muttering curses under his breath. It was nothing short of tragic that a man could not even find sanctuary from the pain of life in his own office. He glanced around the small, cluttered room, with its cheap, mismatched furnishings and broken wall clock. It was not a suitable office for a feng shui master and he knew it. No clients were allowed to visit.

The only consolation was that the desk which normally housed his beyond-irritating assistant, Joyce McQuinnie, was empty. The young woman had been inflicted on him by Mr Pun, the property developer who kept Wong's business going by paying a regular retainer. She had arrived as a 'temporary' intern, but had become horribly, scarily permanent. Wong spent a significant amount of his time dreaming of ways to get rid of her without upsetting his paymaster.

Ignoring the spitting, hissing Winnie, he marched past his desk and headed for the meditation room—a rather grandiose name for what was really an ill-designed room, too small for any purpose beyond being a stationery cupboard. When Wong had initially leased the premises, he had made sure that that room had been kept completely empty except for a meditation mat and a flickering candle—red, electric, purchased from a Roman Catholic trinket shop. Then he had placed a hand-carved hair stick from an ancient branch of the Qidan tribe on the altar, a small table at one end. The hair stick was a sort of ugly, miniature totem pole topped with thick, dreadlock-like tresses. Its purpose was to dismay evil spirits, and to that end it had wide staring eyes and a sticking-out tongue. Wong was fond of it for a number of reasons. First, it reminded him of his mad Uncle Rinchang, who lived in a cabin in the Kunlun Mountains. Second, the Qidan people were reputed to have used real gold leaf in their objets d'art, so he felt it might be valuable. And third, it was so ugly that it put the women off entering the space or using it for anything.

The idea of having a meditation room in the office was well-intentioned but had proved to be impractical. There was always so much pressure to make money to pay the rent that he rarely used the room, and neither Winnie nor Joyce appeared to be interested in meditation, although Joyce occasionally went to yoga and some sort of church. Winnie's only interest in life was nail varnish. She used the office computer to subscribe to RSS email alerts informing her of the launch of new nail colours or appliqués. In contrast, Joyce's main interest was wearing iPod headphones and nodding her head up and down to *tsch-chika-tsch-chika-tsch* noises while idly scanning celebrity magazines.

These two women had grossly tainted the purity of his office—after all, it was supposed to be the headquarters of a practitioner of an ancient, mystical, male-dominated spiritual art. But what could be done? Mr Pun paid the retainer and had given him no choice but to accept McQuinnie as an assistant. And Winnie Lim had organised the files under a system so arbitrary she was the only one who could find anything. He was stuck with them. His temporal life was cursed. He needed to retreat to a better place to recharge his spiritual batteries. If there had ever been a time when he needed the meditation room, this was it.

He opened the door and peered inside. He hadn't entered the room for several weeks and expected it to be stuffy and smelly. But something was wrong. It was full of something.

He turned on the light. The room contained two foul-smelling mops, three red plastic buckets, and a solid wall, taller than Wong himself, of what looked like several hundred toilet rolls. He backed out of the room and turned to face his office manager.

'Winnie,' Wong barked. 'What is in my meditation room?'

'Mops and toilet rolls and those things,' she replied, without looking up from her hands. She was applying miniature representations of Old Masters onto her fingernails.

'I know that. But why?'

'Because I need to use the toilet cupboard for something else. All full up. No room for that stuff.'

'Why do we need two hundred toilet rolls?'

'Is not two hundred.'

'Well, how many is it?'

'Five hundred.'

'Why do we need five hundred toilet rolls?'

'Special offer. Twenty per cent off for orders of five hundred rolls. Cheaper to buy five hundred than to buy four hundred. Also we get a bonus ten thousand points on our loyalty card.'

'But we don't need five hundred toilet rolls. We don't need four hundred. In one week, we only need one or two.'

'Well, then, we have enough for a long time.'

'Ten years.'

'Right, ten years.'

'But the lease for this office only has eight month left.'

'We can take them with us to the next office.'

Wong was speechless, incensed by the image of his having to hire a van and a driver merely to transport several hundred unwanted toilet rolls from one set of premises to another. Then something occurred to him: where was his ancient gold leaf Qidan hair stick? This worry caused the power of speech to return. 'Where is my totem?'

'What?'

'My totem. My hairy totem.'

'You mean ugly toilet brush thing? In the toilet.'

He opened his mouth, and then shut it again. Sometimes there were no words.

'You always complain, even when I save you money,' Winnie muttered.

Wong would not put up with that. 'You buy five hundred toilet rolls we don't need and you say you are saving money? You are one crazy woman. You waste all the money.'

'We got ten thousand points on our loyalty card,' Winnie thundered. 'That's not a waste.'

Wong thought about this for a moment. Ten thousand points might actually be enough to buy something with. What did he need? So many things. For a start, the office clock was not working. It was not just mildly embarrassing, but utterly humiliating that a feng shui master's office clock had not worked for two years. A standard part of the introductory feng shui speech he gave to clients was an exhortation to make sure the premises contained no stopped clocks, no dark light bulbs, no dripping taps and no dead plants. Yet he had examples of all four in his office. This was not magic, but an important symbolic change he made his clients go through. It was simple psychology, really: you take control of the tiny, physical things in your life, and you find yourself subliminally sorting out all the big, non-physical things, too.

'Go back to store,' he barked at Winnie. 'Use ten thousand points to buy new clock for the office. We need clock. Our clock broken.'

Winnie looked sideways at him, a guilty, furtive stare. 'Very busy,' she said. 'Too much paperwork today.' As if realising that her argument was rather weakened by the fact that she was sitting at her desk doing her nails, she gestured vaguely at the pile of papers and envelopes on her desk.

'Open envelopes. Then you go buy clock.'

'Cannot,' she said quietly.

'Why not?'

Winnie paused reluctantly from her operations and looked up. She cast her eyes around the room as if she was seeking advice from the wobbly desks and rickety chairs on how to reply. In truth, it was pretty obvious to Wong that she was having trouble deciding just how honest she should be. Eventually she turned to face him with a hardened expression, daring him to object to what she was about to say: 'Already spent the ten thousand points.'

'What?'

'You hear me. Already spent ten thousand points.'

'Buy what?'

'This.' She gestured at the lamp on her desk. Now that she had pointed it out, Wong noticed that it was unusual—it looked vaguely like a miniature version of a light you might see over your head while you were in a dentist's chair.

'Lamp?'

'Not a lamp. A Pro-Manicure Set.'

'What is pro-manicure set?'

'This.'

'Why you buy that?'

'This office has no Pro-Manicure Set. So I buy. Besides, special offer on pro-manicure sets this month. Fifteen per cent discount if we buy two.'

'You buy two?'

'Of course. Fifteen per cent is good discount.'

Wong drew himself up to his full height, which was one point six metres. 'You go back to shop. Return pro-manicure sets. Buy clock.'

'No exchanges, no refunds,' she said. 'But I go out anyway. You in bad temper. I need a break.'

She blew on her nails, gathered up her handbag and headed out of the door, slamming it hard as she left. He heard the frosted glass crack. One day, very soon, it would fall out. That would be another expense he'd have to deal with. *Aiyeeah.*

Well, look on the bright side. Both women were out of the office. At least he'd get a few minutes' peace.

He went into the meditation room/sanitation cupboard and decided to rearrange the stacks of toilet rolls into some sort of seat. It took several minutes and a fair bit of exertion—bags of toilet rolls were surprisingly heavy—but he had soon made himself a rather comfortable throne. At his age, he found it easier to sit in a Western-shaped, legs-dangling chair than to squat or sit cross-legged.

He began to meditate. To start with, he performed triangular breathing.

You breathe in slowly, counting to six.

Then you breathe out slowly, counting to six.

Then you stop breathing, stop thinking, stop *existing* for a count of six.

Then you are reborn, you start existing again, and repeat the cycle.

Breathe in, one, two, three, four, five, six.

Breathe out, one, two, three, four, five, six.

Cease to exist, one, two, three, four, five, six.

After a few minutes of this, he started to regain his composure. Triangular breathing was an easy technique, yet it worked like magic. That six-second gap between breathing out and breathing in again became a satisfying moment of pure, delicious non-existence. In that short period of nothingness, one really did seem to physically vanish. Your body was not breathing, yet for some reason you felt no panic or discomfort or craving.

He gradually increased the count of each part of the triangular breathing exercise to seven, eight, ten, twelve and then fifteen seconds. And finally he raised it to twenty seconds, with each three-part cycle lasting a full minute. He kept it up at that level for several minutes.

Now he was calm. His spirit was still. His heart was subdued. His worries had been temporarily discarded.

The toilet roll throne was surprisingly comfortable. He was relaxed, and his eyes were shut, but he was dimly aware of being in a soft, rather comfortable, all-white atmosphere. It reminded him of something. What was it?

He thought of the time he had made a snow chair for himself as a child. When was that? Could he return to that moment? He emptied his mind and allowed the memory to fill it. But the first thing that came into his mind was a picture of a grey-planked cabin on a snowy mountain.

He recognised it immediately. It was the home of his great Uncle Rinchang, who lived in the west of China for many years until his death in 1993. Rinchang had lived in the mountains south of the Takla Makan desert, on the edge of the Tibetan plateau. Wong had been sent there in 1963, when he was twelve years old, during a period of political upheaval in the main cities of China. He had not wanted to go to a place that was so cold and remote and lonely, but the year he had spent in the mountains had been a life-transforming experience for him. He had learned from his uncle and the other mountain people that life could be lived to a different rhythm, a much slower, deeper beat than the shallow, stuttering music of life in the cities.

Uncle Rinchang was not much of a talker, rarely needing to say anything. The quiet seriousness with which he did his regular tasks—working with yaks, gathering foodstuffs, trading in the markets, spending time with friends, worshipping the mountain gods—had impressed itself on Wong, who had grown hardy and thoughtful in those twelve months.

He connected his visit to the mountains with the first time he had heard the legends of The Immortals, who were sages and mystics said to have lived in the high hills for centuries. The oldest were reputed to be eight hundred years of age. They lived on a diet of rare herbs and secret elixirs, which gave them magical powers.

There were several experiences he had had with Uncle Rinchang he would never forget. One was a walk the two of them had taken to a sheer cliff, some two hours' trek from the cabin. It was one of the most dramatic scenes Wong had ever seen. You walked along a misty, icy plain towards what looked like the far horizon. But as you moved forwards, you became uncomfortably aware that the horizon was actually oddly close, that it was only a short distance in front of you, and you were indeed getting very close to it. The human mind is used to the horizon being a long distance away; the effect of seeing it just a few steps away was highly disturbing. It was as if one had become a giant and had walked to the very edge of the world.

Despite the bravado of being male and twelve, he had wanted to turn back. But Rinchang had taken his hand and made him walk onwards. They had slowed their steps and come to a halt within a few metres of the edge. To Wong, it really seemed as if they had come to the edge of the planet. Everything seemed to just stop. Existence itself seemed to finish at that point. There was only a great misty nothingness ahead of the packed snow at their feet.

As they stood there, a wind sprang up. The clouds began to drift to one side and it became clear that it was not the end of the world after all. Across a huge valley there was a distant mountain range, a massive, craggy, fist-shaped outcrop in white, grey and blue.

Things he had never quite understood became clear to him. The people here worshipped the mountains as if they were gods. They talked about the biggest mountain as the Holy Mother. Wong, who had hardly ever known any sort of mother, now realised why. The mountains did have a divine presence about them: something magical and parental. They seemed to be watching. They seemed to be listening. They seemed to be guiding.

Also from the mountain people he had heard stories of creation. Heaven was above, Earth was below. The highest mountains of the Earth were sacred pillars that supported Heaven. High peaks were thus quite literally close to the divine realm.

Another unforgettable experience he had had that year was a walk along a ridge leading to a plateau Uncle Rinchang knew; a cloud-hidden path that ran to a plain some two kilometres long between two of the mountains in the area. The old man called it the Fire Dragon's Back, but the villagers simply referred to it as Uncle Rinchang's Walk. There were several narrow points along this snowfield trail where the sojourner could get a full view of the valleys on each side simultaneously—they were so different they seemed to belong to distinct worlds. On the left were the snowy wastes and high mountains of the Tibetan plateau. On the right were green fields and rolling, verdant hills, which eventually become the yellow grey of the plains of the Takla Makan desert. Winter on one side, summer on the other. Cold and heat. Yin and yang.

'We call this the Point of Balance,' Rinchang said.

Again, Wong had felt he had learned something really important, but without really understanding what it was. All he knew at that moment was the world was a strange and wonderful place, more curious than he had ever imagined in his childhood in the dirt-poor rural village of Baiwan in Guangdong.

As daylight disappeared, a fierce wind blew across the ridge. It took hours to walk its length and return to their cabin. But they were warm when they reached home. Wong had been intrigued to discover he could be in one of the coldest places he could imagine, and yet be sweating in bright sunshine under a summer-blue sky. His toes were almost frostbitten and his cheeks sunburned.

And then there had been the time Rinchang had taken him to the Great Mother of All, visible from the foothills of the Himalayas, a long journey through Tibet towards Nepal. As they approached their destination, Rinchang had pointed ahead of them.

'There. Can you see it? That is the greatest mountain in the world. Qomolangma: the Mother of the mountains.'

Where? Where?' The young Wong had scanned the horizon ahead of them but could see nothing but sky and a few low hills. Surely one of those hillocks could not be the tallest thing in the world? He had heard much about the mountain on the borders between Tibet and Nepal. Rinchang had explained that the place was known as Devgiri, 'Holy Mountain', to the Indian peoples, and Qomolangma, 'Mother of the Universe', to the Chinese and the Tibetans.

'There. Look. Keep looking. There are clouds in the way, but the Mother shines through them.'

Wong had continued to scan the scene ahead of him, but could still only see gentle hills. And then he looked upward and realised what he was supposed to be looking at. He had been looking at the wrong part of the sky, entirely too low. The Himalayas were high in the air, far higher than anything around them. Indeed, they seemed to belong to the sky, not the earth. They stood as jagged shapes in the upper part of the sky, far above the clouds.

That was when he realised how the concept of the divine came from the majesty of mountains. Their immensity and power and *personality* were things that commanded total respect. Now he knew why the local phrase for 'making a pilgrimage' was 'paying your respects to the mountain'.

More than four decades later, as he sat in a toilet-roll cubby-hole in his office, Wong fell into a deep trance, his old, creaking body lost to him as he became a child, wandering the mountains of the Kunlun Shan. Why had his meditation led him to this place? Could the answer to the quandaries of his life be here?

His heart started thumping.

He felt himself shake.

There was a Presence.

A booming voice started to groan. It was the voice of God, deep and low. But what was He saying?

'Git on down and shake shake shake. Move your booty and break break break. Sock-it-to-me sock-it-to-me sock-it-to-me, yeh! Uh-huh, uh-huh, uh-huh.'

He opened his eyes. Pounding rock music was playing in his office and shaking the floor of his tissue nest. This could only mean one thing. Joyce McQuinnie was back.

Aiyeeah. Why did the gods hate him so?

❀ ❀ ❀

'Oh hi, CF. What were you doing in the toilet roll cupboard?'

'Meditation room. That is the meditation room.'

'Whatever.'

'I was meditating.'

'Cool.'

'Hard to meditate with loud music on.'

'What? Oh sorry.' She turned the volume down. 'This is the new CD from The Rogerers. It's called *Biscuit Dunked in Death*. Cool title, no?'

Wong was no expert on rock album names and was disinclined to offer an opinion.

'I bought it to celebrate our new assignment.'

'Oh.'

He pondered for a moment on whether he should try to return to his place of transcendence but he quickly dismissed the thought—it would be futile. Whether her music machine was on or off made little difference; Joyce herself was intrusive in every way—physically, aurally, visually and spiritually. Dressed in shapeless, garishly coloured clothes, and stinking of expensive perfume and bitter coffee, her arrival immediately tainted every centimetre of the office. His vision of a mountain idyll was gone, swept away as if a flood had burst into a valley and pulverised a village made of paper.

What to do? Life was hard. He owed money. He shared an office with unhelpful people. He had received no high-paying jobs for weeks. He may be knifed to death by the friends of the world's only Indian Chinese triad in ten days' time. This was not shaping up as one of his better months. He needed distraction. He needed something else on which to focus.

An idea struck him. From his top drawer, he pulled out his journal, deciding to spend a little time writing some notes on stories he remembered from his days in Kunlun Shan. An hour or two lost in his book might help him regain his composure. Then he noticed Joyce was still staring at him. She was restless about something. She seemed to want his attention.

'Did you hear what I said? I bought the CD to celebrate *our new assignment*.'

Wong looked up from his tatty volume with undisguised irritation. 'What?'

'While. You. Were. Out,' she said, spacing the words like a nanny speaking to a newborn, 'on that ship this morning, someone called with an assignment. A majorly nice one. We're going to make some dosh.'

'Dotch? Dutch?'

'Dosh. Moolah. Greenbacks. *Money.*'

'Someone call with a job?'

'Yes. Winnie was late this morning, surprise, surprise, so I took down all the details. It was such a nice one I went out to HMV to celebrate. It's classified as "urgent" so we can charge the express service surcharge. And the guy giving us the assignment sounded totally swanky. So I think it could be like *major* bucks. You should be happy. This is a good news day.'

Wong listened without getting excited. It was too much to hope that easy money should arrive just when he needed a massive injection of cash. The fact that something had got Joyce excited did not fill him with confidence. She sometimes got things so muddled that good news was bad and vice versa. Nevertheless, he might as well hear her out.

'So, this assignment, easy and big bucks, is it?'

'Not only. The guy had been given our number by the British Trade Commission. He wants us to feng shui something for them in Hong Kong on Thursday. They'll pay the airfares and the hotel and everything—and our fees, of course. They reckon it will take between six and ten days.'

Wong, despite himself, started to become interested. The British Trade Commission sounded like a proper organisation with proper budgets. And international trips could often be profitable, if one spun out the expenses on top of the fees.

'Thursday? This week? In Hong Kong? Better be plenty big money. I don't have time to go to Hong Kong just for small thing.'

Joyce theatrically raised both thumbs. 'Trust me, boss man, it's *biiiig* money. It's gotta be. I told him we only travelled business class and he just kept talking. Didn't faze him at all.'

'Business class? We don't travel business class.'

'I know, but I wasn't going to tell him that.'

Wong scratched his chin. 'Good. You tell him to give us money for business class tickets. We go economy and I keep the other money.'

'I knew you'd say that. But can't we go business class just this once? I've never been business class anywhere—well, except with my dad, but I was too young to remember.'

'We go economy.'

'Okay, okay.'

Wong was wondering whether he could let his hopes rise, just a little bit. Perhaps there was some potential money here? How rich was the British Trade Commission? 'The assignment is what?'

She started rifling through her shapeless bag—a knock-off Louis Vuitton from Shenzhen—and brought out a copy of *Time* magazine. 'It's this,' she said. She opened the magazine to a double-page spread showing a picture of a large passenger aircraft.

'Airplane? We don't do feng shui of airplanes. Airplanes are moving transports. They have no feng shui.'

'I know. I've been in this game a while now, haven't I? But we do feng shui of venues, don't we? Listen to this. The British Trade Commission is having an important meeting on that plane and they want it to be perfect. They're meeting reps of airlines from east Asia, mostly Chinese, and they wanna make sure there are no protocol mistakes or cross-cultural errors. This is the most expensive aircraft in the world—that's what this mag says, anyway.'

Now Wong was interested. *The most expensive aircraft in the world.* There had to be a way of turning this into a big ticket assignment. People in aircraft sales are always dealing in amounts of hundreds of millions of US dollars. His humble fee of a few thousand Sing dollars would be small change for them. He could surely milk this for a good return.

'Maybe we make exception and do feng shui reading of this aircraft for them,' he said generously.

'That's exactly what I told the guy.' Joyce read out a paragraph from the magazine. 'Listen to this: "The British party, which includes several members of the aristocracy, is flying in and out of Hong Kong on a specially adapted A380 called Skyparc, which they like to describe as a flying business park, 'Your office above the clouds'. The meeting is not only an aircraft sales presentation, but the launch of what the chief executive of Skyparc, Sir Nicholas Handey, calls 'a new vision of flying'. Instead of the usual rows of seats, the plane has a network of multi-use spaces, including lounges, conference rooms, a theatre, two restaurants, a bar and a coffee shop. The event is combined with the launch by MB Dutch Petrochem of a new 'green' aviation fuel, which, the company claims, significantly lowers the carbon footprint of the traditional passenger aircraft".'

Wong leaned back in his chair and considered the prospect. It had potential. But still, it was only an aircraft, which was a single, rather cramped tube. How could it be spun out into a high-earning assignment? Just one aircraft? Get it ready for just one meeting? Will not take six to ten days.'

'They want us to feng shui the aircraft before the meeting in Hong Kong. And then they want us to go with them in it on a journey to London.'

'Go to London? *Aiyeeah*, no, no, no, cannot go to London. Too far. Too busy.'

'What busy? We got no work. Besides, London's not far. Just thirteen hours from Hong Kong.'

The feng shui master pulled a face. 'Full of foreigners.'

'Well, I guess it is full of Londoners. It would be kind of hard for it not to be. But there are apparently some *major* cheeses on the plane. Aristocrats. They want you...um...us to go with them and feng shui their places in London.'

Wong considered this. 'So rich Londoners want me to do readings of their apartments?'

'Not apartments. People in Britain don't live in apartments. Houses. And mansions. And *castles* and things.'

Castles sounded good. One could charge a lot for a castle. Castles must have lots of rooms. Wong rose to his feet: 'You call man back. Make arrangements. We go tomorrow afternoon to Hong Kong. Book two economy class airfares. Tell man we invoice him for two business class airfare. Also, he pay for hotel, et cetera. I'm going out. I will start work on invoice when I get back.'

'Where are you going?'

'I'm going to the Ah-Fat's. Get some lunch.'

He did not want to show too much enthusiasm for Joyce's news, but inside he was feeling distinctly excited. Daswani wanted his money in ten days. A big assignment lasting six or seven days, plus travel expenses—it might just fit the bill perfectly. Indeed, it was possible that today's bad luck was evaporating and a period of good fortune was coming his way.

As he trotted down the stairs of his office block, he reflected on the downside of the deal: going to London. He dreaded the idea of going to the Western world—everything he had seen of Western culture had been repulsive. The people were annoying, the culture baffling, the values shocking, and the food inedible. If he was going to have to deal with revolting Western meals for several days in a row, he would need to be well fortified.

And that meant as many visits to Ah-Fat's Kopi House as could be squeezed into the allotted time.

❖ ❖ ❖

Rice was God's comfort food. There was nothing like the taste of a piece of soft, curried potato, pressed gently with the fingertips into a ball of rice. Somehow, the creamy appeal of the spiced potato combined with the comforting taste of the white rice produced an incomparably satisfying mouthful. And then balance the hand-fashioned rice-potato ball on a piece of poppadum, add a touch of mango chutney, and toss the whole construction into one's mouth... Joyce referred to Asian food in general as 'carbo heaven'. Paradise it was.

Of course, eating with one's fingers did not come naturally to Wong; it simply wasn't a Chinese thing, too unrefined and indelicate. But many hours of observation of the enthusiastic dining habits of his friend Dilip Kenneth Sinha had persuaded him to adopt some south Asian techniques.

Wong was powering into a mammoth, lip-blisteringly hot curry lunch when Dilip Kenneth Sinha arrived. The feng shui master greeted his friend with a flash of his eyes, his mouth being too full to use for speech.

'Aha. Practising the use of digital dining.' The angular, black-dressed Indian astrologer clearly approved. 'Far superior to the use of chopsticks and inestimably better than the use of forks and knives.'

Sinha had a habit of philosophising for some minutes about any scene in which he found himself before actually becoming a participant in it. He thus eased himself gently into situations with a sort of introductory lecture.

'It truly astonishes me that the gourmand around the world takes inordinate care about his drinking utensils, but almost no care at all about the tools with which he takes solid food. I mean, think about it. There has been much written for decades, if not centuries, about the importance of using a good china cup for one's tea. And there are entire books written about how slight alterations in the precise curve of a wineglass can alter the taste of the wine therein. Yet these same people, who take so much care over their drinking vessels, will taint every mouthful of food they eat throughout their long lifetimes with the taste of cold, hard metal—and never notice. For someone brought up in the south Asian tradition of dining with the fingertips, the addition of the taste of steel to curry is a tragedy. The Chinese habit of using wood or bamboo chopsticks is hardly better. Indeed, a significant number of chopsticks carry splinters, so that the wood not only spoils the taste of the food but actually adds itself to it. And then there are lacquer chopsticks, with their inherent chemical dangers.'

As he spoke, he lowered himself onto a stool and felt inside his pockets. He pulled out an antiseptic wipe, which he used to carefully rub his fingers, and then he flexed his fingers in the warm, midday air to dry, before wiping them with a silk handkerchief from another pocket. At last, after a short period of silence to mentally prepare his oesophagus and stomach for what they were about to receive, he was ready to eat.

Sinha surveyed the dishes in front of him: white potato curry, siya fish, brinjal, daal and several other lurid-coloured dishes, some of which appeared to be glowing radioactively. 'Hmm. I see you are feeling entirely south Asian today, Wong. What gives? In need of spice in your life?'

'Spicy food clears my head,' the feng shui master replied. 'Need to think about lots of things.'

He may have had much on his mind, but he did not share any of it immediately with his friend and fellow member of the Singapore Union of Industrial Mystics. For both of them, eating was a serious business, and the activity did not benefit from frivolous distractions such as conversation. Both concentrated fully on the task ahead of them: to empty the dishes on the table in the shortest possible order with maximum possible pleasure. Talk could come later.

Less than five minutes had passed before Joyce McQuinnie arrived at Ah-Fat's with her news literally bursting out of her: 'CF! CF! Just wait till you hear this. I called the guy back about the Hong Kong trip. Just *wait* until you hear this.'

Wong looked up, chewing.

'You know I said, like, there were some, like, aristocrats coming on this trip?'

'Ah, Ms McQuinnie, how lovely to see you.' Sinha half stood up and then lowered himself back into his seat and returned to plundering the dishes. The protocols of civilised behaviour had to be followed, but should never be allowed to distract one from the important things in life.

Before Joyce could launch into her announcement, there was another distraction: the arrival of Ms Xu Chong-li, a fortuneteller, who threaded her way carefully through the tables, anxious to avoid staining her clothing. Although she was a rather grand fifty-something lady who was always expensively upholstered (she had been a banker before giving it up for astrological pursuits), she loved cheap kopi house meals and was delighted to slide onto the seat next to Sinha.

'Sit, sit,' she said, waving her hand to Joyce, who was too excited to do so. 'And then tell us about these aristocrats. I have hobnobbed with a great many aristocrats in my days, and it may be that I am a personal friend of the ones who are due to visit you.'

'Er...I don't think so. But I'll tell you about them anyway.'

'Sit first.'

'Okay, but I don't think I want to eat anything.' The young woman flopped down onto a stool and by habit placed her left leg through the straps of her handbag. She leaned forwards conspiratorially.

'It's a member of *the royal family*,' she revealed. '*The* royal family. Or maybe two. He wouldn't say exactly who it was, but it was someone very high up—security reasons, you know— they can't tell us exactly. *The royal family.*' Joyce vibrated like a washing machine on spin-cycle.

Sinha gazed thoughtfully at her over the piece of fried brinjal he was just about to slip into his mouth. 'There are many royal families on this planet, but one in particular seems to hog the headlines internationally, whether for right reasons or not, so I assume you are talking about the Windsors?'

'I mean like the *Queen*. A member of the Queen's family.'

'Indeed, there are a great many queens on this planet as well, including several thousand in Indonesia and even more in Africa, but the Queen of England is the lady you have in mind, I take it?'

'The Queen is coming?' Chong-li asked.

'It's not the Queen. It's a member of her family. It could be Prince Charles, or...or one of his sons.' Joyce's eyes instantly glazed over.

'Prince Charles coming to visit you?' Chong-li was impressed. 'My. That *is* a coup. Well done. How did you set that one up? I have often invited him, but have never had the pleasure. I thought after he lost his wife he might be tempted, but he resisted my blandishments.'

'Or his sons.'

'He has boys, does he? No girls? What a pity. A pretty wife he had. Girls would have been nice.'

'The boys are pretty nice, too,' said Joyce, and then blushed.

Sinha at once noticed the reddening of her cheeks. 'Aha. Instant scarlet. I do believe you have designs on the boys, is that right? Are you planning to let CF do the work so that you can devote yourself to seducing one of the princes from the tower for yourself?'

Chong-li started singing: 'One day my prince will come...'

'No, of course not,' said Joyce, looking down at the table, as if there was something in its cracked vinyl-coated surface of great interest. 'But I wouldn't mind meeting Prince Will. He is a bit of a dish, although I don't know if he's really my type.' She uttered this last phrase with patently false nonchalance.

'Talking of dishes, why don't you sample some of these?' suggested Sinha, sweeping his hand over the plates.

Joyce shook her head. She lived on processed snacks and coffee, and only occasionally forced herself to eat actual food. She scanned the array of weapons-grade curries with suspicion. Although she could enjoy a mild tofu tikka masala with some white rice and a poppadum if she was feeling adventurous, the more exotic dishes repelled her British-Australian palate. They kind of had *too* much taste, sort of thing.

'Mm...no thanks. I think I'll just have a poppadum.'

While the rest of them were eating, Joyce explained to them that she and Wong had just landed an assignment involving something that was going to be front-page news all over the world. A revolutionary new European aircraft called Skyparc had just flown into Hong Kong. It was a British version of a giant plane built by Airbus Industrie, a European consortium, and was being offered for sale as a luxury skyliner to Asian airlines. One of the group of organisations responsible for the meeting, the British Trade Commission, was assumed to know most about Chinese conventions, because of Britain's long official history in Hong Kong. There were aristocrats on board, and an executive called Mr Manks, who was something to do with the royal family, had suggested the conference rooms aboard the plane be inspected by a feng shui master before the meeting.

'You have been asked to feng shui an aeroplane,' said Sinha. 'Surely a moving craft by definition cannot be feng shuied? Items of transport have no north and south, no east and west. And in the case of an aircraft in particular, it spends much of its time in the air, and thus has no direct relationship to the ground, so no up or down. Surely it is the mountains and rivers and topography that define the macro-feng shui of a place? A moving aircraft...well, every minute, its relationships with the surrounding geography change.'

The others knew Sinha was allowed to engage in technical, even adversarial discussions about feng shui, as he was a master of vaastu, the Indian equivalent.

Joyce agreed. 'But we're just doing a feng shui reading for the aircraft's main conference room while it's in the hangar. This is not your ordinary airplane. Skyparc is "your office in the air".'

She pulled out the copy of *Time* magazine and showed them the photograph. 'We just have to make sure there is nothing that can go wrong for this particular sales meeting. Easy. Airplane sales deals are big money. They can't take risks. They have to get everything right.'

'Quite so,' said Sinha. 'I imagine a craft like this would cost hundreds of millions of US dollars. So, if there is some deal where they are selling a fleet of these, we must be talking very large amounts indeed. A single purchase of a small fleet of aircraft can add up to more than a billion US dollars.' He turned to Wong: 'I hope you're getting a good slice.'

Now the subject of money had been broached, the feng shui master was happy to turn his attention away from the food and deign to join in the conversation. 'Normal fees, I bump it up a bit, maybe sixty or seventy per cent, plus big surcharge for express service. But one bad thing. The man wants me to fly to London to do some work for someone else after.'

Sinha looked puzzled. 'You are invited to go on a free trip to the United Kingdom, all expenses paid by a wealthy organisation, but you are reluctant to do so? Is this logical?'

'I think I will not like UK. Too many foreigners.'

'That's true. There are a lot of UK people in the UK. Odd, that. But you could always hang out in Gerrard Street. You'd feel at home there. They do an excellent *cha siu bau*, and you can even get a good plate of *dau miu*. Indeed, Cantonese is the main language of Gerrard Street, as it now is for large swatches of Vancouver. London might be fun. I haven't been there myself for, oh, half a decade or more.'

The feng shui master shook his head. 'Too much trouble. Besides, I have plenty of worry on my mind. Maybe should stay here, raise some money. I have to make a payment of big, big bucks to Arun Asif Iqbal Daswani in ten days' time. Harmoney deal turned out to be big, big trouble. *Aiyeeah*.' He grimaced at the memory of the morning's meeting. Daswani messed up plenty but still he wants me to pay. Not fair, but what can I do?'

Sinha put his elbows on the table. Ah. You owe money to Arun Daswani? That's bad news indeed. He's not the sort of person to get on the wrong side of. That alone might be a good reason to get out of town and on to the other side of the planet as quickly as possible. Anyway, if you need big bucks at high speed, surely the London deal is what you want? The royal family, no less! Surely it will be easy money?'

Wong scowled. Given his long history of loathing all things Western, it would be hard to reconcile himself to having to spend several days there. And he always felt long-haul trips were bad value because of the travelling time. 'Maybe they pay full fees, but overseas trips take so long. I get maybe two-three days' pay, but have to travel one-two days to get there, another one-two days to get back. End up wasting seven-eight days for only two-three days' money. Too much time, not enough cash.'

Sinha dismissed this with a wave of his hand—which unfortunately sent a piece of onion into Joyce's hair. 'Nonsense. You have to factor the travelling time into your bill. Make them pay for it. Better still, with the royal family, there is no need to hold back when you are writing an invoice—so just make up a number. They can afford it. They're as rich as Croesus.'

Wong had no idea who Crease-Us was, but it occurred to him Sinha might be right—he was dimly aware that a royal family in the West was likely to be super-wealthy. He had encountered non-rich royals several times in places such as Indonesia and Malaysia, but the royals of London should have money, one would think.

Joyce enthusiastically backed up Sinha's assertion. 'He's right. They are *totally* loaded. Filthy rich.'

'Filthy?'

'It means, *really, really*.'

Wong couldn't hide the lust for money that was beginning to sparkle in his eyes. 'I can charge them three-four times usual rate?'

The Indian shook his head. 'No. I think six or eight times the normal rate would be more like it. Just think of the Queen's property portfolio. It's massive. Remember, Britain is one of the richest countries in the world—it's up there in the top ten with America and Switzerland and all those places. And the Queen is one of the richest people in Britain. That makes her one of the richest people on this planet.'

'Oh. She has much property?' asked Wong.

Sinha gave a scornful bark. 'Much? *Much?* "Much" is not the word. Let me tell you about the Queen's property portfolio,' he said, counting on his fingers. 'She owns England. And Scotland. And Wales. And Northern Ireland.'

The feng shui master was astonished. 'All those?'

Sinha leaned forwards. 'Yes. *And* Australia. *And* New Zealand. *And* Canada.'

'She owns Australia? And Canada?'

'She does.'

'I think Gibraltar too,' Joyce put in. 'That's in Spain. And the Falkland Islands, which are part of Argentina really, but...'

'Quite,' said Sinha. 'And she used to own Hong Kong. And India. And Sri Lanka. And what is now Bangladesh.'

Wong was stunned. 'What did she do with them? She sold them?'

'Yep. Pocketed the cash. Money in the bank.' Sinha leaned back in his chair. 'Now *that* is a serious property player.'

Wong's brain was now ticking away at high speed. He had thought he knew all the names of the big players in property: from Li Ka-shing in Hong Kong to Donald Trump in America. But he had never realised the Queen was in the game. Respect dawned in his eyes.

Sinha, having satiated one appetite, was now happy to lean back and indulge a second great love: the sound of his voice. 'Of course, the British Empire has shrunk from its glory days, but at one time it spread across one-third of the world's landmasses. One-third! And the Queen of England was ruler over all of it. As I say, her empire is not as large as it was, but she still holds sway over a large part of the civilised and uncivilised world.'

The geomancer was impressed. It was indeed an impressive property portfolio. He had a vision of himself and the Queen sitting in a palace having a long chat on the subject of property arbitrage, square-foot pricing comparisons, hottest tips for emerging property markets, et cetera. And, better still, she would be paying for it—at any rate he chose. Perhaps she would retain him as the royal feng shui master. It would be more fun doing palaces than doing scenes of crime, which had kept him busy for much of the previous three years. 'So I can charge big extra premium, for sure?'

'Make up a number. Ten times the normal rate should be no problem at all.'

Joyce was excited. 'So we're doing it for sure? We're going to London, too?'

Wong grimaced. 'Maybe *one* of us go. But only for a short time. And very hard work. Work hard, collect big bucks, go home.'

The young woman stuck out her lower lip. 'They wanted both of us. I told them we were a team. Besides, you can charge more for two operatives.'

Sinha turned to her. 'What exactly is the United Kingdom part of this assignment? Does the Queen want Buckingham Palace feng-shuied or what?'

'I'm not sure. He didn't say—the man who called up. He's some sort of consultant. His name is Robbie Manks and he's a PR man or lobbyist or something in that line. I don't even know which member of the royal family he's working for. It may not be the Queen.'

This worried Wong. 'Not the Queen? Other members of the family, are they also rich? All share the family fortune?'

'I'm not sure,' said Joyce. 'I mean, yes, they're all rich. But they're not much of a family, if you know what I mean.'

He looked at her blankly.

'According to the papers, the family members don't really like each other all that much. And they all hated Princess Di and Fergie, who never behaved like royals are supposed to. So I don't know if they do all share the money or what,' Joyce explained.

'Don't worry about it,' Chong-li told Wong. 'The Queen has Buckingham Palace, Prince Charles has Highgrove House, they all hang out at Windsor Castle and Balmoral—there are more than enough places for you to feng shui in UK. And you can charge the earth for each one.'

Wong looked comforted. 'I need the money quick-quick. You think the Queen pay cash?'

Sinha thought about this. 'I should think so. After all, her face is on all the cash. It's on all the coins, and all the notes. She owns all the cash, in a sense. They are all just portraits of her. I think she probably won't personally hand you an envelope stuffed with fivers but she can arrange for one of her staff to do just that. She has teams of men and women to do that sort of thing for her.'

'Ladies-in-waiting, they're called,' Joyce put in.

Chong-li agreed. 'Yes. They flit around with wads of money in their handbags to hand to people just like you.'

Wong allowed himself a slight upturn of the lips. It was possible that Arun Daswani may get his money on time after all. And if the Queen was as rich as his fellow members of the Singapore Union of Industrial Mystics believed she was, then there would be lots left over to go into his pocket.

This was worth celebrating. He held up his hand to get the attention of Ah-Fat, who was walking past with a steaming dish of something that smelled like a small animal marinated in mouth-searing chilli. 'One more of everything,' Wong yelled.

Chapter Two

Wednesday

IN THE DAYS OF *the supremacy of the southern kingdom, a man with an iron hammer told the people of north Yunnan that he was stronger than any of their village leaders.*

He approached a village made of wood and smashed it with his hammer.

He approached a village made of bronze and smashed it with his hammer.

He approached a village made of stone and smashed it with his hammer.

Soon, everyone worshipped the man with the hammer.

But not the hermit who lived in a small bamboo grove.

Knock down my home, and I will worship you too,' said the hermit.

The man swung his hammer at the bamboo grove. But the rods of bamboo bent with the blow and then sprang upright again. Many times, the man with the hammer swung at the bamboo grove. But he could do it no harm.

Blade of Grass, weakness is a type of strength. When an oxcart passes through a village, everyone sees it coming and gets out of the way. But when a blind man is crossing the road, the oxcart driver has to stop.

From *Some Gleanings of Oriental Wisdom*
by CF Wong

It was restlessness personified. Hong Kong was a frenetic, shaking, entrancing, annoying, gorgeous, mad city perched on the edge of the South China Sea. Gloriously asymmetrical, it was a splat of angular glass excrescences scattered arbitrarily over a series of giant rocks on the edge of the ocean. Everything in it was a statement, and always a loud one: the harbour was jammed with boats; the waterfront crammed with skyscrapers; the pavements packed with people; the sky chock-a-block with aircraft, helicopters and advertising blimps; the air filled with noise, noise, noise, noise. And at the heart of it was the main island, bursting with office buildings, apartment blocks and company headquarters carrying names that were visionary, boastful, grandiloquent and crass: Tycoon Court and Wealthy Mansions and Rich Genius Limited.

Then there were the hotels. What magnificence. What style. What opulence. What grandiosity. What tastelessness.

Joyce screamed as soon as she entered the hotel foyer, a short sharp yelp of sound bursting from the fists at her mouth: 'IIIEEEE!'

Robbie Manks, the royal consultant, seemed to jump out of his skin and then stared at her. Wong stepped smartly away from his assistant, a much practised manoeuvre on his part. The hum of conversation between hotel guests and staff at the lobby desks instantly vanished. Everyone turned to look at the newcomers.

Manks, a PR man who clearly loathed attracting attention to himself, was the first to react. He scanned the room. 'What had she seen that could have caused such a response? 'What is it? What's wrong?'

Joyce stared around her, an insane grin on her lips. 'What do you mean?'

'You just screamed?'

'Oh, that. I was just—I was just happy. I can't *believe* we're staying here. This is *so* amazing. I only ever get to stay in YMCAs or with mates if I come somewhere expensive like Hong Kong. But this—this must be the sheeshiest hotel in the place.'

Wong tried to give Manks a knowing look, as if to say: *See what I have to put up with?*

'Well, if there's no problem…er…let's check in, shall we?'

Joyce squealed again (a little less dramatically) when she saw the luxurious black marble check-in desk and staff wearing black silk uniforms with gold trimmings.

Manks's expression became anxious, probably anticipating the shriek of excitement that would erupt from her on catching sight of their, no doubt to them, extravagantly appointed rooms.

The PR officer was forty-six, suave and impeccably well-dressed in a Gieves & Hawkes suit. He was handsome, despite an over-large forehead and thinning straw-coloured hair, and he had a warm smile and engaging manner. He had met them at the airport with an exaggerated Ian Fleming Englishness, which may or may not have been ironic: 'The name's Manks. Robbie Manks.' He'd quickly explained that he was not officially retained by the royal family, but had his own PR company, which did a lot of work for them because of its reputation for quality, efficiency and discretion—the three things the royals sought above all else. Some of the stories he told Wong and Joyce during the taxi ride from the airport to the hotel suggested that his past twenty years had been professionally rather challenging, as it had more or less coincided with a long period of loss of face for the British monarchy. (He referred to them as 'The Family' with something in his tone of voice assigning capital initials to the phrase.) Manks clearly loathed the British press, whom he blamed for the majority of the problems. He saw the journalistic profession as low-life scum desperate to sell newspapers and make a quid at the expense of ruining people's lives and damaging the dignity of 'the world's finest monarchical institution'. But he stressed that The Family had a good friend in him, and his inventive programmes had been a key element in their success in managing to hold on to much of their personal popularity through these difficult times. But he did admit that one of his previous innovative ventures for The Family—to get a phrenologist to look at their head shapes and make recommendations—had been only a partial success. (Wong was wise enough to interpret this carefully chosen phrase as an admission that it had been a total disaster.) But his latest venture, to get the palaces feng-shuied, vaastued, dowsed and exorcised, was sure to be an even bigger success.

'You will get a vaastu man?' Wong asked.

'If I can find one who speaks good English. Still looking, I'm afraid.'

Joyce interrupted: 'There's a good one we know in Singapore. We'll give you his number. I'm sure he could jump on a plane and catch up with us.'

The geomancer noticed that Manks had a habit of popping white tablets into his mouth. At first, he had thought they were sweets, but when Manks failed to offer them around, Wong deduced they must be something medicinal. Spying the small circular package in which they were contained, he realised they were homeopathic remedy tablets of some kind.

The roads were wide and clear for most of the journey and they had travelled from airport to hotel in little more than forty minutes. Five minutes after checking in, the three of them were up on the eleventh floor, inspecting the rooms they had been assigned. As expected, Joyce had squealed at the opulence of her room, and then yelped again on peering into the marble and glass bathroom.

Manks ('Call me Robbie') had suggested that as soon as they had their bags sorted, they all move to his room to talk through what needed to be done. But once the two visitors from Singapore had filed into the royal consultant's chamber, he received a call on his mobile phone, which made him very agitated. It was clearly a disturbing conversation, although all they could hear of it were his cries of disbelief: 'What? You don't...you're serious? I just...but that's incredible. You're sure? You're absolutely sure? I'm...I'm stunned. I don't know what to say. Are the police there?'

Wong was vaguely aware he should leave the room during what was clearly a private call, but was too nosy to do so—as was Joyce. They continued to stand and eavesdrop, even as Manks glared at them and moved towards the window. After a minute, the conversation drew him in so deeply he seemed no longer to register their presence, and then he suddenly marched out of the room and into the corridor to finish his chat.

For a moment Wong was tempted to follow him, but manfully resisted. Two minutes later, Manks strode back into the room, his face white and voice unsteady.

'There's been a terrible accident...er...incident at the hangar where Skyparc is. I think this may change things. We need to stand by for further instructions.' He breathed in and out quickly, like a small dog.

'What do you mean? What sort of incident?' Joyce asked.

'I'm not at liberty to say at this moment.' He sat down on the bed in a daze. 'We need to stand by for further instructions. You folk can take a break. I need to make some urgent calls.'

Joyce headed to the door. 'I'm going to change into my swimmers,' she told her boss. 'If the rooms are this fab, can you imagine what the hotel swimming pool must be like?'

They had barely left the room when Robbie Manks followed them out, his phone back at his ear. 'Okay. Understand.' He rang off and turned to face Wong, who was standing in the thickly carpeted corridor. 'I've just been in contact with Sir Nicholas Handey at Skyparc. We are going to continue with the preparation of the venue. There's too much riding on this for us to change the schedules now.'

'So we go to the plane tomorrow morning?' the feng shui master asked.

'The visit will be as scheduled tomorrow morning.'

'Ten o'clock.'

'Correct. But there's one thing…'

They both looked expectantly at him, but his voice trailed off. For a moment, he said nothing, merely staring at the backs of his hands. Then he turned to face Joyce squarely. 'I'm afraid you can't go. Only Mr Wong.'

'What?'

'The vetting people have been doing a secondary search on visitors after…uh…an incident, and the level of security has been raised a notch. They've dug up something in your profile, Ms McQuinnie, that means we have to ask you not to accompany Mr Wong to the venue tomorrow.'

'Me? What have I done?'

'Don't take this too badly. It's nothing serious. It's just that…well, in certain situations, extra care has to be taken—and this is one of them.'

'But can you at least tell me what I've done?'

'You've done nothing, I'm sure.' He gave her a smile. 'It's just bureaucracy.'

The lines between Joyce's eyebrows arranged themselves into an angry little grid and she pouted, suddenly an upset little girl about to have a tantrum.

But then her face relaxed and she turned to leave them.

'Where are you going?' Wong asked.

'Swimming,' she said. 'If I'm not allowed to do any work, I might as well enjoy myself. I'll do some shopping and stuff, after a swim. I can't wait to see the pool. It's going to be a scream.'

❀ ❀ ❀

An hour later, Joyce had finished her swim and started to phone some local friends, hoping to meet them at the mall. There was one young man she was particularly longing to see: Paul Barker, a former classmate of hers at Island International School during the period in her mid-teens when she had lived in Hong Kong. But he was not at home.

The phone was answered by a nervous domestic helper, who was clearly anxious to discontinue the conversation.

'Can you take a message to give to him?' Joyce asked.

'I take your number give his mama,' came the answer.

Joyce left her contact details and rang off. Only then did it register how odd the reply had been. Paul was twenty years old. Why on earth would a domestic helper give the message to his mother rather than to himself? Was he ill? Or away? Surely if he had been away, the helper would just have said, 'He's out of town.' There was something curious about it.

She phoned another friend, Nina Madranini, and got through to the young woman's mother instead.

'Nina can't talk to you just now,' the older woman said. 'But she's meeting Jason at Starbucks in Jardine House at ten tomorrow morning. You know Jason McWong, don't you? Why don't you join them? I imagine there's lots for you to talk about just now.'

'Fine, thanks, will do, Mrs Madranini.'

Joyce rang off, intrigued. What did she mean by saying they had lots to talk about? What had happened? She was sorry not to have been able to arrange a meeting with Paul, but it would be great to see Nina, one of her favourite chat partners on her instant message list. Nina, a school friend of Joyce's, had been born into an Italian family that had emigrated to Australia, and then moved to Hong Kong for work. She was twenty, and was studying law at Hong Kong University. Like Joyce, she was into global justice: her real love was campaigning for the environment, and she was chair of the city's branch of Pals of the Planet.

Her boyfriend Jason was twenty-one, but somehow seemed younger, despite being large and hairy. His father was Scottish, and his mother Chinese: they had humorously combined their surnames (McCann and Wong) into McWong at their wedding. Jason was a gentle giant who had become a stalwart of the local environmental activist scene. Certainly, his heart was much more focused on activism than on his day job—he was a computer programmer for an animation company.

But Paul—oh, what a shame it would be if she spent two days in Hong Kong without managing to see him, Joyce thought. Paul had once been the most important of her friends in this city and, at the same time, had always been the one she knew least well. Joyce got to know him at school during a period when they were both outcasts sitting near the back of the classroom (it was the same as other schools all around the world—the good kids sat in the front half, the bad kids sat in the actual back row, but the nonentities filled the gap near, but not quite, at the back). She had been a shy new girl who had never been good at making friends. He had been a loner with little interest in anything except music and green politics, and had been known in class as an 'environmental Nazi', criticising teachers for not turning off every light when leaving the room. Both of them were children of busy, divorced parents who had given them plenty of material possessions but little in terms of affection or attention. Unsettled at home, neither managed to relax enough at school to make friends. Finding themselves unable to muscle into any of the cliques, they fell in together and fashioned a sort of low-temperature relationship by default.

It could not even be called a half-hearted friendship: quarter-hearted at best. It had grown with glacial slowness, and they really only got to know each other in Joyce's final year. That period was known in the lore of their social group as The Year of Masterbrain. Paul, an obsessive character, knew a great deal about what he called 'classical music'—a term that included all pieces of popular music composed or recorded in the two decades before he was born. His favourite period was the 1970s, a period about which he had encyclopaedic knowledge. That year, a teacher had arranged for him to be lined up as a contestant on a touring schools version of a UK television show called *Masterbrain*, on which he would be asked questions about his specialty topic.

There were a dozen or so members of the Music Appreciation Society in school at that time, and a few of them, including Joyce, Nina and Jason, had undertaken to meet after school at regular intervals to spend an hour drilling Paul with questions about the music of the 1970s. By the time the show was due to be recorded, Paul was an expert on the subject, and so were Joyce, Nina and Jason.

On the day of the show, the Music Appreciation Society got seats in the studio audience to cheer on their creation. The cameras started rolling and Paul got an almost perfect score on music of the 1970s. But he performed atrociously in the general knowledge section. He didn't make the final cut for the next round, and that was the end of it.

After the show, the four of them had broken off from the other group members to start a subset of the Music Society called the Obsessive-Compulsive 1970s Music Trivia Group, or Obcom 70s for short. They had entire conversations about class-mates that consisted only of references to song titles and artists of pop songs issued between 1969 and 1980.

'Joe Jackson, 1979?'

'"Is She Really Going Out With Him?" I don't know. I think it's more a case of Doobie Brothers, 1979.'

'"What a Fool Believes."'

While the friendship between Joyce, Nina and Jason had gathered depth, none of them became particularly close to Paul, who seemed to find it difficult to put as much effort into his relationships as he did into his campaign to fashion a life for himself out of idly collecting music tracks and complaining about other people's wastefulness. Joyce and Paul drifted apart, and on her last day in Hong Kong, they had not bothered to seek each other out to say goodbye.

What had failed to blossom face-to-face had thrived remotely: a more solid friendship between them grew by email. Joyce had often wondered whether they would meet again and actually move on to an actual face-to-face friendship with a bit more depth to it—or even something deeper: a relationship. He wasn't bad looking. He was clever. He didn't have much person-ality, but he might grow one. It was as if she had known two Pauls—one an uncommunicative face across a classroom, the other a likeable email correspondent whose letters were filled with passion about music, movies and global warming.

Paul, like Joyce, had refused to go to university. He had instead taken a job at a rare records company, where his encyclopaedic knowledge of rock stars had been useful. But then he'd changed. He became the first chairman of Pals of the Planet Hong Kong and had become more obsessive about that than he had ever been about his fabled music collection (which was so extensive it was eventually held across three separate iPods). In the past six months, he had hardly written to Joyce. He had become secretive, complaining about people intercepting his email and spying on him. He had not replied to her last two emails.

The only way to re-establish the friendship would be face-to-face, she decided. Nina and Jason would know where he was. And whether he had gone right off the rails, or was worth pursuing, for friendship or just possibly something deeper...

In the meantime, what? She was on her own for the evening. How to occupy herself? A bit of shopping perhaps and then another visit to the pool? Shopping was more fun with buddies, but was still enjoyable as a solo pleasure. She skipped down the stairs and was soon heading to the Lanes, a little network of bargain stalls and barrows off Des Veoux Road.

Just as she turned into an alleyway of stores selling fashionwear and cheap watches, something caught her eye: a shape, a man, a tall, stocky figure of some sort who seemed to be following her from a distance. But as she turned and scanned the crowds behind her, she couldn't see anyone looking her way. She must have imagined it. She turned back to the Lanes, and allowed the tightly packed Aladdin's cave of good things to suck her in.

Chapter Three

Thursday

WONG STEPPED TENTATIVELY into a small motorised buggy as a PR officer from the airport staff minced around to the other side of the vehicle. He had never been invited to step into a car indoors before. There seemed to be something incongruous about vehicle tyres nestling into thick carpets. It seemed wrong for a car to brush past people in corridors. Was this not illegal? Or immoral? Or at least uncivil? Or had he been living in Singapore too long? He reminded himself that in China, his homeland, the rule was that anyone who owned a motorised vehicle was above the law, and vehicles often pushed people out of the way.

Airport spokeswoman Nicola Teo set the vehicle in motion by grinding it into gear. As they jerked forwards, she prattled on with her eyes fixed on the passenger-strewn concourses ahead of them. She spoke so quickly her strings of over-rehearsed sentences turned into a wordless drone in his ear, and Wong soon became lost in his own thoughts.

He had spent less than an hour looking around the airport, but had already been impressed by what he saw. It was not so much an airport as a medium-sized city. As he gazed around, the young woman touched his arm to emphasise a point.

'We process forty million people a year,' she said. 'That's more than the population of New York, London, Hong Kong and Tokyo combined.'

He wondered what she meant by 'processed'. Was that not something Westerners did to food?

She turned briefly to him and flashed him a smile to give him a chance to react. When he did not, she continued unabashed with her flow of conversational factoids, gently easing the small vehicle around groups of straggling passengers. 'The long-term plan sees us growing to a maximum passenger through-load of eighty-seven million people.'

The feng shui master still did not visibly react, but he let the numbers enter his consciousness. Eighty-seven million people! Where would they put them all? If the city was built for seven million, what would they do with the other eighty million?

He scanned the floor plans on his lap. They showed that the airport was shaped like a giant letter Y. When you looked at photographs from above, it looked like a two-headed centipede, with lots of little leg-like protrusions attached to the main body and the two necks sticking out of one end. Of course, there was no need for him to do a feng shui reading of the airport itself, as his assignment was merely to look at the conference facilities on the Skyparc super-jet. But most modern architects tried to acknowledge the principles of energy flow in their buildings these days, and he was pleased to have an opportunity to see how these elements had been handled at this vast and futuristic new mini-city in Hong Kong, one of the few places on the planet which took feng shui completely seriously.

As they skittered along, Ms Teo pointed out the stairs leading to the internal railway station. 'The building is so large— more than one point two-five kilometres from end to end—that we have an internal railway system taking people from one end to the other, speedily, safely, and in comfort.'

Wong wondered what it meant in practice to have railway trains inside a building. Probably it led staff to have ridiculous conversations: 'Excuse me, I have to take the 2.50 to the kitchen, then the 3.05 to the toilet before catching the 3.10 back to my desk.'

'This new airport at Chek Lap Kok is nine times the size of the previous one at Kai Tak,' she continued. 'We have more than one hundred immigration arrival counters, so we can minimise the queuing time for passengers who have come in after a long flight.'

As she slowed the vehicle down, nearing their destination, she turned to look at him: 'Do you have any questions you'd like to ask? I know everything there is to know about this place...well, nearly. I'll be glad to answer any queries you have. Incidentally, in case I didn't mention it earlier, we handle fifty-three flights an hour at peak time, which is equivalent to almost one per minute.'

The feng shui master turned to her: 'I have a question.'

'Good.' She was delighted. Most of her victims were so stunned by her torrential onslaught of facts they were barely able to speak.

'Where's the front door?'

'The front door?'

'Yes. Where's the front door? I want to know which way it faces.'

For Wong, it was a natural question to ask: how could you understand the feng shui of a building without knowing where the front door was? The main door of the house had to be aligned with the most positive direction for the director of the group of people who used the building. For example, if the most senior man had a kua number of seven, a northeast facing door would make the house prosperous, while a southwest door would see the property expanding in size; other directions would be less positive.

Nicola Teo was momentarily silenced. No one had ever asked that question before. But the confusion in her face suggested she was surprised to be unable to answer such a simple question. She pointed to his diagram.

'Well, that's easy. The front door is, well, at the front. And, well, I would say the front was this bit, where the airport express train arrives—at least, it is from the passengers' point of view. The passengers on the trains, that is. But from the air passengers' point of view...well, they arrive at gates mostly down that end, so they would probably see that end as the front. But then the car drivers...well, there are five car parks—well, two main ones, you could say. And they come in sort of from one side or the other. So they would probably think the front doors were probably at this side, or that one. Did I tell you, we have a total of two thousand four hundred car parking bays? So, let me think, where exactly is the front door?'

Wong let her chew over the question and returned to his study of the plans. It became clear over the next few minutes that his question had more or less silenced the young woman, although she still spewed forth a fresh factoid at irregular intervals, like a short-circuiting copy of a child's talking dictionary. 'Did I tell you there were ninety-eight separate elevators in this building alone?' she gushed. 'Did I tell you we serve the passengers from two hundred and ten thousand, one hundred and twelve flights a year?'

Wong smiled. The sun was starting to shine in his life again. Over the past day, the feng shui master had become increasingly enthusiastic about this assignment. Everything had gone well. The client had said he was happy to reimburse them for the business class tickets they had not purchased. The hotel was comfortable and had good Chinese food on its menu. Joyce had been banished from the task, so he could work efficiently and without interruption. The schedule was relaxed, with him doing the on-board conference area today, and then flying off to London for more work tomorrow.

And then there had been the icing on the cake: the murder.

Once Joyce had moved out of earshot at the hotel, Robbie Manks had filled Wong in on the details of the 'incident' that had so upset him. Apparently an environmental activist—a well-known extremist in greenie circles—had broken into the plane while it was parked at the airport yesterday morning. The man had shot and killed a petroleum executive, and then tried to escape. But airport technicians had seen the whole thing through the aircraft windows and had alerted police, who pounced on the killer as he was trying to leave the hangar.

For the feng shui master, the incident was proof that the gods were going out of their way to make things up to him, having been so mean over the past few months. A murder undeniably introduced a massive amount of negative energy into a space. It meant that his role was far more important than would otherwise have been the case. More importantly, it meant that he could jack up his fees. Best of all, the murderer had been caught, so he didn't have to do the difficult part of the job, which was to work out who did it and gather proof for a legal case. That particular ball was firmly in the court of the law enforcement people. All he had to do was check out the space, alleviate the negative vibrations, and collect his fee. Life was sweet.

Wong and Teo abandoned the buggy, went down an escalator, and then stepped outside into the bright sunshine, whereupon they boarded another small vehicle, which trundled them towards the hangar where the fabled visiting aircraft was housed. Minutes later, they stopped at a security gate and Teo had a long and earnest talk with security staff, producing a long series of papers to justify Wong's presence on the site. Clearly, the murder had brought down the shutters heavily, and officers had become hostile to allowing anyone into the hangar who had not been born and raised there.

After three sets of people had examined the papers, Teo and Wong were allowed through.

'Hard to get in here,' he commented.

She agreed. 'That was the problem. It wasn't hard enough, before. We used to just have two staff at the barrier. I guess one was in the toilet, or fetching coffee or something, and the perpetrator got past the other one.'

'He sneak past?'

'No. He tricked her. That's what I heard. He said he was a local environmentalist and he didn't have a pass but he wanted to go in and take some pics, do an environmental assessment on the new plane. He was cute and charming, and she was a bit of a greenie, you know vegetarian and all that, so she let him slide through.'

'I know this type of woman. Very troublesome. Too bad.'

'It was a very naughty thing to do. You should never let anyone past security like that. But it was hard to blame her. She wasn't a trained security guard or anything. More like a receptionist or PA.'

'Very bad to let a bad guy in.'

'True. But we felt a bit sorry for her. I mean, she was quite young, and it all seemed innocent enough.'

'What happened to her?'

'She was sacked on the spot, of course. I think she'll be lucky if she's not prosecuted.'

'And this bad guy. He did what?'

'You don't know?'

'Mr Manks told me a bit. But not too much. He shot somebody.'

'Well, it was in the newspapers this morning, so I guess it isn't a secret any more. He got into Skyparc and then shot a guy working there. Then he tried to escape but the techies saw it all through the windows, and tipped off the guards, who came running. They grabbed him before he was even out of the hangar.'

They had reached a long corridor and she ushered Wong into a room on one side. In it, three men were waiting. One of them, a tall man with a walrus moustache, stepped forward to greet them.

'Mr Wong. Good morning. My name's Handey. Most people call me Sir Nicholas. I have the honour of being chairman of Skyparc Airside Enterprises. Now you understand that your role has become rather more important than we had expected, due to the highly regrettable incident yesterday morning. We hired you because we wanted to make sure everything was correct for the meeting; so we didn't make the sort of protocol mistakes that we would have been unable to see without the help of a...er...specialist such as yourself. But since yesterday, things have become more serious. A death on the plane is bad luck to the superstitious of any country, Mr Wong, Britain or China or anywhere else. We're going to make damn sure we don't have any British or Chinese bad luck signs around—fortunately, for the British, that's a simple enough affair. We make sure we don't have thirteen seats at the table, we check the calendar to make sure it's not Friday the thirteenth, we chuck a bit of salt over our left shoulder, hope it lands on a black cat, and that's pretty much that. For the Chinese, though, we understand it's all a bit trickier, a bit more detailed. That's where you come in. We want to be able to say to our visitors we have one of the world's finest feng shui masters on our team, and we can assure them on your behalf that any negativity has been completely excised.'

'Very hard to do this in one day. Better you have the meeting in another place,' Wong said.

'That would seem to be the obvious answer. But, Mr Wong, we are selling a place. A building. A very fine building that happens to be a flying building. A flying building that we are saying is the very best place to hold a meeting in any city in the world in which it lands. Thus, it stands to reason that the meeting has to take place in Skyparc. It would be absurd for it to happen anywhere else.'

Sir Nicholas clasped his hands behind his back and thrust his chest forward. Clearly, he was a former military man.

'One of the sales angles for Skyparc is that it has the sort of first-class conference rooms that is ideal for top-level summits, be they business meetings or political ones. We have to demonstrate that that is true. We have to imply that now that Skyparc has landed in Hong Kong, the best meeting room in the city is not at the Mandarin Oriental, or the Four Seasons, or the Grand Hyatt, but inside an aircraft on the apron of Chek Lap Kok airport. Furthermore, Skyparc is unique in being a meeting place beyond the concept of national boundaries. We can organise a summit on this aircraft and fly it to a place where it is subject to no jurisdictional boundaries of any kind. It will be the only place in the world ideal for inter-governmental summits dealing with tricky territorial issues: the Israelis and the Palestinians can meet here, as can the Singhalese and the Sri Lankan Tamils, and so on and so forth. Do you understand?'

'Understand.'

'Fine. Now Ms Teo will take you into Skyparc itself. She will arrange for you to have access to the parts you'll need to go into.' He dismissed them with a short bow of his head.

As they walked out of the hangar and onto a gantry leading to the aircraft, Wong decided to ask Teo about the murder. After all, she was clearly talented at memorising facts. 'Who died? Who killed the man who died?'

'There's not much we can say,' she said. 'The whole thing is *sub judice* now. A man from BM Dutch Petroleum was shot, and an intruder was caught red-handed. An environmental activist. Someone who has been waging a war against the petrol company for years. That's it, really.'

The feng shui master nodded. 'But if I do a reading of this airplane, to make sure there are no bad vibration there, then better you tell me more detail about exactly where the man was shot, how he was shot. Or let me talk to someone who knows about it.'

'I see. Well, there are a couple of cops still here. Would you like to meet them? I think you'll find them in the aircraft.'

As they approached the enormous, double-decker plane, Wong was curious about how much it appeared to differ from other aircraft. The entry door seemed wider, and seemed to be made of wood and brass. The windows were not a line of small portholes, but were long, thin and rectangular.

The PR woman noticed his surprise, and gave a laugh. 'Strange, isn't it, the first time you see it? They've gone to town to make this different. It's the iPhone of the aircraft world. It is amazing what a difference you can make, just by getting the designers to think outside the box for a change.'

As he got closer, it became clear that the wood and brass were faux artistic surfaces laid onto a rather conventional aircraft door. Close up, he could see the door was neither over-sized nor materially different in any substantial way. But the rectangular windows were genuinely eye-catching. And much more pleasant to look through, he imagined, than the tiny, too-low oval windows that were standard in every other aircraft on the planet.

Stepping onto Skyparc, he was pleased to turn to the right and find himself in a relatively large, open space, rather than the usual narrow aisles. The rows of seats that normally filled the body of an aircraft were missing. Instead, comfortable armchairs, which would not have been out of place in a gentle-men's club, were scattered around the room in clusters. As he walked through the room into the next, he was surprised to find himself in a space that was not the normal tube-like space in a curved fuselage, but had straight walls like a normal room. He soon realised there was a series of interlocking rooms, some of which had staircases leading to an upper floor.

The aircraft really was revolutionary. Instead of first, busi-ness class and economy cabins, there were multiple rooms on two levels, each with different designs and seating arrange-ments. One was built for a cabaret and featured a tiny stage. Another was a bar, a third was a modern coffee shop, a fourth was called Gourmet Boulevard and had multiple eateries, and so on. One of the lounges on the upper deck looked like it had come from a discotheque, another appeared to have been lifted from a colonial 1920s sitting room, complete with Chesterfield sofas, and a third was a cinema with a relatively big screen. The chairs were varied and cleverly designed. Each had a matching seatbelt built into it.

Teo led him into an upper-storey space, where the delegates for the meeting would gather. 'They'll stop here and have some drinks and canapes before the meeting proper,' she said. In the place of the usual narrow galley, there was a counter with a lit display of pastries and cakes. On the wall behind the counter, bottles of alcohol and optics were suspended. She turned a switch and mood lighting gently started glowing. She flipped another switch and a slow-swirling light effect started to paint patterns on the walls on all sides of the room.

'Very…different,' said Wong, a traditionalist who did not like mood lighting, and would have preferred an uncarpeted floor and cushion-less, hardwood, black-lacquered furniture: simple and elegant and sturdy (and cheap).

'Then, they'll go into the conference room, which is here.' She opened a pale pine door to show him a large room with a round table and minimalist panelling, which no doubt slid to one side to reveal projector screens.

Then she led him back down the stairs to what she called 'the back office' rooms. 'These are the executive offices, where Mr Seferis was when…yesterday.'

'Mr Seferis is the man who was shot?'

'He was. Ah, and here's a police officer.'

She explained to the officer who Mr Wong was and why he was here. The policeman introduced himself as Chin Chun-kit from the Hong Kong police. Clearly bored by his task, he seemed torn between sticking to his brief to repel anyone who approached, and being pitifully grateful to have someone to talk to. In the event, he decided to compromise and let Wong put his head into the crime scene, but not step into the room further than the doorway.

'We are very careful with evidence these days,' the officer said. 'You drop one invisible fibre on the floor, big trouble.'

The room was an elegant office with several desks, one of which was rather messy. Mr Seferis had obviously been in the middle of paperwork when he had been interrupted.

'We're not a hundred per cent sure which door the assailant entered through—there are two ways in,' Chin explained in Cantonese. 'We haven't been able to find a video record showing his exact approach, and there are no other clear signs. There were a lot of fingerprints and fibres, which have been sent off by the SOCOs—scenes of crime officers—for examination. They'll eventually answer the question for us. It's my belief the perpetrator entered through this door.'

'He come in and surprise Mr Seferis and shot him?'

'I think not. I think he must have entered and talked to him for a little while. As you can see, the door is on that side and he was shot by someone standing over here. So the two of them must have talked for a little while, moved around a bit. Seferis stood up from his desk and moved slightly, facing away from his desk. The assailant, judging by the angle of the bullets, stood here. The discussion turned into a row. It was so loud a group of technicians working outside heard them shouting. Then the man shot four times at point-blank range. Some technicians were actually working on this window here, just behind where the killer stood, and saw what happened. He fired off four shots one after another, all at the same angle. The first hit Seferis just under his heart. He slid down the wall, and the second hit him in the shoulder as he fell. The last two shots, probably fired in panic, went straight into the wood panelling. It's mahogany, which is bad luck for the hardwood conservationists, but good luck for the aircraft people. Mahogany is a very strong wood, it absorbed the bullets, preventing any harm being done to the aircraft walls.'

Wong leaned forwards and peered at the wooden panels. There was a single hole in the wood, apparently made by two bullets hitting the same spot.

'What gun?'

'Not sure yet. We have an expert working on it. He reckons it was a Beretta. A PX4 Storm pistol, probably, with fine bore ammo; maybe a bullet of seven millimetres or so. Smaller than normal, probably to minimise the sound.'

'You catch the bad guy already?'

'Yeah. We caught him. We're fast workers.'

'So my job is to clean up here.'

'No,' said Chin, looking alarmed. 'We've got more SOCOs coming in to do some tests later today. It's still a sealed-off crime scene. You can't touch it, I'm afraid.'

'I do not mean that sort of cleaning. I mean cleaning up negative forces coming out from here. I do not need to touch anything in this room.'

'Oh, that. Yes, well, you can start that any time you like, as long as it doesn't interfere with police work.'

'Thank you.'

Wong asked to be escorted back upstairs, and he started work on the conference room.

❀ ❀ ❀

Jason McWong jumped up when he saw Joyce arrive, spilling his Venti-sized coffee over the table. He gave her a hug, and refused to let go, even though a pint of tepid latte was spilling down his trousers and into his left Doc Marten.

'Wow,' said Joyce. 'Why such a warm welcome? Did I win the lottery and nobody told me?'

Jason answered only with a long watery sniff. Below him, the paper coffee container, now empty, rolled to the floor and disappeared under the table. Joyce realised he was in an emotional state, his heavy body a-tremble. She pulled away from him just enough to look at his face. His eyes were red.

'I just want to be held,' he whimpered.

She glanced at Nina and noticed she too had been crying. 'What's wrong? What's happened? Has something awful happened?'

Jason nodded, but was too overcome to speak. He sniffed again and eventually let go of Joyce. He lowered himself back into his seat, and reached towards the table for his drink. 'Where's my latte?' he said, baffled and annoyed.

'In your left boot,' Nina told him.

Jason wiggled his toes, heard a squelching sound and realised she spoke the truth. 'How'd it get in there?'

'Something awful has happened,' Nina said to Joyce. 'It's Paul.'

Joyce's hand had flown to her mouth. 'Paul? What? What? Tell me.' Nina's tone could only imply death or dismemberment. Jason seemed to be occupied with wondering whether he could get his coffee back out of his boot and into a cup.

'He's been arrested,' Nina said.

Joyce relaxed slightly. Most members of the group had been arrested at least once in their lives, and Paul had already been arrested at least once this year. It was an activist's life—indeed, it was what several activists lived for. 'Is that all?'

But Nina looked so worried Joyce snapped the look of concern back onto her face.

Joyce knew this brush with the law had to be much worse than usual. 'What is it? What's he done now?'

'Murder,' spat Nina angrily. 'He's been done for murder. They say he killed someone. It's ridiculous. It's totally ridiculous.'

'*Murder?*'

Nina nodded.

'He wouldn't murder anyone,' Joyce said, a tone of outrage in her voice.

'He'd never murder anyone,' Nina agreed.

'Except maybe a veal farmer,' put in Jason.

Joyce considered this and decided it was a fair comment. 'Or a mink farmer,' she added.

'Or a battery hen farmer,' added Nina.

'Or a fox hunter,' said Jason.

'Or pet shop owners.'

'Or people who kept caged birds.'

'Or a big-scale polluter.'

'Nah,' said Nina.

'I mean, if it was a *really* big-scale polluter.'

'Maybe,' Nina conceded.

There was a palpable ripple of discomfort at the way this line of conversation was running and they dropped it by unspoken mutual consent.

'But he wouldn't kill anyone else,' said Nina.

'Too right,' said Joyce.

There was a pause in the conversation.

'So who did he…I mean, who did he not…I mean, who did they say he killed?'

'An oil guy from BM Dutch Petroleum,' Jason said. 'An official.'

'He wouldn't kill an oil official from BM Dutch Petroleum,' said Joyce, wondering whether he would.

'He wouldn't,' said Nina. 'He wouldn't kill a fly.'

'Now that's true. He definitely wouldn't kill a fly,' Joyce echoed. Most of the gang would far sooner kill a nasty polluting human than an innocent bug of any kind. 'Where did it happen? I mean, where do they say it happened?'

'On that plane. That special plane at Chek Lap Kok.'

'Skyparc?'

'Yeah.'

'Skyparc. That's *so* weird. I was supposed to go up there today. I had an appointment at…well, just about now, actually.'

'You did? On Skyparc? Geez, you some swanky high-class lady dese days, Jojo.'

'Yeah, I…' Joyce stopped. Her mind raced. Of course! Now the pieces fell into place. That's why her authorisation had suddenly been withdrawn. A man had been murdered on the plane, and a member of Pals of the Planet—her sort-of buddy Paul—had been accused of doing the dirty deed. The security people must have gone through their database and instantly barred access to everyone on the list who was registered as a member of the Pals.

'I was supposed to go and like feng shui it this morning— with my boss—but yesterday afternoon they suddenly said I couldn't go. I think it's because I'm a member of the Pals of the Planet. I was *negatively vetted*,' she said, knowing that such a phrase would impress this group. 'I must have been.'

'We're all going to be negatively vetted,' said Nina gloomily. 'For the rest of our *lives*. Paul's going to be done for murder and the Pals will be made illegal,' she said, bursting into tears.

Over the next twenty minutes, all the details came out. The story was electrifying. Joyce realised that odd, quiet, obsessive Paul, by becoming part of a major news report, had become part of history, at a stroke overtaking all the noisy, clever, ambitious kids in the class.

She listened in a daze, her mind running on multiple tracks at once. She felt she was part of the discussion but at the same time merely an observer, little more than an astral projection that happened to be in the room. The young woman could not escape the feeling that life was rolling too fast, too many things were happening in quick succession, there were too many problems to solve and too many paths to choose from.

Nina did most of the talking, with Jason nodding and Joyce listening silently, with her hand to her mouth, as they sat knee-to-knee around their Lilliputian table at Starbucks.

'I still can't believe it,' said Jason. 'Our Paul, locked up for murder.'

Joyce felt they were becoming permanently bonded together by the horror story they were sharing. This is what life was, she semi-subconsciously decided: an endless series of conversations in which people tried to make sense of their lives by chopping them up into stories and trading them with each other; some funny, some sad, some shocking, some exciting, some endearing, some boring, some tragic. Emotional, shared tales created strong bonds; shallow, trivial ones cooled relationships and caused them to drift apart. The power of a story was not related to how much drama or death there was in it, but in how involved the listener was. A nuclear bomb on the other side of the world could be ignored, but a firecracker at the next table could not.

And the fact that Paul was only a kid—twenty, maybe twenty-one—was also a factor. A man of forty being arrested was not really news: such tales were just grey paragraphs in grey newspapers. But a young person being thrown into jail—that was different. You wanted to find out more. What happened? What led up to it? Who should be blamed? Was it the parents? Did he fall into bad company? Children were always seen as blank slates. Anything that turned them into news items, whether as victims or perpetrators, were stories that demanded to be pored over.

Then there was the money. Wealth was always a factor, whether or not it should be. Paul was a spoilt upper-middle-class brat who had gone to an international school: one couldn't listen to a tale of someone like him coming to grief without an emotional reaction, whether it was 'he deserved it' or 'I blame the parents'.

Joyce knew the beginning of the history Nina was relating: that the remaining members of Obcom 70s had decided to march alongside Friends of the Earth at a demonstration against pollution in Hong Kong, and had eventually dropped their focus on music and become the local branch of Pals of the Planet. From pop music to environmental activism may seem a stretch, but they were sister subjects for politically correct teenage rebels at the time. The metamorphosis had been organic and natural. After their star performer's dramatic failure on *Masterbrain*, the group had lost its focus, and the wave of concern about the mess adults were making of the planet became their new uniting emotion. The skill they had developed in collecting, processing and distributing trivia was useful, and they sent out dozens of fact-packed press releases about the effects the deteriorating air quality was having on the health of residents.

Everything had run along predictable lines for the first year of the existence of Pals of the Planet Hong Kong, with the group making local-paper headlines with their campaigns against idling engines, wasteful air-conditioning and other crimes against humanity. But Paul had become increasingly secretive. He was the original chairman of the group, but after a visit to London had decided to hand the title to someone else. Nina had taken it. He had become a 'special operative' for head office instead, working on various international schemes, some of which he darkly hinted were 'top secret' and could not be shared.

'For a while, we thought he may have become an Earth Agent,' Jason said.

Joyce gave him a puzzled look.

'Earth Agents—it's a new extremist group that likes to shut down facilities.'

Nina added: 'It's an interesting group. They reckon what's happening is that there's a war-to-the-death going on between Planet Earth and the human race, which is kind of true, if you think about it. Anyway, they reckon Planet Earth is in the right, and the human race is in the wrong, which is also true if you think about it. So, they are a group of people who have "changed sides", sort of thing. They're on the side of Planet Earth and aim to destroy human projects that damage the environment.'

Joyce liked the sound of this. 'Interesting idea,' she mused.

'Interesting, but not practical,' Nina explained. 'The first few operations they've done have been completely illegal and very dangerous to people on both sides. A security guard was badly injured at one of their break-ins at a power plant. And they even put out a statement saying they considered themselves at war, using phrases such as "collateral damage". It all got a bit too nasty.'

'So you reckon Paul became one of them?'

'We worried about it. But I asked him directly, and he claimed he wasn't. He said he was in special operations for Pals of the Planet.'

'Do you believe him?'

Nina thought about this. 'I do. I think I do. Paul's not quite insane enough to be an Earth Agent. Almost, but not quite.' Jason nodded his agreement.

Nina went on to explain how Paul had become interested in BM Dutch Petroleum's new, supposedly 'green' fuel and had researched it obsessively for weeks. It was a complete scam, he had announced. This was hardly an original discovery. Every environmental group in the world, from Greenpeace to Friends of the Earth, had said the same thing. And even *National Geographic*, which could hardly be described as a group of wild-eyed activists, said it was 'a scheme widely accepted as an attempt to fool the public'. And then, when Paul heard that the

Skyparc plane was due to touch down in Hong Kong, he'd told the others that he was going to pay it a visit.

'By that time, he almost seemed to be not part of the group any more,' Nina explained. 'He hardly came to the meetings, and we kind of resented the fact he had all these other so-called projects going, which we didn't really know anything about.'

Jason nodded. 'Yeah. He seemed to have gone a bit extreme, over-the-top.'

Joyce blinked. If Jason, who was said to have anti-nuclear symbols tattooed on his buttocks, was describing someone as extreme, Paul must have been several kilometres beyond rational thought.

When the group had heard of Paul's arrest the previous day, it all seemed to fit. Their former leader had tried something daring, getting on to the airside of the terminal at Chek Lap Kok, and then breaking into Skyparc itself. That was pretty impressive. They would have expected him to adorn the plane with pro-environment banners or spray-paint his favourite slogan, 'Combat hunger, eat the rich', onto its fuselage. But when they learned he was a murder suspect, it was clear something had gone horribly wrong.

All of them had talked with mock-seriousness of how much better the world would be if someone would 'take out' George W Bush, or any other members of the iconic class of big business leaders, but none of them would dream of actually harming anyone. They were the sort of people who took spiders out of their baths rather than wash them down the plughole. And actually shooting a stranger in cold blood? It couldn't happen. He wouldn't do it. Such a thing would not only be temperamentally impossible, it would clearly achieve nothing except to get Pals of the Planet into a heap of trouble—trouble it might not even survive.

'It's really bad,' said Jason. 'I've been crying all night.'

'Yeah, Jason's taking it really bad.'

Joyce stood up.

'Where are you going?'

'To find Paul.'

'He's in jail.'

'They must have visiting hours or something. Let's go.'

There was silence.

'Don't you want to come and see him?'

'My mum won't let me,' said Jason.

'Mine's the same,' said Nina. 'They'd go ape if we went to jail to visit Paul.'

'You guys! You're adults. You're over eighteen. How can you let your parents stop you visiting a member of the gang in jail? That's ridiculous.'

'Sit down.'

Joyce sat down.

'There's something else,' said Nina. 'Abel went to see him last night.'

'Who's Abel?'

'Professor Abel Man Chi-keung. A friend. A law professor. A member of Pals of the Planet. Abel said Paul had taken a vow of silence. He's not saying anything to anybody. And he wrote a message saying he didn't want any visitors. He didn't want to talk to anyone. And then he snapped his pencil to show he wasn't going to talk in writing, either. So it would be a waste of time going to jail, anyway. He won't see you.'

'Paul just sits there in silence?' Joyce asked.

'Well, Abel said he sometimes hums tunes from the 1970s, or lists names of artists from that period. But that's all.'

'Maybe he was talking Obcom. Abel wouldn't have understood.'

'You can't talk Obcom when you're about to be done for murder. Especially not to your defence lawyer.'

Joyce sat in silence for a moment, and then stood up again.

'Where are you going now?'

'I'm going to see this professor guy. We can't just sit here drinking coffee. We've got to do something. You coming?'

'I need another latte,' complained Jason. 'My first went in my shoe.'

'Nina?'

'I've already talked to Abel, for ages. But you go talk to him. I'll give you his address,' she said, starting to write it on a napkin.

❀ ❀ ❀

In the reign of the Tang, the people of Lower East Lake did not allow anyone imperfect to stay in the village.

After some years, there came to be two settlements there: the village of the perfect, and the village of the blind, deaf and lame.

Every year, the two villages each sent a representative for a one-on-one competition. And every year, the representative of the perfect won.

Then one year, a passing monk said he would organise the competition between the two. 'But this time, we will have two from the village of the perfect and two from the village of the rejects,' he said.

From the village of the perfect came two representatives: both strong, brave and healthy. From the village of the rejects came two representatives: one blind and one deaf.

The first test was for the contestants to sit in the dark and hear the approach of the monk from three li distance. The blind man won the competition easily.

The second test was for the contestants to look at a field of red blood-berries and find a single purple nut-berry. The deaf man won the competition easily.

Blade of Grass, it may seem that some people have disabilities, but the total amount of perception that each person has is the same.

From *Some Gleanings of Oriental Wisdom*
by CF Wong

Travel just twenty minutes away from the centre of Hong Kong and an extraordinary transformation meets your eyes. The shoulder-to-shoulder crowd of mismatched skyscrapers disappears. The world's most densely packed layer cake of miniature, overlapping residences thins out. The yellow-grey haze vanishes.

But they are not replaced by a pristine wonderland of green mountains and beaches as the tourist brochures would have you believe (those things do exist, but they are set well off the main thoroughfares). No, what you see is an angular landscape where man and nature are holding an ongoing contest as to who can throw up the most dramatic structures.

There are walls of mountains. There are walls of buildings. Everything is nicely spaced, with gaps in between for light and air. There are natural canyons, lined with green. There are unnatural canyons, lined with washing. There are thick woodlands of deciduous trees and bamboo groves, gently swaying in the breeze. There are forests of television aerials and telephone repeater stations, sternly defying the wind. There are Hakka women, wearing tribal outfits as they pick at crops of vegetables. There are men in denim overalls erecting Coca-Cola hoardings. There are tiny brown stalls from which tiny brown people sell tiny cups of brown Chinese tea, the whole caboodle appearing to have evolved naturally from the soil. There are glitzy, glassy shops offering pizza and internet connections, which appear to have been dropped in place by passing aircraft from a different planet.

At several locations on the road from urbanised Kowloon towards mainland China, there are huge cities that seem to have been built yesterday, or perhaps the day before at the earliest. The areas of green around them are still unspoiled, and look somewhat shellshocked at the fifty towers that have popped up overnight in their midst. Scan the buildings and you note that one-third of the windows have curtains and occupants; the other two-thirds have neither. The roads look new and fresh, and are an even shade of pale grey; they look as if no cars, trucks or buses have yet been allowed to belch their way over them.

Joyce was on a train, chugging its way into what is anachronistically called Sun Gai, or the New Territories. This name is highly politically incorrect. They are the 'new territories' only in the sense that they were an extra bit added to the lands that the British claimed from China after the Opium War. These areas were appended to the pile of British winnings in 1898, more than fifty years after Hong Kong island had become a crown colony in 1842. So, in a real sense, 'new territories' is short for 'new British territories added to the old British territories'. The name should have been changed at the time of the handover of Hong Kong to Chinese sovereignty in 1997. But memories were short in this city. People didn't even remember the last stock crash, which was no more than a few years before, so it was unlikely they would take note of anything that happened more than a century in the past.

Joyce was travelling through a place still called the New Territories, heading for an address scribbled on a piece of paper in her hand. She was feeling uncomfortable because she was at a disadvantage, not being able to read Chinese characters. Nina had asked one of the staff at the coffee shop to rewrite the address on the napkin in Chinese.

She left the train at Tai Wai station and stopped from time to time to show the address to people, who nodded and pointed. Something felt wrong about her mission, and after some minutes, Joyce realised what it was. What was a lawyer doing out here, working in the rural areas? The legal professor was a teacher from one of the universities—or had been. He must have retired as you can't run either a law office or a tutorial from the middle of a rural new town. And this was definitely a new town, with all the blandness the phrase implied. A dull cluster of identical white residential towers seemed to stretch almost to the horizon in three directions—the fourth was occupied by a steep, craggy hill.

Joyce had been in east Asia long enough to know what happens when you ask people for directions. In some countries, in the Philippines and Sri Lanka, for example, the person you ask will often walk you all the way to the door of the place you are looking for, and sometimes come in with you. In other places— Hong Kong and Singapore—the person you ask will merely tell you the immediate next direction, so that if your journey is first left, second right, third left, first left, he will merely point you to the first left. He will expect you to ask at the next junction to get the next bit of the puzzle and so on, so you will speak to six or seven people before you get to where you are going.

After fifteen minutes, Joyce had consulted four people and been sent in various directions, along eight streets, all of which looked exactly the same. Indeed, the eight streets could have been the same street eight times over and she would never have known. But she had faith in humanity and believed she was getting closer to her destination.

At the next junction, she asked an elderly woman who was so tiny she barely reached Joyce's chest. The woman stared at the piece of paper and pondered for a long time without saying anything. Joyce was getting frustrated. She was at a T-junction and assumed she needed to turn left or right.

She tried out a bit of basic Cantonese to hurry things along. 'Jor-been? Ding hai yau-been?' Left-side or is it right-side?

The woman thought for a moment longer and then pointed straight up. 'Gor do,' she said. Just there.

Joyce followed the line made by the woman's finger and looked to the top of the block right next to where they were standing. 'Thanks, I mean, mm-goi.'

Five minutes later, she emerged from a lift on the forty-third floor of the building—was there anywhere else on earth where residential buildings could be sixty or seventy storeys high?—and started coughing. The air was full of smoke or dust or something. Was the building on fire? She detected no heat. Instead, Joyce heard a grating, whining noise, and realised workmen were cutting or grinding something.

The door of the apartment in front of her was open and she stepped in, hand held over her mouth and nose. She waved her other hand in front of her eyes and eventually managed to get through the worst of the dust storm. In the small room there was nothing but a man at the top of a ladder, making a storm of powder, all of which was heading towards the front door because of the angle at which he was holding his tools.

'*Mm-goi,*' she said, grateful for the fact that 'thank you' in Cantonese was a useful portmanteau word that also meant 'excuse me', 'please', and so on.

The man looked down from his perch.

'Professor Man? I want to see Professor Man.'

The worker just stared at her, saying nothing. She decided to try it in Chinese. '*Man Sin-Saang hai bin do?*' Mr Man is where?

The worker's head changed angle but he still said nothing.

Bother, thought Joyce. She recalled that many manual workers were mainland immigrants, legal or illegal, and spoke only Mandarin. How do you say Professor Man in Mandarin? '*Man Lau-sher?*' she attempted.

The worker put down his electric sander. 'You've bravely attempted three languages. Out of the three of those, I think I prefer the English,' he said. 'The others were hopeless.'

'Oh. You speak English.'

'Just a bit.'

'I'm looking for Professor Man. He's a professor of law.'

'You're not.'

'Yes, I am.'

'No, you're not.'

'*Yes, I am.*'

'You're *not* looking for him. You were, but no longer. You have found him.'

'Ah. Right. Doing some DIY?'

The Professor laughed. 'Certainly not. This isn't my apartment. Wouldn't catch me living in a small box at the top of a tower at cloud level.'

'Oh. Helping out a friend?'

'Goodness, you are polite, aren't you?' the Professor said, coming down the creaky ladder. 'You cannot conceive this sort of manual labour might be my actual job, can you?'

Joyce merely smiled, not knowing how to respond.

'I run a company called Fat Man Interiors—*Fat* being Chinese for "prosperous", as I expect you know. This is my day job, so to speak.'

'Oh. I thought you were a professor of law. That's what Nina told...'

'I am trained as a professor of law. Did that for some years. It doesn't pay too well, so I starting doing a bit of construction and interior design on the side. I discovered the whole builder thing works rather well. So I do rather more of that than the legal lecturing these days.'

'But I thought lawyers were rich?'

He pulled off his goggles and shook his head. 'Never make the mistake of confusing professors of law with practitioners of law. Working lawyers earn the big bucks. We professors are merely another branch of the teaching profession. Poor as church mice.'

'Really?'

'Well, probably not really. I don't actually have any data on the disposable income of church mice, so I shouldn't be so cavalier with the statistics.'

'How come you sound so English?'

'The British legacy. Most legal people of my generation trained in London.'

He gestured at her to follow him onto the balcony. 'Come. There's air over here which we can actually breathe. Nice stuff, air. Don't get much of it in my line of work.'

A few short strides took them to a minuscule balcony at a dizzying height above the street. Joyce noticed the little old lady she had asked for directions below them, having tottered just twenty metres further along the road.

'Now what can I do for you?'

'Sorry to disturb you, Professor, but I'm here to ask about Paul Barker.'

He looked out into the sunshine, his eyes half-closing in the glare. 'Thought so. You can call me Abel.'

'Thanks. Have you spoken to him? Nina said—'

'I spent some time with him last night.'

'How's he doing?'

'As well as can be expected.'

'That's a cliché.'

'So was your question.'

'But how is he? I mean, is he okay? He must be so shocked. I mean, what an awful thing to happen to...to be accused of something like that. *Jeez*.'

He nodded. 'It is, as you say, an awful situation to be in.'

'Can we get him out on bail?'

Abel shook his head. 'On a murder charge?'

'But his parents could pay a big bail bond. They're rich.'

He shook his head again.

'Is he estranged from them?' Joyce asked.

'No, I spoke to them. I think they rather admire him. His father does, anyway. But I think bail is unlikely, given the charges...and the evidence.'

'Trumped up, of course.'

She expected Abel to enthusiastically agree with her, but he said nothing.

'I've known Paul for years,' she went on. 'He wouldn't hurt a fly. I mean...' She decided not to go down that avenue again. 'I mean, he's a good guy. He would never murder anyone. What sort of evidence do they have? This has *got* to be some sort of frame-up.'

Again, there was a gap during which time Joyce expected the Professor to agree with her, and once more he said nothing. She started to feel affronted—how come Abel Man wasn't rushing to Paul's defence? An unwelcome thought struck her. 'Do you...do you think he's guilty?'

'That's a question you cannot ask a lawyer. Or even teacher-lawyers. Or even builder-teacher-lawyers.'

She waited for him to explain himself.

'One of the things that happens to your brain in the first few years of practising law is that you get a logical disjunct. You learn how to marshall any number of facts together without drawing any conclusions from them.'

'I don't get it,' she said.

'If lawyers didn't have that ability, they couldn't work. They would be constantly researching the facts, discovering the client they are defending is guilty, or the person they are prosecuting is innocent, and then they're sunk. They have to abandon the case or continue with it, hoping they fail to prove what they have set out to prove. If they win their case, they get kudos for themselves, but have caused an act of injustice to have occurred. It's an impossible situation.'

'I see...I think.'

'That's the heart of it: you think. We don't. We just get as many facts as we can, and we put ourselves into the shoes of the judge and the jury and try to process the odds. Lawyers count rather than think. Are the number of facts implying guilt higher or lower than the number of facts implying innocence, in the eyes of people listening? It's a largely mathematical computation. It takes place in the lawyer's head. It never translates to the natural next stage, which is: do *I*, personally, think he really did it or not?'

'Is that what happened in the OJ Simpson thing?'

'In that case, there was only *one* crime and only *one* possible offender at the scene—a suspect who acted in an unmistakably guilty way straight after the murders. If the defence lawyers had allowed such an inconvenient little fact to penetrate into their souls, they would have been unable to defend him. So they turned it into a mental game. How can we amass enough circumstantial facts to prompt the jury to react in a particular way? As for the question of whether he did it or not, the defence lawyers would not have allowed themselves to even think about it. Otherwise they would have been unable to operate honestly. Either that or they thought about the question, reached the unavoidable conclusion and decided they would be happy to continue in spite of this, thus to operate dishonestly.'

'Eww. They sound like bad guys.'

'Exactly. People like you and I wonder how others can stand up and lie in front of people, speak the opposite of what is in their hearts—but there are people who can. Most lawyers, I like to think, cannot. Again, I have no empirical evidence for that claim. It's probably more a wish than an assertion.'

He stopped talking and gave her a friendly smile. Construction work in a new town must be a lonely job for someone as bright as he was, and Joyce imagined it must be pleasant for him to take a break and chat about something he had obviously thought a great deal about. She let the silence surge around them for a while. But then it occurred to her he had avoided answering her question. What exactly did that mean? Was he gently letting her know Paul might actually be guilty?

'What *is* the evidence against Paul?' she asked at last.

The Professor looked down at his feet for a while before answering. 'It's a long list. They have a confession from a staff member who allowed him to get past the security doors and enter the aircraft hangar where the plane was parked. She claims he told her he just wanted to take pictures—he apparently charmed her.'

'He can be very charming, in an odd, quiet sort of way.'

'They have a security video of him entering the aircraft minutes before the shooting. The victim was killed in a room on the lower deck of the craft.'

'Couldn't we argue it was circumstantial evidence? Someone else may have been there?'

'I haven't finished. They have people working on the aircraft who saw him pull the trigger—they were watching him and the victim through the plane windows.'

'Oh. That's bad.'

And they have a video of him leaving the aircraft a few minutes later. He was caught almost immediately. At least one eyewitness has made a positive identification of him. And the security videos are nice and sharp—you can see his face clearly.'

'*Jeez.*'

'Yeah.'

'But have they got any record of him actually *murdering* the guy? The other guy may have pulled a gun first. I mean, as far as I know, it would be unlikely Paul even owned a gun. Maybe the other guy tried to kill Paul, and Paul grabbed the gun and shot back in self-defence.'

'Hah! Now you're thinking like a lawyer. I like it. Instead of acknowledging that the evidence strongly implies he did it, you are adding up the facts and looking for gaps and loopholes.'

'But maybe it was like that. Or maybe he was framed.'

'None of this is impossible.'

'Maybe there was someone else on the plane, who looked like Paul if you were peering through the plane windows from a distance.'

'Yes,' the Professor exclaimed. 'A good argument. Except for the inconvenient fact that there was no one else on the plane. Various technical staff were working in the hangar, but they were all on the outside of the plane. And the windows on this aircraft were unusually large and clear. So the engineers got a good view.'

'So he is the only suspect,' Joyce said.

'Like OJ.'

'Can we get OJ's lawyers? No, forget I said that. But I know Paul wouldn't have shot anyone in cold blood. There must be something else to it. What does he say happened?'

The Professor sighed. 'That's the problem. He's not saying anything.'

'What do you mean?' Joyce asked, although she knew the answer.

'He's not talking to anyone. Not to his friends, not to his parents, not to social workers, not to me. When he has to say something, he just recites lists of songs or singers from the 1970s. Songs from before he was born.'

'He's a collector. He loved the 1970s, and wished he had been born earlier. The whole song titles thing—it's a game our gang used to play all the time. We called it Obcom, from obsessive-compulsive.'

Abel nodded. 'I gathered it was something like that. Nina told me.'

Joyce sighed. 'So he's not defending himself?'

The Professor shook his head. 'Nor giving me the information I could use to organise some sort of defence for him.'

'It doesn't look good.'

'On a murder rap, it's very bad indeed. Indeed, I would call it a hopeless case. Unless of course a friend, a good friend, could persuade him to open up a little.' He turned to face her and lifted his eyebrows, setting her a challenge.

'I could try. I don't know if I'll be able to do any good. What are you going to do?'

'One does what one can, when one can. I have certain things planned.'

'Such as...?'

'I'm going to finish sanding the ceiling.' He slipped his goggles back on and raised his electric sander to shoulder height. 'This has to be finished by seven o'clock.'

Joyce left the room as the machine began to scream.

Half an hour later, she was on a different train, this time on her way to prison. She had decided to visit Paul anyway. It didn't matter whether he was guilty, whether he would receive her, or whether he would talk to her. They'd been friends, he was in big trouble, and she felt it was her duty to show herself, and make herself available as a shoulder or listening ear, whatever he chose to respond to.

Perhaps the fact that she was sort of an investigator, if only a feng shui man's assistant, may cut some ice with him. Wong's agency specialised in scenes of crime. It may be that Paul didn't want to talk to a social worker or a lawyer or his parents, but would talk to her, as she was in a unique position of being both a friend and a professional investigator.

And she hadn't missed the message in Abel Man's closing words: perhaps the only thing that could save him would be if a friend could persuade him to abandon his vow of silence. And anyway, she knew she wouldn't be able to rest until she'd at least tried to be that friend.

Caught up in her own thoughts, she did not notice the man following her all the way to the prison gates.

❀ ❀ ❀

When organising your work space, it is important to position yourself and your colleagues in a configuration that correctly takes into account each person's role, place in the hierarchy, focus of activity, personality, birth date, temperament and ambitions. In a conference room, where one individual guides a group of people in discussions and decision-making, one concentrates primarily on ensuring the chairman's position is clear and strong. At home, the patriarch can have a chair with its back to the door, but in a business situation this should never be the case: he needs to know what is behind him as well as what is ahead. He needs to make sure no one stabs him in the back, metaphorically or otherwise. Further, the leader's chair must not have a window behind it: such a position subconsciously creates an image of lack of support. The leader has to have something strong and solid behind him—a wall, representing a mountain of strength.

Using details of Sir Nicholas Handey's birth—he was born in the Year of the Monkey, 1944—Wong decided west-southwest was his most positive direction. He was able to make slight adjustments to the room easily, to give power to the chairman's seat. Fortunately, the conference table was round, so simply changing the relative positions of all the seats and moving the table itself a quarter turn, gave Sir Nicholas's seat control over the others.

After strengthening the positive, Wong's next job was to alleviate the negative. The room where the man had been shot would remain off limits to everyone, including the VIP visitors touring the plane. So all he had to do was to provide evidence that any bad luck that came from that room, in any direction, had been alleviated professionally. His function, he understood, was merely to allow the Europeans to boast that the work had been done.

While unschooled practitioners of the art would merely hang a mirror outside the door, the geomancer preferred to use a mixture of physical and psychological remedies. For immediate effect, he asked for rugs and carpet runners in certain colours to be placed in the room and a harsh piece of modern art on the wall to be removed. Pots of cacti and floral displays of dried plants tied to angular sticks were taken out; replaced with live, flowering houseplants. Dead light bulbs were renewed, with the fittings adjusted so that light did not glare directly onto the occupants or their paperwork and was reflected, instead, at least once before it softly reached desk level, the energy therefore gently dissipating.

He ordered that mirrors be hung at certain places, and the spot directly above the place of murder was assigned powerful elements that would absorb negative energy. Fish and other animals, apparently, were not considered suitable for aircraft in flight, but Wong ordered that a tank of miniature turtles be installed just for the day, for the duration of the meeting, to be removed when the plane was due to take off the following day. He also organised a calming oil-painting of a Suzhou garden to be installed close to the entrance of the conference room. This would introduce a natural earth energy into a space that was in danger of being affected by the over-strong fire and metal energies of the gun that had been used in the room beneath.

To get the details straight, the geomancer had asked for more information about the victim—Dmitri Seferis. He had been born in Germany to a Greek family, and was a thirty-four-year-old corporate finance executive who had been at BM Dutch Petroleum for about four years. Born in 1974, he was a Water Ox.

Any murder is a sad story, of course, but there seemed to be something particularly poignant about this one. He had been working quietly at his desk when he was interrupted. He seemed to be a nice man: Wong remembered from his visit to his room that there were plants on his desk and a photograph of his family—a pretty, dark-skinned wife and two attractive small children. Wong liked murders: they raised his fees. But this did not make him feel guilty as he was doing something worthwhile in return. By efficiently compensating for the negative energy created by the incident and introducing positive energies, he would help the victim's co-workers recover more quickly.

After making these and other short-term changes, the geomancer sat down with the aircraft's senior interior design executive, Sammy Bulowski, and made a list of long-term alterations that would further improve the space inside and outside the conference room: a change of colours for the walls and carpets, for a start. He told her that the normal layout of an aircraft was extremely bad feng shui—long, straight aisles with blocks of seats on either side. The design of Skyparc, though, was far superior.

'Should always avoid straight lines,' he said. 'You have straight lines, energy moves too fast. People feel unsettled. Good fortune disappears. Dead ends are also bad. Energy stagnates. But if you have curves, wavy lines, energy flows slow-slow. Like a river. A river has a main channel, but is never straight. Always it curves. Always there are side branches. Always there are rock pools.'

The feng shui master explained that although you could not see ch'i energy, anyone could feel it. 'It is the life energy... Inside you. Outside you. In every space. In spaces with a lot of people, you feel the people energy. In spaces with no people, you feel the land energy.' Mixed layouts were ideal. Good ch'i moved like a stream of water or a gentle breeze or even a river of humanity. It flowed, it meandered, it sometimes settled and circled for a while in a single spot before moving on. 'When you design things, think of invisible rivers,' he said. An awareness of invisible energy could be found in the wisdom literature of every major society. In Chinese, it was feng shui. In India, vaastu. In European culture, they spoke of ley lines.

As the afternoon wore on, it became evident there was nothing left for him to do: he was merely killing time to justify describing this as a full day's work. And then there were more important decisions to make. He wondered whether to prepare an invoice on the spot—he always carried a book of them in the pocket of his dark, box-shaped Mandarin-collared jacket. Could he ask for the first half of the money now? Or should he wait until the entire two-part assignment had been done, including the London leg? One needed to do a bit of strategic thinking here. Getting money in multiple small lumps sometimes resulted in getting more of it than asking for a single chunk. It seemed to the payer he was paying less. On the other hand, dividing the bills allowed an opportunity for the payer to default on later parts, so perhaps it was better to get it all at once.

Normally, Wong asked for a fifty per cent deposit before he started work. But this assignment had arrived so suddenly they were in Hong Kong on the job before contracts had even been drawn up. Yet he decided he needn't be too worried. It was unlikely someone as famous as the Queen of England would write a bouncing cheque. She had her credibility to think about. Would she be insulted if he refused her cheque and demanded cash? How would he phrase the question: 'If Her Majesty does not mind, please pay cash, thank you?'

As he struggled with this issue, he saw Robbie Manks approaching him.

'Just step this way, Mr Wong, I'd like to talk to you about something,' the PR man said. He grabbed the feng shui master's arm and drew him to the exit of the aircraft.

Wong was immediately worried. Whenever anything unexpected happened as he approached a pay-off moment, he was put on edge. Was Manks trying to wriggle out of his financial duties?

The Englishman certainly looked uncomfortable. But this was not surprising: everyone had looked miserable all day, as was only to be expected at a location where a murder had taken place.

Outside the aircraft, Manks pulled him into the sort of flat-topped truck that carried bags and cargo around the runways. And then he slipped into the driver's seat and set it in motion. Manks noticed Wong's raised eyebrows. 'Don't worry. I can handle it. I've got an HGV licence, you know. HGV—heavy goods vehicle. Was in the army for a while. Done all sorts. I have an advanced driving licence, too. Anyway, prefer to talk while driving. Safer. Less chance of being overheard, and you know me, like to be super discreet. Secret of my success.'

As they drove around the back roads of the airport, keeping well away from the runways, Manks spoke conspiratorially about the London assignment. 'As I said, I wanted to talk to you about doing the next bit of the job, which will involve you heading to London with us for a couple of days.'

'For the family.'

'That's right—The Family. They refer to themselves as The Firm, but that's an in-joke for members of The Family only. We humble workers don't use that term. It's just for members of the monarchy.'

The monarchy—the King and so on.'

'The royal family, actually, which does not have a king at the moment.'

'That's right, no king.'

'Only a queen.'

'She is not married?'

'She is married. She's married to the Duke of Edinburgh.'

'Ah. A queen can marry a duke?'

'Yes, yes, a queen can marry anyone she wants. Even a commoner. Even a foreigner. But not a Roman Catholic. That makes things awkward.'

'Understand,' said Wong, not understanding at all. 'If the queen marries the duke, does the duke become king?'

'No. He was actually a prince—Prince Philip—before she married him. After marriage, he became a duke. The Duke of Edinburgh.'

'So a duke is bigger than a prince?'

'Uh, no, not really. It's all rather hard to explain. He's still a prince, as well as being the Duke of Edinburgh.'

'Oh. He is Scottish?'

'No, he's Greek.'

'Edinburgh is in Greece?'

'No, in Scotland. But he's not Scottish himself. Although they do now live in Scotland. For some of the time. It's a bit complicated.'

Wong was alarmed when the truck they were in skimmed too close to some sort of fork-lift baggage vehicle, nudging it to one side, and causing it to tip over with a loud crash. 'Aiyeeah,' he said, putting his hands to his ears.

Manks did not appear to notice, continuing to talk. 'I've got some very good documents explaining it very simply and clearly. They're in my bag at the hotel and I will be very happy to give you one. It's a short book, really, but admirably clear. Explains everything you need to know about the royal family. I wrote it myself, actually.'

Wong nodded. 'What sort of job is it and how much you pay? I am very, very busy this week.'

'I think the money should not be a problem. We'll pay your usual fee, of course, plus the usual expenses. We pay promptly and discreetly. Indeed, discretion is our middle name. This is what I want to talk to you about at this moment: the importance of discretion.'

'I see.'

'I want to impress upon you the importance of total, utter discretion at all times in this affair. We want you and Ms McQuinnie to do some work with The Family and their main London residence, Buckingham Palace, while regarding this job as entirely private. You will get a lengthy briefing about this, and you will be asked to sign a succession of documents, some of which are very lengthy. Everything related to this assignment must be kept discreet and private. Indeed, I would go so far as to use the word *secret*.'

'Why secret? Something bad happen in Buckingham Palace? Someone murder someone there?'

'No, no, no, no, no! That would be preposterous, not at all.

'It's just that *anything* that the royal family do—well, if the press gets hold of it, that's the end of it. While the royal family is held in high esteem by the vast, vast majority of the public, the press in my country is rather anti-monarchy. Extremely anti-monarchy, you might say. Especially the damned columnists. Evil nightmare monkeys, every last one of them. Anything that leaks out is used against them. If people were to find out that money was being spent on a feng shui master, they would likely raise an enormous fuss—the headlines would say, "Despicable royals use public purse for financing nutters" or something.

They'd say that even when the Queen uses her own money for something.'

'Nutter?'

'A nutter—it's British slang—it just means "crazy person", really. The press would assume anyone who believed in feng shui would be mentally deranged, that's all. No insult intended or anything.'

'No problem. Many of my clients are Asian businessmen. They also like to keep everything secret.'

'Well, this is exactly the same as that.'

'Mostly because they are crooks.'

'Oh. Well, perhaps not exactly like that, in this case.'

They drove around another hangar and began a second circuit of the same trail. But this time, the truck hit a fire hydrant, pushing it over and causing pressurised water to gush out in a fountain behind them. Once more, Manks appeared not to notice—although he did look surprised at the drops of water which fell onto his windscreen. 'Rain out of a clear sky. That's good luck in British superstition,' he said approvingly.

Wong shuffled along the bench seat, closer to the middle of the vehicle, realising it would be safer to stay away from the sides. It was a wise decision. Seconds later, they clipped an airport bus, knocking off its wing mirror.

Manks was lost in his own world, unaware of the results of his erratic driving. He wanted to move on to matters of detail. 'Now, The Family has had a great deal of bad luck in the past couple of decades.'

'Yes, I know.'

'You follow royal news?'

'No, somebody told me.'

'There have been an unwarranted number of high-stress events, tragedies even.'

'Yes, being born with such big ears and long noses—this very negative.'

'I wasn't really thinking of that. I was really referring to the string of bad marriages, the death of the Princess of Wales and so on.'

'Princess of Wales die too?'

'Too...?'

'Lady Diana died in car crash.'

'Oh, I see, no...there isn't *another* princess who died. The Princess of Wales is the formal title of Lady Diana...er...Princess Diana, to be more correct. They are one and the same person.'

'She was a princess from Wales?'

'No, she was a commoner from England. But her title was the Princess of Wales.'

Wong decided it would be wiser to not try and make sense of any of this. He took a small notebook out of his jacket. 'I will need their full names, date of births and place of births. Then I can start research immediately. Take a long time to do full feng shui reading for each member. How many person?'

'Well, I'm really just thinking of the immediate family, so no more than eight or ten people. Perhaps twelve.'

'You know their names, ages, date of births?'

'Of course.' He tapped his temple. 'I've been working with them for years. It's all up here. Who would you like to start with?'

'Head of household. Queen's husband.'

'Ah, Prince Philip. Well, he may be the man of the house, but it would be a protocol problem to consider him the head of the household. So let's start with Her Majesty. Tell you what. Let's pause for a minute.'

He stopped the truck at a forty-five degree angle across the road, opened his briefcase, and pulled out a laptop computer, which he had left on standby. Bringing it to life, he called up a photograph of the Queen. 'Okay. There she is. Elizabeth Regina, born in 1926.'

Wong jotted it down. 'Her family name is Lagina?'

'Regina. Elizabeth Regina. That's not really her family name, but that is the formal name she carries. The women are Regina. Kings are Rex.'

The feng shui master's eyebrows wrinkled at this. 'But Joyce told me that "Rex" means "dog" in England.'

Manks considered this. 'That's true, in a manner of speaking. In the West, the Latin word *Rex* is used as a name for dogs, but also is the word for kings.'

Wong slowly shook his head. No wonder Western civilisation was in such a mess. There was no sense of propriety.

The PR man continued: 'Technically speaking, members of the royal family only have first names. But they are known colloquially as the Windsors, as if it was their surname. But when they have a need to sign their full names on any document, they normally write Mountbatten-Windsor.'

Wong wrote it down. 'So her surname is Mountbatten-Windsor. That was name of her father?'

'Actually, no. I think one could not accurately say that that was her father's name.'

'Oh. You don't know who the father was?'

'Of course we know who the father was!' Manks looked horrified. 'We know her father and her father's father and so on, all the way back to Egbert, King of Wessex, who reigned from 802 to 839 AD. Creating a long and distinguished line stretching back over one thousand years—just think of that, Mr Wong. One thousand years!'

'In China, one thousand years is not long. I come from line of Yellow Emperor, nearly five thousand years ago.'

'Well, that's China. A thousand years is a long time in England.' He stopped. 'I've lost my train of thought.'

'You say you think her father's name not Mountbatten-Windsor.'

Ah, yes, that's right. Well, it's like this. The surname of Queen Victoria's eldest son Edward VII was actually Saxe-Coburg-Gotha, which was the family name of his father Albert, a German. When war broke out between the British and the Germans in 1914, Edward's son George assumed a name that sounded less Germanic and more English.'

Wong nodded. 'I see. Double agent.'

'No. King George V was not a double agent.'

'So why he needs a fake name?'

Manks thought about this for a moment. 'It was sort of for PR reasons. I like to think he was an early example of an individual who instinctively knew the power of good branding.' He puffed out his chest and looked rather proud of this notion.

'Anyway King George v decided to call himself Windsor. That was the name of their castle. Many people these days, of course, assume the castle was named after the family. Not so. The family was named after the castle.'

'So they are going by fake name Windsor, but really they are the, er, Sexy-Cobber-Goater family?'

'Er, not sure if I would call it a fake name. Maybe we should think of it as an adopted name. And it's Saxe-Coburg-Gotha. Hmm. Perhaps I am giving you too much information. Let's go back and start again.'

'Understand. This information top secret.'

'No, it's not exactly secret. But let's just think of them as the Windsors.'

'Queen Windsor.'

'No, we don't say Queen Windsor. Traditionally we only use first names.'

'Elizabeth Vagina.'

'Regina.' Manks started to look seriously concerned at this point. 'Look…let me make it as simple as I can. The most senior members of the family go by first names only. But they do have surnames, which they only use on certain occasions. The family as a whole abandoned their German name and adopted the name Windsor. But in the 1960s, the Queen and Prince Philip decided to call their immediate family Mountbatten-Windsor, to differentiate themselves from the other Windsors.'

'They had a fight?'

'No, they did not have a fight. They just did it because… well, I don't know if there is an official reason. They just did it. Are you following me?'

'Yes,' Wong lied.

'There's one more thing. On some occasions members of the royal family use their title as if it was a surname. For example, His Royal Highness Prince Harry, when he joined the army, was known as Cornet Wales. See how it works?'

The feng shui master thought long and hard about this. 'So for his family name, he uses the name of the country his mother was not born in.'

'Exactly.'

Wong shook his head. 'Very suspicious. All this use of fake names. Must be hiding something.'

'Um. I think you'll find that's not really the case. Anyway, you won't be looking for anything fishy there. You will merely be doing a feng shui reading of the main living area of Buckingham Palace. Do you understand?' Manks was starting to look thoroughly disaffected.

'You want me to find out what is causing bad fortune?'

'In a nutshell.'

'In a nut shell? What nut shell?'

'It's just a figure of speech. It means, well, never mind. Check out the bad fortune in the palace. Alleviate the situation. Stop the bad...what do you call it...bad ch'i, or whatever it is from flowing. Now you will not be working alone. I contacted the gentleman you mentioned yesterday. Mr DK Sinha, the expert in vaastu. He's flying into Hong Kong from Singapore as we speak, and will be joining us on the flight.'

'Wah! Sinha is coming too. This is good news. He is very good man. We are both members of the same union.'

'Very good. Next week, we're flying in Shang Dan, a gentleman based in Shanghai, a medium called Elsa Dottvik from southern Germany, and we've also booked a couple of English people to look over the premises, including Edward Alaine, a famous dowser.'

Wong nodded. 'You are taking good care of your Queen. These sound like good people. Shang Dan is also old friend of mine.'

'Well, I like to do things properly, Mr Wong. You will soon find out that when Manks is involved in anything, every detail is covered. So, do you have any questions for me?'

'When will I be paid?'

'I've slotted you in for three days in Britain. At the end of the third day, you can be paid immediately.'

'The full amount, before I leave Britain?'

'Yes.'

'Cheque or cash? I need something I can cash immediately.'

'We can arrange a cashier's cheque or a bank transfer, if you wish.'

'Good.'

'But we want good service out of you. We want all negative energy banished from The Family and their premises. We want wonderful good news, nothing but good news, from here on in. Do you get me?'

Wong nodded. 'Can. But will cost more. Royals more expensive than people.'

Watching from a distance was a tall stocky man with dark skin and short hair. Wong did not notice the man watching him as he got out of the truck and headed back towards the hangar, nodding politely as Robbie Manks continued to talk.

❀ ❀ ❀

'Hi, Paul, it's me.'

She was shocked to see him. He looked years older. He looked sick. He had purple bags under his eyes, which stood out against the pallor of his dumpling-coloured skin.

Joyce had turned up at prison unannounced and had been flatly refused permission to see him. It was only when she pretended to be his sister and explained she did not live in Hong Kong and would be leaving the territory the next day that the officer at the gate had become fractionally less intransigent. From her time spent living in Asia, she knew she could pull the 'irrational, emotional white woman' trick: for some reason, Asian males seemed to have an inbuilt terror of Caucasian females, and she could always get rules bent if she pretended she did not understand the regulations, or indeed the concept that rules existed, and gave the impression she was about to become screechy and unhinged.

The exhausted door guard had eventually sent her up the ladder to the duty warden. He had consulted a woman who turned out to be some sort of social worker assigned to Paul's case. The woman had argued that the prisoner had refused to speak to anyone, and she was inclined to give Joyce brief contact with him, presumably in case she had a positive effect on him, but only if the prisoner personally consented.

The warden had then relented and allowed her five minutes. 'When I say five minutes, I mean five minutes only,' he said. Unsmiling, he handed Joyce into the care of a guard who had walked with her through five separate layers of lockable gates before she was shown into a cold, empty room painted hospital green, and told to wait by an internal glass window.

Almost ten minutes passed before Paul Barker, looking haggard and unhappy, had been shown to a chair on the other side of the window. In reply to her greeting, Paul merely touched his lips with the tip of his left index finger and waved his right index finger from left to right like a metronome. The message was clear.

'You're not talking?'

He dipped his chin in affirmation.

'Not even to me?'

He said nothing. But his eyes seemed to tighten their grip on hers.

'Paul.' Joyce felt she had been aching for this moment for a year, but now it was here, she didn't know what to say. If they could not use words, how could they communicate? They could not touch, hug or squeeze each other's hands. Would a one-way conversation work?

'If you won't talk to me, that's fine. I believe in you, Paul, and whatever you think is right, that's what you should do. Perhaps I'll just talk anyway and you can listen. We've only got five minutes.'

She looked at his face, and a flicker of a smile crossed his lips.

'Well, what shall I tell you? Shall I tell you what's going on in my life and you can listen, and then I'll ask about you, and you can reply or not reply or nod or not nod or whatever you like, okay?'

He said nothing, but seemed to relax slightly in his chair.

Despite what she had just said, she couldn't think of anything in her life worth talking about in comparison with the drama of the situation he was in, so she turned the subject back to him.

'How are you bearing up? Could you tell me that, at least?'

He spoke, his voice little more than a whisper: 'The Cure, 1980.'

Joyce blinked. Okay, so he wanted to play Obcom. It was better than silence. She thought about it for a few seconds. 'Is it "Boys Don't Cry"?'

He nodded.

'Two can play at this game. Stevie Wonder, 1974.'

A genuine smile.

'So you got that, hey?' Joyce said. '"You Haven't Done Nothin".' What about Billy Swann, 1974— "I Can Help". Will you let me help?'

He shrugged his shoulders. 'Robert John, 1979. Barbra Streisand and Donna Summer, 1979.'

Joyce thought about it. 'Robert John I don't know. Barbra Streisand? Was it "No More Tears"?'

Another smile. Again, a phrase from Paul, spoken in a whisper: 'Gloria Gaynor, 1979.'

'"I Will Survive". Ha ha ha. Very funny. But Paul, this is not a joke. I mean, look, I'm sorry to bring this up, but, well, you're bringing it up yourself. *Will* you survive? This is part of China now. I don't even know what they do to people on murder charges…I mean, maybe there's a death penalty here. I'm sorry to talk about all this, but you have to face the facts. This is really, really serious.'

'Blue Oyster Cult, 1976.'

'"Don't Fear the Reaper",' she offered.

He nodded, pleased with himself. 'Queen, 1975.'

'1975? Was that the year of "Bohemian Rhapsody"? No, it can't be that. *A Day at the Races?*" I know— "You're My Best Friend".'

He raised a thumb.

'This is crazy. We're playing Obcom when you are about to be charged with murder. You have to fight back. You have to talk to the lawyer. That Abel guy. You have to give yourself a chance.'

'Billy Joel, 1976.'

'I'm not playing any more.'

'Billy Joel, 1976.'

'Can't we just talk normally for a minute?'

'Billy Joel, 1976.'

'"Only the Good Die Young". I want you to answer this question for me. Everyone says you are a Talking Heads, 1978. Are you?'

He thought for a second and then shook his head.

'So you're not a "Psycho Killer". Did you shoot—did you Bob Marley and the Wailers, 1974?'

He shook his head again.

'You didn't shoot the sheriff. That's good. At least we are making a start. Was it self-defence? What actually happened in that room?'

He said nothing but looked away briefly.

'Can't think of a song?'

The guard approached. 'Time's up.'

'Please, Paul, say something.'

'Jimmy Buffett, 1977.'

'What? I don't know that one. It's too obscure. Paul. Paul.'

A guard grabbed Paul's arm and started to hustle him away. 'Finish,' the man said.

Paul called out: 'Jimmy Buffett, 1977.'

'James Taylor, 1971,' she shouted as he disappeared. '"You've Got a Friend", Paul. "You've Got a Friend".'

❀ ❀ ❀

Wong sat in a dream on the top deck of the tram as it trundled slowly towards Central. He loved the trolley-cars of Hong Kong island, which moved only slightly faster than the walking speed of an averagely impatient Shanghainese. And it was cheap. Just a couple of Hong Kong dollars, flat fare, to anywhere you wanted to go. Even then, he was always tempted to go further than he needed to and walk back a bit—flat-fare journeys always made him want to do that, keep on going, get more money's worth, even at a cost of inconvenience to himself.

Having said that, trams were not easy vehicles on which to relax. They trundled slowly through the busiest parts of town, and often skimmed close to busy building sites and factories—top deck passengers were frequently in danger of being skewered by pipes swung languidly across the road by half-asleep crane operators. There was no air-conditioning, so the upper windows were left open, allowing a cacophony of jack-hammers and road diggers to reverberate through the seating. Yet despite the pandemonium on both sides, Wong was a happy and relaxed man.

Things were looking good. Manks clearly wanted him to do the feng shui of a huge mansion owned by one of the richest families in the world. The aircraft job had been quickly finished, and would also prove lucrative. The two jobs together would push him well into profit for the year, even after paying Arun Asif Iqbal Daswani.

The only bad thing: he would have to go to London. He had never been out of Asia and had no desire to visit the West. Oh, he knew all about the West. He had seen it on TV enough times to realise that it was a place best avoided. From his under-standing of Western life, gained largely through accidentally watching bits of American sitcoms and Hollywood movies on televisions in Chinese cafes, the West was highly dangerous. It was a place where:

(a) police cars crash into each other and explode on a daily basis;

(b) women are tall and beautiful and like to wear torn clothes while firing machine guns with one hand;

(c) all moving trains have two men grappling hand-to-hand on top while approaching tunnels;

(d) people are rich and live in huge houses but argue all the time, and the more they fight, the more the audiences laugh;

(e) there are many tall buildings, but they all have something strange at roof level: caped men in red costumes, giant animals, gangs fighting, or men chasing each other and jumping from roof to roof;

(f) at street level, cars generally contain one person driving and another who shoots at vehicles in front or behind. Westerners frequently jump from one fast-moving vehicle to another, and they often chase each other in the wrong direction down motorways;

(g) everyone is beautiful, tall and slim—ugly women are beautiful women with glasses and their hair in a bun;

(h) helicopters usually have a person clinging to a landing strut;

(i) it is the norm to drive vehicles into buildings through shop windows.

Similarly, weddings climax with espionage agents driving cars through the wedding cake. And so on, and so on. In short, he had become convinced the West was a violent, unpredictable place full of explosions and drama—much too much excitement in every way.

But the grim screen images suggested there were a few things he would recognise. Police officers in the West were usually corrupt, he considered, and could be bought off with a wad of cash. This gave him comfort—at last, something a person from China could understand.

❀ ❀ ❀

Joyce was also sitting on a tram. She called Jason McWong on her mobile.

'Yeah?'

'Jace, it's Jo. I've just been to see Paul. I have a really, really important question for you.'

'Hit me.'

Did Jimmy Buffett have a hit in 1977?'

'Er. I don't know. Probably.'

'Called?'

'Er, not sure. Was it something called "Attitudes"? Lemme think. I might need to look it up on the internet. Give me five minutes.'

He worked at a computer and didn't need five minutes. He phoned back in less than two. *'Changes in Latitudes, Changes in Attitudes.* It was the title of an album released in January 1977, got to number twelve in the Billboard pop chart. A single too. What does it mean?'

Joyce said nothing, her mind ticking over at high speed.

'Jojo?'

'"Changes in Latitudes, Changes in Attitudes": I think it means Paul was on the top deck of the plane, not on the lower deck where that guy was killed. This is some sort of set-up by the Skyparc people. I'm going to report them to the police.'

She was thrilled. 'This is a breakthrough, Jace. At last, we've got something to work with. Paul's innocent.'

'Cool.'

❀ ❀ ❀

Wong was jarred out of his reverie when the tram he was in pulled level with one going in the opposite direction. Someone inside waved to get his attention. It was Joyce.

'Hey! CF,' she called. 'It's me.'

'You going wrong way. Hotel this way.'

She leaned out of the window of the tram. 'I'm not going to the hotel. I'm going to the police.'

He jerked upright. Now what was the mad *mui-mui* up to? 'What police? Why police?'

'It's Paul. I went to see Paul.'

'Paul is who?'

'Paul Barker. He's the guy they said killed someone on Skyparc. He didn't do it. He's innocent. Totally innocent. He was upstairs, not downstairs where the guy was killed. I'm going to report all this to the cops. I mean, they're charging him with *murder*. I think it's some sort of frame-up. I think the Skyparc people are doing the dirty on him. Maybe even Robbie Manks is involved.'

'No, no, *no*. Do not make trouble. Skyparc is paying us plenty big bucks. I think you should not interfere. Very important. We need the money. Manks has not paid yet. Will pay in a few days, I think.'

'This is murder, CF. He's been charged with murder. He's innocent. He could get sent down for life. I don't know the laws here. He could maybe get executed or something.'

Wong was furious. 'You cannot do this. Very important we receive this payment from Mrs Elizabeth Queen Windsor. We cannot risk this. Maybe after one-two week, you can go and see if you can get your friend out of jail.'

Joyce was angry. 'This is a murder charge, CF. We can't risk wasting time. I'm going to the police station *now* and you can't stop me.'

Wong stood up, his face thunderous with rage. 'Yes I can. I am boss of CF Wong and Associates Private Limited. You are forbidden from doing any assignment to help your friend. Must keep low profile until the Queen job is finished.'

'I quit,' shrieked Joyce, her face turning red and her eyes filling with tears. 'Keep your stupid frigging job. I'm going to the police and you can't stop me.'

Wong was horrified to hear the tram doors click shut on the lower deck. In seconds, he would be whisked westwards, unable to escape, while Joyce would be taken to the east—in the direction of the police station, where she would pour out slanderous thoughts about the company associated with his soon-to-be paymaster, Robbie Manks. This could not be allowed to happen.

He leaned out of the window and tried to shout down to the driver. 'Stop, stop.' He switched to Cantonese: '*Ting che! Ting che!*' But he couldn't be heard above the rumble of the traffic and the racket from the nearby building sites. From below he heard the heavy click of the tram driver engaging the engine. Trams had no steering wheels and the only action the bored drivers did was to pull or push a flat lever that made the vehicle move forwards.

What to do? Wong pondered for a moment whether there was any way he could stop Joyce's tram leaving. If this was the West and he was a Western person, he would leap out of the window of the tram in a single bound, landing squarely in Joyce's tram. That's the sort of thing everyone did over there. But no way would an intelligent man such as himself ever contemplate such a dangerous move.

Out of the corner of his eye, he saw the tram was close to a building in the process of being covered with green netting and bamboo scaffolding. Impulsively, he stretched his body as far as he could out of the window and reached out with both hands. He grabbed a piece of bamboo and tugged with all his might. It barely moved. He pulled again, his skeletal but wiry limbs aching. This time the thick stick budged and came loose from its position. It had not yet been securely tied into place. He jerked the head of the rod into the tram and kept pulling.

The people around him started shouting at him in Cantonese: '*Mutyeh se?*' What's happening? Why was this mad man pulling a piece of bamboo into the tram?

He kept pulling until the long strand of bamboo went into his tram window, right out of the other side, and in through the window of Joyce's tram. She ducked just in time to stop it from braining her. The look on her face told him she knew what he was doing. He was using the bamboo to bind both trams together.

Wong, using his anger to give himself strength, tugged at second and third pieces of bamboo and yanked them from the building site: these, too, he threaded through both trams.

Some of the passengers on his tram started to laugh. The man was crazy, but entertainingly so. Why was he so angry with the foreign girl? And would he really manage to skewer the two vehicles together with long bamboo scaffolding rods?

At that moment, both tram drivers clicked their levers into gear and the trams started to move apart.

The bamboo rods that united them creaked and splintered against the window frames. The passengers on the upper decks of both vehicles shouted at the drivers to stop. With multiple voices working at once, a curious physical resistance, and strange cracking noises from the wooden window frames on the top deck, the drivers got the message and yanked back on their levers. The trams ground to a halt.

Joyce grabbed hold of the bamboo rods and tried to push them back out of the window. 'Don't try and stop me, CF, I have to tell the police what I know.'

'Do not tell the police. You tell police and cause trouble for Skyparc. This will be big trouble for me. I need this money.'

'I don't care about your money. That's all you care about, money. You can have all the money in the world, for all I care. I've got to tell the police about Skyparc before Paul gets locked up for murder or *hung* or something. Murder is serious, CF.' She bashed ineffectually at the rods.

'You tell police to get Skyparc in trouble and you will murder me,' Wong complained, pushing the sticks further into Joyce's tram.

The construction workers on the building site, realising that someone was stealing parts of their bamboo scaffolding, started to yell.

'I'm telling the police and you can't stop me,' shouted Joyce, pushing at the rods again. A powerfully built young man on

Joyce's tram stood up and started to help her push them back out of the window.

'Thanks,' she said.

'I'm doing it for myself,' he replied. 'I'm late for work.'

Wong could hear shouting from downstairs: the driver of his tram was hanging out of the window, looking up and complaining in loud Cantonese: 'Get those sticks out. Get them away.'

Now the men from the building site had clambered spider-like down to the level of the tram and had grabbed the ends of the stolen pieces of bamboo. Far more muscular than Wong, they effortlessly started dragging them out of the trams. The feng shui master ducked out of the way just as the rods flew free and disappeared back into the green scaffolding nets.

'I quit,' Joyce screamed.

'You fired,' shrieked Wong.

Even though they were no longer sewn together with bamboo poles, neither tram moved. This was typical Hong Kong traffic accident behaviour. Any incident on any road, even if it caused no damage, would be followed by all vehicles concerned stopping for twenty minutes until police came and took photographs from every possible angle.

Knowing they were going nowhere for a while, the impatient passengers surged downstairs and raced out of the vehicles' front and back doors—Wong sneaking out with them. He crossed the tracks as quickly as he could, but his newly sacked assistant was younger and faster. She had also left her tram and was already more than one hundred metres away. She was light on her feet: he would never be able to catch up. Fortunately for him, she did not have his sense of direction or his familiarity with Hong Kong: she was running as fast as she could in the opposite direction from the police station.

The feng shui master looked around. They were in Wan Chai. An idea struck him and he turned towards Lockhart Road.

The door of a taxi which had been hovering behind the tram swung open. A heavy, dark-skinned man climbed out and followed.

❀ ❀ ❀

The Village of Seven Pines was a peaceful mountaintop settlement most of the time.

But four or five times a year, typhoon winds would strike and threaten to send villagers over the edge of the cliff.

The wisest men in the village could never guess when the next typhoon would come.

One night, the old dog man who lived with animals in the poorest part of the village started shouting: 'The winds are coming.'

The villagers raced down to the safety of the valley just before the typhoon came.

From that day on, the dog man always gave a successful warning of the approach of a typhoon.

One day, the leader of the village asked the dog man how he knew when the winds were coming.

'The early winds whistle at a pitch that only dogs can hear,' he said. 'When the wind starts to blow, the dogs hear the whistling and wake me. And I wake the rest of you.'

Blade of Grass, messages from the highest of the high are often delivered to the lowest of the low.

From *Some Gleanings of Oriental Wisdom*
by CF Wong

J Oscar Jackson Junior wondered why anyone would be insane enough to open a sauna in Asia. Surely it contravened the whole supply-and-demand principle? The whole damn place was a sauna, wasn't it? Asia was the world's biggest, free of charge, open-all-hours, outdoor hothouse. The air was unbearably hot and humid from morning until night, so why would anyone assume people would pay hard cash to enter a man-made indoor re-creation of the horrible climate outside? But apparently people did.

Perhaps they didn't go in these places for the hot air. Perhaps it was a sex thing. Lord knows that sort of thing was reputed to happen often enough in Asia. The scary thing was that this was apparently winter in Hong Kong. Which meant the air was cooler and less humid than normal. Yet to him it was horribly uncomfortable. How could people live like this?

The man he was tailing had just entered a large building bearing the name 'Diamond Lotus Sauna' so he dutifully followed. He couldn't wait outside. The sauna appeared to be part of a large collection of services sharing an ugly rectangular building the size of a city block, close to where Wan Chai blurs into Causeway Bay—there were clearly going to be myriad exits. It was almost time, anyway.

The tall African-American strode through frosted double-doors and found himself in a rather gloomy, under-lit reception area staffed by two women who would have been pretty, had they been wearing an eighth of the amount of make-up they had on their faces.

One of them immediately shot around the counter and raced to where Jackson was standing. She took hold of his arm. 'Come this way, sir,' she said.

'Er, no, thanks, I'm just having a look,' he stuttered.

'Come, have a look-see, no problem. Sauna, massage, we have everything.' She pulled him through a pair of doors into the main massage centre.

He saw a large room lined on one side with curtains—hospital-style screens that had been wheeled into place around raised beds. On the other side were armchairs and foot-stools. Several men were sitting in these, having their feet massaged. At first glance, it seemed legit.

'Your friend is getting changed. He will be on massage bench number six,' she said, pointing to one of the curtained-off areas.

'My friend?'

'You came with Mr Wong? We will put you in number seven. Next to him.'

'Er, I don't think so. Look, thanks, but—' Then Jackson made a snap decision that surprised even himself. He would go for it. Why not? 'Okay. Just for a while. A quick massage. Short one only, okay?'

His feet were sore. His back ached. He was hungry and tired and overworked. He had had only scrambled eggs with no toast for breakfast—a desperate bid to use the Atkins diet to curb his spreading midriff. What better way to keep an eye on the man he was tailing than to have a massage in the cubicle next to him? The fact that the walls were thin, fabric sheets gave him comfort. This meant: (a) this was real massage, no dodgy stuff (a man in his position could not afford to be seen entering a sex establishment); and (b) if Mr Wong got up and left, he would know about it. He'd be able to thank the woman, get into his clothes at the same time as the man he was tailing, and resume his mission. It was kind of odd though that the women assumed he was 'with' Mr Wong. Had Wong noticed him following, and told them someone would be coming into the sauna in a few seconds? Or had they just made the assumption, since he and Mr Wong had arrived within a minute or so of each other?

'Come, get changed here,' she said. 'Leave your clothes there.'

He stepped into the screened area and stood in front of a full-length mirror, turning to look at himself in profile.

Suit by Barney's.

Shirt by Van Heusen.

Watch by Seiko.

Underwear by Calvin Klein.

Waistline by Dunkin' Donuts.

'Damn,' he said. He slowly removed his clothes, folding them neatly and tucking them into a transparent plastic chest of drawers.

A minute later, he was in his too-tight Calvin Klein boxer shorts, feeling depressed. He had bought the pricey underwear because they were supposed to be flattering. Certainly, they looked wonderful in the advertisements. But a grim truth about fashion was beginning to filter through to him. If you have the right physique, almost everything looks good on you. And if you look like Adonis, the most curious, misshapen garments just make you look even more striking. However, if you have the wrong physique, everything looks bad on you, and things designed to be flattering were the worst of all. 'Damn,' he repeated, looking at his bulging belly. 'Damn, damn, damn.' He'd had a waist, once. Where had it gone? He'd left it at a Taco Bell somewhere. He'd left it at a hundred Taco Bells.

A young woman, who was a little less pretty, a little more businesslike than the receptionist, entered the room. She gestured to him to get on the bed, face down.

He climbed up on the structure with some difficulty. It wasn't just that it was higher than a normal bed. It was his general lack of energy. Today was his eighth day without carbohydrates. This morning, he'd risen early and skipped breakfast, having only that unadorned portion of scrambled eggs. According to the book, the diet was supposed to get easier, but that did not seem to be happening. He felt tired and listless all day, every day.

The bed creaked alarmingly as he climbed on top of it, and only stopped swinging when he was in position. He guessed it was designed for small Asian men with their flat stomachs and no hips. He noticed there was a gap in the padding at the top, and guessed that was where he was supposed to place his face. That way he could lie straight and continue to breathe while whatever was going to happen happened.

'You are having forty minutes or one hour or two hours?' he heard the voice of the woman behind him ask.

'Same as Mr Wong, next door.'

'Okay. You have four-sprinkle service, one hour.'

He lifted his head from the hole in which it was held and looked around at her. 'Four sprinkles? What's that?'

She pointed upwards with her index finger.

That's when he noticed for the first time there was a pulley system affixed to the ceiling containing several suspended bowls. What was in them?

'First sprinkle,' she said, and pulled a tiny string at the side of the first bowl. It tilted and a dollop of something warm, yellow and perfumed fell on his back. She started rubbing it into his skin. It smelled beautiful—*ylang-ylang* or something equally heavenly.

Her hands glided around his back, expertly kneading his tense shoulder muscles and teasing the spaces around his vertebrae. She used her knuckles to get deep into the knotted flesh and her fingertips to smooth and soothe. Within seconds, Jackson was so relaxed he was almost asleep. Man! Now *this* was living. This was what earning your bread and butter should be all about. He was technically working, and doing a very demanding job, yet at the same time he was enjoying the most wonderful massage of his life. Until this minute, he had not realised just what a miracle a good masseuse could achieve. He could feel the stress dissolving from his tired bones, as if tiredness was a thick, oily liquid clogging his engines, and this woman had pulled out the sump plug and let it flow away.

This part of the massage session went on for a good fifteen or twenty minutes; it was hard to tell, since he was drifting in and out of sleep for the entire period. He hadn't realised he had dropped off until he heard a voice cutting into a dream he was having of being at home with his children and ex-wife: happier days.

'Now turn over on your back,' the masseuse said.

He languidly shuffled his heavy body over. He noticed that while he had been sleeping, she had gently removed his shorts, leaving his nether regions covered only by a soft white towel. All his personal bits were covered, so there was nothing improper about it—yet it was kind of exciting to be more or less naked with this stranger.

Lying on his back, he could stare above him, at the suspended row of bowls, each of which seemed to contain some form of aromatic oil or cream. The masseuse then gave a brief bow and left the room. He craned his head to look out through the crack in the screens. Next to him, in screened area number six, he saw a scrawny ankle—Wong, who was having the same treatment.

A minute later, another woman appeared and gently tapped the next bowl, which tilted, slopping a dollop of some other delicious-smelling substance on his body. The first one had been yellow, warm and silky. The second was cold, orange and sweet. It smelled of jasmine, ginger flowers and lavender.

The second massage was, if anything, even more enjoyable than the first. Instead of relaxing him, it invigorated his skin. This time, the woman used her fingertips, knuckles and elbows to dig firmly but gently into his flesh. It was as close as possible to being tickled, without actually making him laugh or jerk around. The experience lasted for a delicious ten minutes or so, before this masseuse also bowed and left the room.

The 'sprinkle service' was great—and there were two more rounds to go. J Oscar Jackson Junior closed his eyes and gave a short snort of a laugh. He did not know how much this was costing, but it would be worth it. *And* he was going to charge it to his expense account. He must find an Asian massage service near his office in London. Get into the habit of doing this once a month, or once a week or something.

After a minute, a third staff member appeared and gestured for him to roll over. She immediately reached up to tip a third bowl, which slopped a purplish substance on his back. This was scratchy, full of gritty bits. After an unsure beginning, Jackson decided the feeling it gave him was a positive one; one which should be classified under the heading 'hurts so good'. The scratchy stuff was slightly painful, but undeniably satisfying. After doing his back and thighs, she worked carefully on his wrists and arms.

'Now for final sprinkle, number four,' she said and bowed. As she left, she gestured to someone just out of his range of vision.

He craned his head to note a man entering the room: a thin man wearing dark round glasses. It must be one of those blind masseurs, he decided. The lights were very low, so it was hard to focus on him, but the old man looked a bit like Wong.

'What's the next bit?' he said. 'I don't want to take too long.'

By this time, a good forty or forty-five minutes must have passed. It would be bad news if the man he was tailing finished before him and made good his escape. Jackson angled his head in the other direction and saw a pair of thin, bony ankles between the cracks of the curtains: the feng shui master appeared to be still in place.

'Okay, let's get the fourth sprinkle done, and then we'd better stop,' Jackson said, turning himself over. 'This better be my last one.'

The old masseur stepped forward. He flicked a bowl very gently with a fingertip, and a tiny splash of red liquid flew out of the bowl and descended to Jackson's flesh. It landed on his stomach—and immediately began to burn.

'Ow, ow, owww!' he squealed. 'That hurts. I think I'll skip this one.'

He tried to sit upright, to move his body out of the way of the bowl, to try to wipe the burning liquid off his stomach, but he found himself trapped. His wrists and ankles had been tied down with some sort of light, silky material.

'What?' He tugged hard at the material, but couldn't move. It was a strong fabric, some sort of reinforced cloth.

'Hey? What's going on? Untie me. Now.'

'Relax,' said the man, wiping the drop of red stuff from his stomach. 'This won't hurt. Maybe.'

He took off his glasses. It was CF Wong.

With one movement, the feng shui master whipped Jackson's towel upwards, leaving his genitalia exposed. Then he yanked at the pulley apparatus holding the essential oils. The whole system moved backwards, so that the bowl of red fiery stuff was now positioned right over Jackson's private parts.

'Hey man, what are you doing? Get that stuff away from my, my, bits. Gimme my towel back. Look, I don't want that stuff on me. And I want to be untied, right now, right this minute.'

'Why you follow me?' Wong barked.

'Me, I'm nobody, I just wandered in here. I don't know you from Adam.'

The feng shui master lifted up his long bony finger and stroked the bowl.

'No, no, don't drop that stuff on me. No, please.'

'Why you follow me?'

'I don't even know who you are, I—'

Wong tipped the bowl and a tiny drop of red liquid flew out.

'No-no-no-no,' screamed Jackson, trying to move his hips out of the way.

The geomancer flicked the towel he was holding and intercepted the drop.

Jackson let out a gasp of relief. 'What is that stuff, anyway?'

'Finest Hainanese chilli sauce,' Wong said, putting a drop of it from his fingertip into his mouth. 'Very tasty. Very strong. Very burny. Why you follow me? Who are you?'

'My name's Jackson. I'm an envoy for—for—for someone.'

Wong let his index finger drift back up towards the bowl.

'For a powerful man. A rich man. A man who can pay you. Pay you lots and lots of money! Please. Really.'

Wong's finger continued its journey towards the bowl of chilli sauce. 'Name?'

'I can't.'

His finger touched the edge of the bowl, which started to tilt.

'No, no, I'll tell you, it's a member of the royal family.'

The feng shui master's puzzlement showed on his face.

'What do you mean? Already I am working for royal family. Mr Manks.'

Jackson squirmed on the table. 'Why don't you untie me? I can talk much better at a table over a nice cup of coffee.'

Wong shook his head. 'I think you talk better under a nice bowl of chilli sauce.' He reached for it again.

'No, no, don't tip it. I'll talk. I'll tell you anything you want.'

'Who are you working for? The Queen? Like Mr Manks?'

Jackson shook his head. 'No. I'm working as a private envoy. There are many groups working for members of the royal family. I work for Prince Charles, in an entirely private capacity. I know Manks—he's a public relations man, he's official, he's listed, he's an employee of a subcontracted company. I work for a charitable foundation and report directly to my boss, but I am on a rather more discreet mission at the moment.'

'Discreet. Always this word—discreet.'

'Yeah, well it's important to the British.'

'You are not British.'

'I'm American.'

'Why you follow me?'

'I was checking you out — trying to get a feel for what sort of person you were—and your partner, Ms McQuinnie. You see, we're interested in using you to do some work for us—some serious investigating for us.'

'But Mr Manks already asked me. He wants me to do feng shui for the family members, for Buckingham Palace and all that.'

Jackson shook his head. 'That's not what I mean. That's something separate. That's some cockamamie scheme that the—that another member of the family has thought up, to try to get all the weir—I mean—get some unusual, er, esoteric sorta people to use their skills to help improve things. It's not what the Prince of Wales asked me to do.'

'He ask you to do what?'

A man was killed on board Skyparc yesterday morning. A young guy, Paul Barker, a member of an activist group called Pals of the Planet, has been charged with the murder.'

'So?'

'Pals of the Planet has a number of major sponsors, some of whom are public, some of whom are discreet. It may be that the Prince of Wales has an interest in the group.'

'You mean he is secret sponsor?'

'I didn't exactly say that. But Prince Charles was told immediately about the arrest on Wednesday and was upset about it. He believes Mr Barker is innocent. I'm an envoy of his, and happened to be part of this mission. He asked me to see what I could do. I asked around and heard about your reputation with criminal cases. I understand you are doing some feng shui work on Skyparc, and Ms McQuinnie is a supporter of Pals of the Planet. We would like you to investigate discreetly and find out who killed the BM Dutch Petroleum executive. So that Mr Barker can be released and Pals of the Planet cleared. Before anyone gets negative ideas about the organisation and traces connections upwards to its sponsors. We want to avoid trouble at all costs.'

Wong nodded. 'I see. So why you following me?'

'Like I said, I just wanted to check you guys out. When you were described to me, you sounded, well, a bit kinda flakey... know what I mean? I decided I shouldn't just hire you, but would try and check you out first.'

'Flakey.'

'Yeah. You know, eccentric. Not in a bad way. Just, uh, offbeat. You know. Distinctive, if you like.'

Wong thought for a moment.

'Not interested. Sorry.' He turned to leave.

'No, wait, wait, wait. Don't you want this case? I thought that's what you did.'

'Very busy. Soon going to be working for the Queen, Queen of England, Queen of Australia, and so on and so forth.'

'We can pay you.'

'I think your boss not as rich as the Queen. The Queen is one of the richest human beings in the world.'

'Mr Wong.'

'Yes.'

'The Prince of Wales is heir to the throne.'

'Air?'

Jackson racked his brain to find the right words. 'Heir. Like, you know, eldest child. What you would call Number One Son.'

Wong was listening.

'Yes,' said Jackson. 'He is Number One Son of the Queen. He will inherit everything the Queen has. *Everything*. He will be the next king, as soon as she dies, or she steps down. She's over eighty. It might not be long.'

Wong was intrigued. 'He will inherit everything the Queen has.'

'Yes. He gets it all. And he has his own fortune, as well.'

The feng shui master's eyes flashed.

'It's really worth getting friendly with us,' Jackson added.

'So he can pay well?'

'Whatever Manks has promised you for feng shuiing Buckingham Palace, we'll pay you the same.'

'How about double?'

'Okay, double.'

'No.'

'Please.'

'Triple?'

'Triple, then.'

Wong nodded. Then, quick as lightning, his hand flicked upwards and tipped out the contents of one of the bowls.

Jackson screamed and tried to wriggle out of the way.

But the stuff that fell onto his genitals was from bowl number five, a soothing, cooling blue-white substance based on cream and vanilla essence.

'Dear God,' said Jackson.

Wong called over his shoulder as he left the room: 'Enjoy the rest of your massage. Meet you in tea room afterwards.'

The pretty young woman from the reception desk approached J Oscar Jackson Junior. She cracked her knuckles and smiled at him. 'My turn.'

❀ ❀ ❀

It had taken almost an hour to find a police station. Hong Kong was really badly signposted. Joyce was walking up the stairs to the main door when her mobile rang.

'Joyce? Is me,' said Wong. 'I change my mind. I think very important we investigate murder in Skyparc. I think your friend innocent. He is good guy.'

'What's going on?'

'Mr Paul not guilty, I think.'

'Is this a joke?'

'No. Very sorry. I make a mistake. I am thinking about it. I am thinking, oh, Joyce's friend, very good man, very innocent, no problem at all. He must be not guilty. We must save him.'

'What are you not telling me?'

'Nothing, nothing. It is important to save not guilty persons. He is not guilty, so we must save him.'

'Is someone offering you money to investigate Paul's case?'

'No, no, not at all, definitely not, no way, indeed.'

'Who is it? How much money?'

'No one. Just a bit.'

Joyce put one fist to her hip and snapped sternly into the phone: 'Look, I don't know what you're up to, CF, but this is no joke. Paul's going to be done for murder. I think I need to go to the police. Tell them what I think. He was on the top deck, not the lower deck. He won't talk to anyone. I'm the only person he's told. I'm the only person who has been given that bit of information. Someone needs to investigate that angle. This is a big deal.'

'No! Don't go to the police. Just let us do it ourselves. I forbid you to go to police.'

'I don't work for you any more, remember? I quit. *And* you sacked me.'

'No, that was only a small joke. You are my number one staff.'

'Now this is really fishy.'

'So? You agree? You not go to police, we investigate murder your friend did not do?'

'So I'm going to get my job back then? I want better pay and conditions.'

'What pay and conditions?'

'That's just it. I get no pay and conditions to speak of. Things are going to have to change. I want a desk by the window.'

'No room for you to have desk by window. Very bad feng shui for you to have desk by window. You are a woman. Bad *shar* to give you desk there.'

'I'm going to the police. I'm actually already at the police station, just going up the steps.'

'No. You have desk by window, no problem. Bad *shar* energy, can fix easily.'

'I'm going to speak to Mr Pun about my salary and holidays.'

'I speak to Mr Pun about your salary and holidays.'

'I'm speaking to him, end of story.'

Wong did not like the new assertiveness he could hear in Joyce's voice. This tricky business was changing the dynamics between them. 'If you go to police, no use. You have no evidence. Does not help your friend. I have some evidence. I went into room of murder victim on airplane today.'

'You did? What did you find?'

'Meet me. I tell you.'

Joyce lapsed into silence. She had to make a quick decision. Should she go to the police? Or should she trust Wong? She realised, if she was honest with herself, she was feeling very unconfident about explaining the whole business to the police. Paul had only told her he was on the wrong deck at the time of the shooting, and he had delivered the news using an Obcom reference. What if the police officer she was talking to didn't get it? Did people in Hong Kong listen to 1970s music anyway? Would they be familiar with the single 'Changes in Latitude, Changes in Attitude'? If Wong had found an easier way to prove Paul was innocent, it would be ideal. Yet she was suspicious. Wong's change of attitude was bizarre. It could only be explained by one thing. Somebody had decided to pay him to prove Paul was not guilty. Well, it didn't matter who was paying who, or how much money was involved. If the outcome was that Paul got off the murder charge, then it had to be good.

Joyce made up her mind. 'Okay. I won't go to the police...
yet. Look, I'll meet you back at the hotel in a couple of hours.
There's one more person I want to see. My friend Nina got me
the address of Kaitlyn MacKenzie. She was the girl who sneaked
Paul on to the aircraft. I want to know if there's anything else
she can tell us about what really went on on Skyparc. If we are
really going to help Paul get off this murder rap, this woman
may be able to tell us something useful.'

❀ ❀ ❀

Joyce found Kaitlyn MacKenzie's address easily, but there was
no one home. It was in a small, old block close to what was officially called Soho, but which she thought of as Escalatorland—a
settlement of restaurants and apartments on both sides of the
long, open-air, moving walkway running up the mountain that
dominated the central part of Hong Kong island. She decided
to wait. 'I'll give you half an hour, Ms MacKenzie,' Joyce said to
no one in particular, finding a step to sit on and shuffling up a
podcast on her iPod. She'd downloaded a long interview with
Stongo of The Rogerers the previous night and was happy to
listen to it for the third time. His voice was soooo sexy.

Thirty-one minutes later, bored and tired, Joyce had just risen
to her feet and dusted the back of her clothes, when an immacu-
lately dressed young woman in her late twenties stepped out of a
taxi on Staunton Street. She was laden with shopping bags.

'Kaitlyn MacKenzie?'

'Yeah. You are?'

'I'm a friend of Paul's. Paul Barker? The guy on the plane?
I just wanted to thank you for what you did for him. I know it
didn't work out, but you were just trying to help—I realise that.
I'm really grateful.'

'Look. I can't really talk. I'm kinda busy right now. I'm sorry
about what happened. But I really just want to forget all about it.'

Joyce scanned the array of shopping bags she was carrying.
'You've just been sacked and you're shopping at Zara?'

'Uh…yeah…just picking up a few things. Essentials.'

'No, I totally understand. I'm the same. When I've got no money and everything's gone pear-shaped, I go out and spend spend spend. I mean, I wouldn't go to Armani or somewhere really expensive, but Zara—I mean, you've gotta have these things for your, for your, self-esteem.'

'Yeah…Hey, I gotta go,' said Kaitlyn, fumbling a key out of a pocket.

'Let me help you.' Joyce snatched the key out of her hand. Any chance of a cup of tea?'

'Look, I don't think I can help you. I think you should—'

Joyce screamed. 'Awesome! Is that a Miu Miu Matelasse handbag?'

'Yes, it—'

'You got taste, girl.'

'I needed a treat.'

'You definitely did. You also need a cup of tea. This week must have been a total nightmare. I'll make you one.'

Kaitlyn MacKenzie paused, and then decided: 'Okay. Quick cup of tea. But then I have to pack. I'm really busy. I'm going on a trip.'

'No worries.'

They took the lift upstairs in awkward silence. The temperature between them warmed when Joyce took several of the shopping bags and made wildly approving noises at Kaitlyn's shopping choices: 'Jimmy Choo, wow. You're an A-grade shopper, I can see that.'

The apartment was small and rather untidy, but Joyce put that down to the shock of the past couple of days. Designer clothes were strewn on the floor. It fitted, she decided. Kaitlyn was so immaculate on the outside, it made sense her having a place where she could slum it, let it all hang out.

''Scuse the mess.'

'It's okay. You weren't expecting a guest. And it's tidier than my place.'

The other woman lowered her shopping bags to the floor and went into the kitchen—actually a tiny indentation in the main room—to put on a kettle.

'I'm sorry to seem unfriendly. It's just that this is a difficult time for me.'

'I can imagine. You just lost one of your colleagues. I mean, it must be awful to know someone and have that person lose his life. Especially with you having played a part in it, so to speak. I mean, how awful. You must feel it's partly your fault.'

'No. It wasn't my fault.'

'I'm not saying it was your fault. I was just saying that you probably feel it was your fault, you know—it's human nature to blame ourselves for things.'

'No. I don't think it was my fault at all.'

Joyce knew when to give up on a line of argument. 'Yeah, you're right, I guess. That's the best attitude to take. I'm right behind you.'

'How do you like your tea?'

The conversation descended into icy bits of small talk for the next five minutes. Kaitlyn MacKenzie was clearly reluctant to discuss the events of the past few days.

Joyce tried to broach the subject of Wednesday from several directions, but to no avail. She decided to just talk honestly about herself and Paul. 'Paul and I have been special friends for ages— mostly just on email, though. I don't live here—I live in Singapore. It's scary to think I might never see him again, if he's going to be locked up for the rest of his life. Is there anything he said to you that you can remember? Anything that might help me get a handle on what happened, and why it happened? I can't believe he intended to kill anyone. He's just not that sort of person.'

Kaitlyn shook her head. 'I hardly spoke to him. He approached me and asked me if I could get him onto Skyparc. I said I could.'

'He's a good guy, isn't he?'

'He said he was an environmentalist and that what he and others were doing would eventually save the earth for us and our children and generations to come. It sounded good. It sounded like the right thing to do. He turned up on Wednesday, and I used my card to get him through the security system. Some minutes later, all hell broke loose. I gave a million interviews to police. I lost my job. That's it. That's all I know. What happened on the plane wasn't anything to do with me.'

'It must have been awful for you when you heard about the killing.'

'Yes. No. As I said, that part of it wasn't really anything to do with me.'

'But you lost one of your colleagues. And your job. That must have been really awful.'

'Yeah,' she replied, absently.

'What are you going to do? Going to take a break? Or are you going to start looking for another job?'

'I've got another job lined up.'

'Already?'

'I'm going to work for the Queen.'

'You never are.'

'I am, actually.' Kaitlyn couldn't resist a grin.

'Wow! How did you swing that?'

'There's lots of people with royal connections on Skyparc. There's even one of the junior royals there. And there's also this lobbyist guy called Robbie Manks, who is a sort of PR consultant to the royal family. He approached me with an offer. I'm going to work with him from now on. It's kinda hush-hush, but it'll be announced eventually.'

'I know Robbie Manks. In fact, my boss is doing some work for him at the moment. When do you start?'

'Tomorrow. I'm flying to London on Skyparc.'

'So's my boss. I was supposed to be going too, but now I don't know for sure.'

'Oh. Well, perhaps if you do come on the plane, it would be better if we talked then?' Kaitlyn put down her teacup and started picking clothes up off the floor. 'I have so much to do tonight.'

It was too obvious a dismissal to miss. Joyce finished her tea and stood up to leave. 'Sure.'

Chapter Four

Friday

FRIDAY DAWNED MILD and misty. The sky was a hazy blue-white. Hong Kong lost much of its sultriness on the more pleasant days in December and the breezes were considerably cooler than those of Singapore. The air was fresh-tasting as Joyce McQuinnie left the hotel and headed in a straight line towards the nearest branch of Pacific Coffee. Halfway down the street she spun on her heel and pointed directly at the man following her.

'Him,' she yelled.

Two men appeared from nowhere and grabbed his arms, pinning them behind his back. One was a large Eurasian youth with straggly hair. Another was a middle-aged Chinese man with small glasses.

'Gotcha,' said the younger one.

'Step backwards and don't cause any trouble,' said the older one.

'Whoa, whoa, whoa,' J Oscar Jackson Junior said. 'Hey! Let me go. I'm not doing any harm here.'

'You are following our friend—an innocent and defenceless young woman, or at least she could be. And that's doing harm in our book,' said Abel Man Chi-keung.

Jackson stopped struggling. 'You know what? I am just not cut out for this espionage lark. I'm going to go back to my office job at the foundation the day I get back—no, the minute I get—no, the minute you guys let go of me. I'll resign on the phone.'

Jackson was so urbane and non-threatening Abel let go of him immediately, but Jason McWong kept his grip tight.

'You're wrinkling my Armani jacket,' Jackson said.

'Like I care,' growled Jason.

'And your Comme des Garçons blouson.'

Jason quickly let go and stepped away.

Joyce approached him. 'What do you want?'

'I want a private conversation with you.'

'Why don't you just ask me?'

'I was about to.'

'You were following me yesterday. I saw you.'

'I was following you yesterday. And Mr Wong. I was checking you guys out before offering you a very important but rather delicate assignment. I spoke to Mr Wong at length yesterday, and I was approaching you this morning with the intention of merely talking to you. He told me yesterday you know more about the matter I have an interest in than he does. So think of me as a friend, or even a prospective employer, a source of paid work, if you like.'

'Most people who offer us assignments phone us up or send emails. They don't sneak around behind us like creeps.'

'I have to work more discreetly than most people. I'm sorry if I scared you. I apologise.'

'Anyway, I'm kind of busy right now. We have assignments up to our ears. And so do my friends. We have a very important case to deal with.'

Jackson knew he had to put his cards on the table. 'We may have something in common. The assignment I want to offer you concerns Paul Barker of Pals of the Planet,' he said. 'My people want to get him out of jail. We think he's innocent.'

Joyce's jaw dropped. 'Talk,' she said.

They all headed to Pacific Coffee, and for the next ten minutes, Joyce listened to Jackson with her eyes and ears wide open. He was saying exactly what she needed to hear. The young people ordered giant coffees and piles of sticky pastries while J Oscar Jackson Junior contented himself with a cup of herbal tea, no milk or sugar. There was a huge row of cabinets filled with food, but he was dismayed to note that every single item seemed to be wickedly, frighteningly carbohydrate-based. But Joyce hardly ate. She hung on his every word as he told her he wanted to get justice for Paul Barker and believed Pals of the Planet was a major force for good.

'But that's incredible. Should I believe any of this?'

'Why shouldn't you?'

'It's too perfect. It's ludicrous. I thought I was the only person on this planet who believed Paul was innocent and then my boss suddenly changes his mind and now you—a big, expensively dressed corporate kind of dude—come along and say the same thing. It's too weird. It just seems so…where are you going?'

Jackson had risen to his feet. He stretched like a cat. His stomach rumbled and he winced. 'I'm going to my hotel to get my bag. Then we're going to the airport.'

'You may be, but I'm not. I gotta stay here and help Paul.'

'I think you're going to come with me. You are going to do no good at all by staying here. You'd be able to visit Paul from time to time, make him feel better, but that's it. He won't even talk to you. He's not talking to anyone. You're better off coming with me. You can meet my team in London, and then we have a chance of springing him.'

'Why London?'

'Listen, lady, I haven't got time to go into everything just now, but here's the deal in a small package. To get someone on a murder charge out of prison, you need big guns. A few of his friends hanging around moping is not going to cut it. You need a top team. You need big lawyers. You need QCs. You need finance. You need strategy. You need people with connections who know what they're doing. We're going to go to London, where I understand you and your boss have an assignment anyway, and, on the side, we're going to have some meetings and get the process underway to get Paul out of prison. We're going to give you some detailed briefings, and then when you get back here, you spend as long as it takes doing research and investigation. The thing won't come to court for months, so you'll probably have time. But we want to work with you to get Paul Barker and Pals of the Planet cleared. Sound good?'

'I can't go on Skyparc. I've been negatively vetted.'

'I can overrule that. My people have higher clearance than security at Skyparc Airside Enterprises.'

Joyce felt torn about leaving Paul in jail and flying away from him, but what this American guy was saying made sense. What they needed most of all was a strong team of qualified supporters together, and if that meant visiting Jackson's mysterious backers in London, that's what they had to do.

'Jojo, you go to London. We'll visit Paul,' said Nina.

'We'll talk Obcom with him,' Jason added. 'If that's what he wants.'

'Your parents won't approve.'

'Hey, I'm an adult now.'

Joyce turned back to Jackson. 'You said you spoke to CF Wong about this? My boss? Are you the guy who changed his mind about Paul?'

'I did. He's cool. We'll all be flying together to London on Skyparc. It all fits together rather well. We leave this afternoon. I'll tell you more about what's going on when we're in the air.'

'But you'll be in business class, I'll bet. Or first.'

Jackson smiled. 'Little lady, we're travelling on Skyparc. It's *all* first class.'

❄ ❄ ❄

Wong and McQuinnie arrived early at the airport so they would have at least an hour to look around and get a feel of what happened—or what was supposed to have happened. Nicola Teo, after a lot of arm-twisting, had agreed to escort the two of them into the Skyparc hangar to talk to the staff.

Their first job, Wong decided, was to talk to the witnesses, which meant the technical staff who had seen the shooting. The feng shui master was soon chatting in Cantonese with several of the engineers.

Teo pointed Joyce in the direction of a woman standing by herself, a thirty-something Chinese woman in overalls who was filling in some notes on an electronic clipboard. 'Speak to that woman. She's a senior member of the team you want to talk to, and she speaks English. Her name's Poon Pik-kwan. I think her English name is Tammy.'

Joyce raced over to her. 'Excuse me, are you Ms Poon?'

'Yes?' she answered, suspicion in her voice.

'Your team witnessed the murder on Wednesday? We're helping with the investigation and we'd like you to tell us exactly what you saw.'

'You a police officer?'

'No. We're from a, er, independent investigating organisation. Teo said I should speak with you.'

'Well, we were working on Skyparc. There'd been some worry about the window seals and we were just checking them. They were fine. A little adjustment on one or two of them, my guys said. Replacing loose rivets, that sort of thing.'

'What did you *see*? You were looking through the windows of the plane when it all happened?'

'I heard the shots. We all did. Hangars are echoey places. I didn't see it myself. One of my men did. Danny Tang.'

'Does he speak English?'

'Yes. He's a Chinese-American intern. Went to school in Texas.'

'Can I talk to him?'

'You a detective? You don't look like a detective. You got proof of identity?'

Joyce shook her head. 'We're not police. My boss and I are from a feng shui agency. We want to make sure nobody gets bad fortune because of what happened. We want to alleviate all the negative energy caused by the death.'

'Oh,' said Poon with a broad smile. 'That's different. Good, good, good. I was thinking we should get someone like you in. I guess someone upstairs had the same idea. Murder is very bad fortune. We should really have a full exorcism.'

'Yes, I guess so. Listen, the windows are big on this plane. Could someone get in or out through the windows?'

The engineer shook her head. 'The windows don't open. But you're right—the windows are unusual on this aircraft.'

'I've never seen rectangular windows on a plane before.'

'That's true. All others have oval ones—every type of plane, every brand, every country.'

'Why is that?'

'It's to do with metal fatigue. One of the first commercial passenger planes of any size was the de Havilland Comet in the 1950s, and it had rectangular windows. But the fuselage kept cracking and depressurising. To find out why, they sank one into a swimming pool. They found out that the corners of the windows became stressed—the constant pressurising and depressurising of the plane caused cracks at the corners of the windows.'

'That doesn't happen with round windows?'

'Correct. You know how hard it can be to rip open a plastic bag, like a bag of crisps?'

'Yeah.'

'But if the manufacturer puts a tiny nick in the plastic bag, it's much easier to tear open?'

'Yeah.'

'The same principle works with aircraft windows. The right-angled corners of square or rectangular windows are like the nick in a plastic bag—the metal tears much more easily there than anywhere else.'

'I see. Round windows are like a plastic bag with no nick. You can't tear them.'

'Exactly.'

'So how come Skyparc's got rectangular windows? Are they dangerous?'

'They would be, except they're reinforced at the corners. The special windows add a bit of weight, but given the scale of the A380 airframe, it's negligible. It's really just a matter of taking advantage of modern design capabilities.'

'Going back to my question: could anyone get in or out through a window? If they took the window right out, for example?'

Poon shook her head. 'No. None of the windows has been removed. They're embedded. It would be a big job to take one out and replace it. We just did some very minor work on the rivets. That's all.'

Joyce was disappointed. She'd hoped to be able to suggest that the 'real' killer entered and exited the plane through a window. 'Tell me again, who actually saw the shooting?'

'Danny Tang—he's over there, doing some paperwork.'

Joyce thanked Ms Poon and approached a young man in blue overalls, who seemed to be in his mid-twenties. 'Er...hello, Mr Tang? I'm investigating the shooting on Wednesday. Can I ask you a few questions?'

He looked up and spoke in a slow drawl. 'Same ones the police asked, I guess?'

'Probably. Can you tell us in your own words what happened?'

'Yep. That's the first question they asked. Well, it was like this. Ms Poon and I were working on the window mountings just in front of the wing.'

'Ms Poon and you?'

'Yeah.'

'She said she didn't see anything—that only you were at the window.'

'Yeah, well, she was around. But she went to work on the wheel mountings. I guess you're right. I was the only one who really saw what happened.'

'Go on.'

'Well, I was standing on the platform checking the window mounting. Most of them were fine, but there were a couple which could have been tighter, which we…which I did some work on.'

He paused and half-closed his eyes, as if trying to recreate the scene in his mind. He spoke slowly and carefully, pausing at intervals to chew the gum he was holding in his cheek.

'Let me see, I had just lowered the screw gun when I heard some shouting. I look up through the window and see some people moving inside the plane—two guys. The shutter is three-quarters down, so I couldn't see much. I didn't want to stare—just wanted to get on with the job. But then there's a shot. That grabs my attention. I put my whole face to the window.'

'Yeah? And what did you see?'

'I saw the dead guy—well, he wasn't dead then, he had just sort of fallen backwards, against the wall. He had obviously just been shot. He was like falling slowly down the wall, you know? Then there was another guy, a young guy. He had a gun. He shot three more times. One hit the falling guy in the shoulder as he fell and the other two went into the wall of the plane. Luckily they were soft-tipped shells and the plane walls in that room are reinforced mahogany panelling. So they exploded on impact, messed up the panelling, but didn't damage the plane itself. They didn't, like, go through the plane walls. Sorry to sound callous but we are trained to worry about the fabric of the plane—that's kind of our focus, if you know what I mean.'

'But did you get a good look at the young man? Did you see his face?'

'I did a bit—just for a couple of seconds. He was a white guy, early twenties, high forehead, biggish nose, wore green socks. Dark brown hair, a bit streaky. Bit of acne on his cheeks, baggy eyes.'

'Thanks,' said Joyce, trying to smile, but with a sinking heart. Paul's own mother would not have been able to give a better description.

The next person she interviewed was the Skyparc chief of security, an Australian named Ryan Drexler, who she found in a room full of monitors on level two of the hangar.

'This is state of the art security,' Drexler boasted, showing a mouth full of Hollywood-white teeth. 'As well as the cameras in the hangar, we have cameras on the plane itself, including one on the only entrances to the lower and upper aisles. They're constantly running. But that's common enough. Our really fancy extra on this particular plane is this. We call it the electric net.' He tapped fiercely on a keyboard and brought onto the screen an outline of the aircraft from above. It was crisscrossed with a fine network of green lines.

'There are circuits built right through the shell of the aircraft which detect moving heat sources—in other words, people. But they would also work if, say, a dog or rat or some other animal got loose in the hold or elsewhere on the plane. Any unwanted presence on an aircraft, human or otherwise, is simply not tolerable these days.'

He tapped the keyboard again, looking through a list of records. 'Now I'm going back to the precise time of the murder. Here we are.'

After a few seconds, a diagram of the main body of the aircraft appeared on the screen, and there was a glowing area close to the back.

'See that? That shows there was one human being, or animal of a similar size, on the plane at that time. We happen to know that that was Mr Seferis.'

He clicked over to another screen.

'These sensors take a snap of the plane every few minutes—we can choose the interval. Now we have the next picture. You see how the glow has spread and seems to have two centres?'

'Two people on board.'

'Right, kid. The murderer has come on board at this time and is in the room with the victim.'

'Could he have been upstairs, or below in the luggage department? At a different level?'

'In theory, yes. The sensors are not three-dimensional but send a beam from the ceiling of the plane straight to the lower floor. They could have been on different floors. But I think it's more likely they were on the same floor, in the same room—given that the technicians saw them through the window, it seems beyond doubt that was what happened.'

Joyce nodded. Things looked very bad for Paul.

'And then we also have the video tapes, showing the perpetrator—'

'The suspect.'

'Hmm?'

'He's innocent until proven guilty, so he's just a suspect at the moment, not a perpetrator.'

'Whatever. Let's just call him the bad guy, shall we? The intruder, if you like. Anyway, here he is.' Drexler pressed a button and a security tape played. It clearly showed Paul coming into the aircraft and going up the stairs to the upper deck.

'Green socks,' the security chief said. 'Makes him easy to identify. Where does he buy them from, I wonder? Not the sort of thing you see around much. Stupid thing for an intruder to wear. We could probably have tracked him down through his socks—had we needed to.'

'He's going up the stairs,' said Joyce. 'But the crime was committed on the lower deck, right?'

'That's true. He must have sneaked down at some point to the lower deck. There are other cameras on the plane, but none of them caught him doing that. There was no camera on the back stairs. Still, you can't escape the timing. Look at this.'

He pressed another button and the digital clock on the tape became more prominent. 'The assailant, er, the suspect, got on the plane at eleven thirty-six and fourteen seconds. The murder was committed at about eleven forty-five, according to the people who heard the shots. At eleven forty-eight and nineteen seconds, we have this scene.'

He clicked with a mouse and the shot changed to Paul, looking worried, coming down the stairs.

'So he went back upstairs before leaving?'

'Yes. Must have used the back stairs again. Clearly he wanted to do more than kill Seferis. He wanted to take something from the aircraft—steal some important papers or something, obviously. But it looks like he couldn't find them. See how he's leaving empty-handed?'

'Could it be possible that he went straight upstairs, spent the whole time there, and left after hearing the shots?'

'It would be possible, except for two things. First, somebody shot Dmitri Seferis, and this guy was the only other person on the plane. Second, the engineering staff actually saw him sneak downstairs and shoot the bugger. I understand they got a good view of the whole thing.'

'Joyce? Joyce?' Someone was calling her name. She looked around to see Nicola Teo waving from the doorway. 'Time's up, I'm afraid, Ms McQuinnie. Time to get on board.'

'I'll be flying to London with you,' Drexler said. 'I'm also in charge of on-board security. So you can ask me more questions if you like, when we're in the air.'

❀ ❀ ❀

From the moment she entered the world's most expensive aircraft, Joyce had had enormous trouble stopping herself squealing with excitement at the extravagance of it all. To her, it was a spectacular flying nightclub, with every room having a different theme. The planet's most daring designers had been given free rein and almost unlimited budgets on each section; as a result, the on-board lounges (they didn't use the word 'cabins') were a wonderland of colours and experiences. There were also several shops and even a swimwear boutique at the back of the lower deck—which was known as The Promenade. The upper deck was officially called The Penthouse.

An hour after takeoff, they were enjoying their first meal in the air. J Oscar Jackson Junior had been right: it was first class all the way. The private envoy sat with Wong and McQuinnie around a table in Gourmet Boulevard on the lower deck of Skyparc.

Forcing his eyes away from the menu's foie gras and beef Wellington, Jackson had ordered a steamed chicken breast and

Caesar salad. But his gaze kept drifting to the meals the others had ordered. Joyce ordered burger and chips and ended up with a veggie patty topped with avocado served in garlic naan with a side order of herb-crusted pommes frites. Wong had asked for plain *cha siu faan*—barbecued pork with rice—and ended up with a tray of Chinese items in almost nouvelle cuisine style. The feng shui master had peered suspiciously at the unfamiliar presentation when it arrived, but seemed happy enough to eat it.

Joyce, ravenous, was speaking with her mouth full. 'How come yesterday I was not even allowed to go near the hangar because of the negative vetting stuff, and today I am fine to actually fly right on this aircraft with all these swanky people?' she asked Jackson. 'Not that I'm complaining.'

'Uh…as I said, my people are a little higher up the ladder than Mr Manks's people,' Jackson said, slipping a forbidden crouton into his mouth and letting it melt slowly in his left cheek. 'When something horrible happens, we go to security code red. Nobody gets in unless they're essential personnel. Anybody who's not like a blood relative of the Queen gets instantly banned. But after a couple of days, things start to get more reasonable. They let us pull rank, they let us make a list of exceptions, they let us pull strings.'

'Does that mean I can now go and see the crime scene? *Jeez*, this burger is like *totally* amazing.'

'No. They're keeping that room strictly off limits. Besides, Mr Wong saw it yesterday. It would be hard to argue that you need to see it as well, given your youth, et cetera. You can see it on screen, though. There's a camera in the room.'

'There is? So did they film the murder?'

'Sadly not. That would have made things simpler for everyone.'

'How do I get to see the room through the security camera?'

'Go and ask Drexler, the security guy. He has all that stuff. He also has pictures taken straight after the murder. He might even print them out for you.'

Joyce took another enormous bite of her burger and spat bits of naan at him as she spoke: 'Are you going to tell us about who you really are and who sent you and what you think happened on Wednesday and why you think Paul is innocent, and so on and so on?'

Jackson finally squeezed the crouton with his tongue and felt it dissolve deliciously in his mouth. 'In good time. I need to eat just now. Not that this is going to take me very long.'

Joyce was looking at the menu again as she stuffed five potato wedges into her mouth at once. 'Wow, they've got chocolate brownies with ice cream for dessert. Ben and Jerry's—wicked. And warm apple crumble with vanilla sauce. And double-thick New York cheesecake topped with fresh cream. How am I going to choose? Can I order all of them, and we'll share? Wanna share with me?'

Jackson closed his eyes, her words causing him physical pain. He knew he would have to leave before she piled all the desserts in front of them. He scooped the final piece of lettuce into his mouth and then threw his knife and fork down. 'I've got to go to the executive offices, make some calls. In the meantime, enjoy the rest of your meal. I'll meet you two back here in half an hour. Then I'll brief you on what we know about what happened on Wednesday. We'll make some plans about how exactly we are going to take this thing forward.'

Sighing at the end of another unsatisfying meal, he sadly left the table without looking back.

'I reckon someone dressed up as Paul sneaked on board,' McQuinnie said to Wong through her mouthful of potato, 'shot the guy and sneaked off. After all, those security heat-detector things only send out their signals every few minutes or something. I think Paul was upstairs the whole time.'

Before she could order dessert she spotted Drexler collecting a cup of coffee from the counter. Joyce dropped the remains of her veggie burger back onto the plate and rubbed her greasy hands on her napkin. Then she raced up to the Australian. 'Hi. Oscar Jackson told me you had a video trained on the crime scene. And pictures. Can you show me?'

'Like a bit of gore, do we?'

'No,' said Joyce, affronted. 'I'm an investigator. I just want to see if there are any clues. There's much more to this than meets the eye.'

'That's true about most of us,' he said, and smiled at her—a somewhat leering grin that made her feel uncomfortable. 'In fact, there are a lot of things on this plane that are not visible to the naked eye. Come.'

'Where are we going?'

'I'll take you to my secret chamber. Mwah-huh-huh-ha-ha.' He wrung his hands together, suddenly a cartoon villain.

'Um...'

'The bunker, we call it. It's the in-flight security centre, really. If you want to see the pictures of the crime scene, you'll have to go there.'

'Okay,' said Joyce, a little warily.

'I'll show you some other cool stuff on the way. This plane has several delightful extra rooms for relaxation and all sorts of activities, karaoke, massage, a director's club-type cinema, even a swimwear boutique—as you know.'

'What do you mean by that?'

He smiled again. 'I saw you prowling around the back stairs earlier, checking out the shopping. I keep a camera there, to see who's checking out the swimwear. On this plane, there's no place to hide from Spyin' Ryan.'

'That could be awkward. What about the shower block?'

'What sort of person do you think I am? There *are* private spots on this plane—one or two of which are well worth visiting. Follow me.'

Halfway down a corridor, Drexler stopped suddenly. 'See this wall?'

Joyce nodded.

'Now watch. You will notice that my hands never leave my sleeves.'

He took out a small electronic device and pointed it at the wall. There was a click in response. Drexler pressed with both hands, and the wall opened, folding up like an aircraft toilet door. Inside was a small room containing two chairs, each of which seemed to have too many seatbelts. The room was cramped, with a low ceiling. It looked like a tiny prison.

What's that?'

'It ain't first class,' said Drexler.

'Is this for people who are naughty?'

'Exactly right,' the security chief explained. 'Welcome to the jailhouse. Normally, if you get someone rowdy and out of control on a flight, we strap them into their chairs and leave them where they are. But that's no fun for people sitting around them. On Skyparc, though, we have our very own little prison built in. We call this room Alcatraz.'

'Do you have a judge and jury as well, to see if they are guilty?'

'Nah. Planes are cities in themselves, with their own laws— really, I'm not joking. We have a lot of laws that don't apply on the ground. It's because of the safety angle. We are allowed to restrain people, even sedate them. All that would be illegal down on the ground.'

'How do you sedate them?'

'Actually, we won't usually need to. Ninety per cent of the problems on planes are caused by alcohol. It might drive them wild for a while, sitting in here, but then they will collapse and fall asleep. If not, we have a gentle dose of sleeping gas built into the chamber—in case we need it.' He pointed to a small canister, attached high up on the wall, well out of reach of anyone strapped to a chair.

'Turn this on and the room will fill with gas. They will sleep off the rest of the flight, whether they want to or not. Now come and see my aforementioned secret chamber,' Drexler said, as he twirled an imaginary moustache like a silent-movie baddie.

Twenty metres down the corridor, they went through a small door into a sunken room filled with monitors. Drexler flicked a switch and a screen showed a bird's eye view of a larger room containing desks and a chalked outline of a man.

'There: the scene of the crime.'

'Jackson said you might be able to print some photos out for me. Can you?'

'Sure, anything for you,' he said as he sent the images to print.

'How come you didn't film the murder?'

'When the plane is empty, we just have the cameras showing the doors and the staircases on.'

'Can you zoom in on the victim's desk a bit?'

'Yeah. He was a pretty messy bugger.'

'He didn't know he was going to attract all this attention. Hey. Weird.'

'What?'

'Look at that CD.'

'A lot of people listen to CDs while they're working.'

'Yeah, but you know what that is, don't you? That red cover—it's unmistakable.'

'Don't care much for modern music, to tell the truth.'

'That's *Biscuit Dunked in Death* by The Rogerers.'

'Any good?'

'Good? It's brilliant. It's the album of the year. Maybe the decade. You *have* to get it. You can hear mine if you like—I have it on my iPod. But…'

'What?'

'It's kinda weird he's got it.'

'You think oil company executives don't have good taste in music?'

'It's not that. It's just that—well, the lead singer is Stongo, you know? Stongo is a mad keen global warming activist. He's always in those concerts for climate change, and he even dedicated the album to "good guy scientists trying to stop us poisoning the planet". It's not the sort of thing you'd expect an oil company man to like.'

'Maybe he was studying the enemy's tactics.'

'Yeah. I guess that would make sense.'

Drexler moved his chair closer, so that he was sitting uncomfortably near to her. She could feel his warm, slightly alcoholic breath on her shoulder. He placed his hand casually on her thigh. 'I keep some drinks in here. I have my own special brew. You like Red Bull?'

'Sure. But—'

'You'll love my special brew. It's like Red Bull to the max. Gives you a real zing.'

'I gotta go,' she said. 'See my boss. Do some work.'

'Don't rush off,' said Drexler, grabbing her arm. His hand was damp. 'We've got all the time in the world.'

'Deadlines, deadlines,' said Joyce, pulling away from him. She snatched the photos from his printer and rushed out the door.

❀ ❀ ❀

Arriving back at their table in Gourmet Boulevard, Joyce was pleased to see both Wong and Jackson waiting for her. The geomancer had his fingers laced together.

'How come you two both say you know Paul not guilty? He look very guilty to me. No other suspect.'

'He kind of told me,' Joyce offered.

'I thought he is not saying anything.'

'He said it to me in a sort of code.'

Jackson stood up. 'Okay, guys. Come with me. We'll discuss this in my private office.'

He led them to what seemed to be the staff toilet. Joyce was surprised when he stopped there and pressed on the door.

'We'll wait here?' she asked.

'No. I want you to follow me.'

Wong explained: 'There's a secret room behind the toilet.'

'You know?' Jackson asked, his eyebrows rising.

The feng shui master nodded. 'Of course. I spent six hours studying plane blueprints. Easy to spot secret rooms. I know every part of this plane.'

'I thought this room was not shown on the plans?'

'It is not shown on the plans. But the rooms around it are shown on the plans. Easy to spot missing section.'

Jackson entered the toilet, used a keycard to open a hidden door in the inner wall, and went into a private chamber. Wong and Joyce followed. They all sat down around a table in the room that was windowless but brightly lit.

Jackson tapped his fingers on the table. 'Story time. Some years ago, the US military's psychological warfare department started a new assignment called RD 13c (i)77. These departments have existed on and off for many years. But in what came to be called Project 77, some very interesting work was done on the concept of subliminal messaging.'

Wong looked blank.

'That's when you show some conventional media to someone—movies, music, television, whatever—but hidden within the media are messages that work on the target at a subconscious level. It may be images or aural statements run at high speed, or it may be material shown at frequencies not normally detectable by our senses working at their normal levels. The curious thing about this project was that it was not aimed at the enemy. It was aimed at our own people. The idea was to combat what was seen as the spreading liberalism in the country, the leftism, the hedonism, the multiculturalism and so on.'

'Sounds a bit right-wing,' said Joyce.

'Very right-wing,' agreed Jackson. 'This was the military, remember? They decided it would be good if the American people were a tad more xenophobic than they were. Obviously, they couched it in positive language. They told their financiers these programmes were vital for ensuring homeland security, but in fact the main thinking behind it was to defend military budgets. If people felt worried about their homeland, military budgets would continue to rise forever more. Project 77 was a clever and innovative plan. It just had one flaw.'

'Which was?' Joyce asked.

'It didn't work.'

'Ah, that must have sucked.'

'It was really a problem of knowing which messages to send. If they sent pictures of death and violence, people got depressed and the fight went out of them. If they sent pictures of children and the American way of life, people felt sentimental and soft. Soldiers who were subjected to the stuff wanted to drop their guns and run home to spend time with their mums. There was no easy way to send a specific message that military expansion had to be encouraged as the only way to preserve the American way of life. They worked for months on getting suitable material. But, even then there were problems: individuals decoded the same images differently. Some people were softened by images of babies, while others were repulsed. Some people were cowed by messages of violence, while others were excited by them. The whole project was too unpredictable and produced such mixed reactions it was eventually scrapped.

'But one of the scientists working on it noticed one constant—pictures of families or similar loving relationships produced a uniform effect of peacefulness and positivity. Similarly, images, sounds or messages indicating green, rural landscapes produced calm, positive effects. This scientist fell in with some psychologists working on psychosomatic effects of emotion and the project quietly restarted—but this time it was in private hands, not the military's. In other words, the project only worked really well when it was used to promote a simpler message, and one opposite of what the military wanted: a message that families, peace, love and a clean, natural environment full of happy humans were good things.

'To cut a long story short, some powerful and well-connected individuals who shared an interest in promoting peace took an interest in this work. Various private meetings were held, and a concept was born: Operation Nice was the nickname we used for it—sort of self-mocking, but that's the kind of people who are involved. We could laugh at ourselves. The idea was to turn this subliminal campaign into a small, hard-to-detect virus and stick it in the places where it would do most good.'

'On TV?'

'On TV At the movies. On mobile video—yes, all of these were discussed as dissemination routes. But there was a problem. However much good it might do, it was borderline illegal. It was possibly dangerous. And it was unpredictable. Everyone agreed it would be wrong to blast it out to the world in general. It seemed wiser to target only the people who needed to be targeted. To see if it could be a weapon that could calm the hawks who had taken over the world. So a very narrow target was chosen: business people in industries associated with global warming, the destruction of the environment, military spending, and so on. A program was designed—this is the brilliant bit—to spread the message as a virus and which then ran in the background on PowerPoint presentations. So while business executives all over the world were talking about profits and GDP growth and annual dividends, they were being reminded subconsciously of a different set of values. These were the people who needed to be reminded of the human and environmental cost of the profits they made.'

'People like the senior executives of BM Dutch Petroleum?'

'Exactly. Paul was one of our operatives. He told us he'd met someone who could get him onto Skyparc, where he could put the Operation Nice virus directly onto the computers on its Hong Kong stopover, just before a meeting at which the top leaders in aviation in Asia were treated to a PowerPoint slide show.'

'I don't get it. Are you really saying they would watch these PowerPoint shows and want to cancel their projects?'

'Oh no, it worked much more subtly than that. Typically, the first time someone sees a presentation of any sort containing an Operation Nice subliminal message, they get nothing out of it at all except perhaps a slight feeling that they should phone their families at coffee break. We've actually measured this result. On test runs, people at conferences do tend to go and phone their spouses or children. The second or third time you are subjected to these subliminal messages, then you might feel drawn to ask questions to the speaker about how human values and profit-centred business values could be brought closer together. Eventually—or so the plan is—business people will start to make decisions that favour humanity and the environment over and above paper profits. That's the long-term aim.'

'It's an amazing project. If it works.'

'We don't really know how well it will work, or whether it will work at all. It makes people more emotional, tugs at their heartstrings a bit—that much is sure. Above and beyond that, we're not sure whether it would really change the way the world worked. But we decided it was worth trying. The world has become steadily more dangerous over the past decade. Someone had to do something. So we greenlighted it. The Nice virus is being rolled out around the world this week. It's really a matter of seeing what happens. The results will not be obvious or dramatic, but should, hopefully, make a difference over the next few months or years. Interestingly, it coincides with a massive rise in the number of women in power, which we think will also have a similarly positive effect on the way the world works. Take the UK or the States, for example. Twenty-five, thirty years ago, less than forty per cent of people going to university were female. Now the figure is fifty-seven per cent and climbing. Similar figures can be found in most developed countries. And there have never been more women in national leadership positions than there are at the moment. It's no longer unimaginable that women will fill the most powerful presidential job-slots on the planet. This is all part of a quiet movement that could see the world becoming a gentler, less aggressive place.'

Joyce leaned back in her chair.

'So that was what Paul was here for. He wasn't here to kill anyone. He just wanted to doctor their computers. So how come he can't tell the police that?'

'He's being loyal. Operation Nice has taken three years to put together. We've also been very successful indeed in keeping it under wraps. Paul is risking his own future to make sure it stays secret. We owe him a tremendous debt.'

Wong, who had been sitting silently listening up till now, said: 'But why did he go downstairs to shoot the other man?'

'I don't know. I don't know what happened. I've spent a lot of time with Paul over the past year, and that is something that doesn't add up. I reckon Paul was somehow framed for the Seferis murder. I don't know how. But I do know this: almost no work was done to find "the real killer". The police assumed they had the right guy, and Paul was saying nothing, not even denying that he was the killer, and the airline company did not want more investigative work to be done anyway, so why bother taking it any further?'

❀ ❀ ❀

An hour later, Wong was in the penthouse office of Sir Nicholas Handey, chairman of Skyparc Airside Enterprises. They had been talking about the business scene in China—or rather, the British aristocrat had been talking, and the geomancer had been half-listening, giving an occasional nod to be polite. Sir Nicholas explained that his people had calculated that between now and 2025 China alone would need some two thousand eight hundred large aircraft.

'China is already the second biggest purchaser of aircraft, after the United States. It may well become the biggest before we know it. Do you know how much it costs to buy two thousand eight hundred large aircraft, Mr Wong? Well, I'll tell you: upwards of three hundred billion euros. That's a considerable sum of money by any measure. Now there have been several statements by the Chinese government about how they intend to finance a state-owned enterprise to build a Chinese large passenger aircraft. Are you familiar with these statements?'

Wong, realising that some sort of answer was expected of him, tilted his head to one side, narrowed his eyes and touched his nose, hoping this would indicate some sort of sophisticated response.

'You may well find such statements provocative. They certainly worry the bigwigs in Toulouse and Seattle,' Sir Nicholas continued. 'But they don't worry me in the slightest.

It has taken forty years for Airbus to have developed its family of super-jets. So, I can't see the Chinese producing anything significant until 2025 at the earliest. Furthermore, we are cementing relationships with the Chinese to ensure they see us as partners. We've already started a programme of assembling the A320 short-haul jet in China. This will ramp up until we are rolling three or four A320s annually off the production line on the mainland by 2011.'

The feng shui master's eyes drifted to the stunning panorama captured in the windows. For some reason, the view of clouds and mountain peaks seemed far more beautiful through a large, rectangular window than the normal, tiny oval ones of most planes. A shaft of sunlight entered the room, making its occupants blink.

'I've always been lucky in business,' the tall, white-haired business leader continued, gesturing at the window. 'I always seem to end up in the office with the nice view. It's nice to be able to enjoy the same privilege in the air.'

Wong glanced out of the window and suddenly looked concerned, his eyes squinting and his mouth twisting.

'Is anything wrong, Mr Wong?'

'This mountain has been moved.'

'What?'

He pointed to a gleaming white peak sticking out of a sea of blue-white cloud. 'This mountain has been moved. Before it was over there.' He pointed to the other side of the plane.

'It can't have been moved. It's probably just a different mountain. Or we're taking a different route.' Sir Nicholas leaned over and looked out of the window. 'Oh, I see what's happening. No need to worry, Mr Wong. We're just taking the northern route over China, that's all. I'll check with the pilots if you want to know for certain.'

Wong still looked agitated, so Sir Nicholas asked one of his staff to call the pilot to the room.

'I think pilot will be busy, flying the plane,' the geomancer said.

'We have three, maybe four trained pilots on a flight like this,' Sir Nicholas explained, smiling. 'It's not unsafe to ask him to leave the controls for a while.'

The pilot, a large Irishman named Captain Eamonn Turlough Daniel Malachy, arrived within a minute to fill them in on details of the altered route. 'Orders from the MOD, sir,' he explained. 'They asked us a couple of days ago to take this route. We cleared it with the relevant authorities, so there should be no problem at all.'

'But why did the MOD want it changed?'

'Nothing serious, I believe, sir. They just thought there would be better security to fly this way, although it takes around ten per cent more time. There's been a bit of unrest in some of the countries we would normally fly over. Not enough to prompt us to change all our routes, but for this plane—a VIP plane carrying VIP passengers, if I may say so—we thought it best to take extra precautions.'

Sir Nicholas turned to the feng shui master. 'How does that sound, Mr Wong? Nothing to worry about, just a technicality, it seems.'

Wong still looked unhappy. 'I was told this was the route,' he said, pulling out a scribbled diagram from his bag. Attached was a map from the inflight magazine.

'That's the normal route,' agreed Captain Malachy. 'But we've only changed it a bit. We still go from the same A to the same B.'

'Does the route matter? Surely the destination is the key thing?' Sir Nicholas asked.

'Every person has directions which are lucky at some times and unlucky at some times. This plane... it is good luck for this plane to travel east or southeast, but bad luck to travel northeast.'

'But sometimes you just have to go directly from A to B, Mr Wong, and there are no choices.'

'There are always choices.'

'What if your clients move office from north to southeast, and that is a bad direction for them on that date? You don't expect them to abandon their new office and buy another one in a good luck direction, do you?'

'I will not ask them to do that. But I will ask them to make their journey a bit longer so they arrive from the right direction. Sometimes I send them right out of town, many mile, and then they come into town from a different place. If their good luck is ensured by them arriving from the southwest, I will tell them to leave their office and travel due south, and then approach their new office from the luckiest direction.'

'I see. Well, it doesn't look like there's much we can do about it now. The decision has been made, and you can't really change these things once you are in the air—unless of course there's a major emergency of some kind. How bad is the bad luck?'

'Pretty bad,' said Wong. '*Shar* number five.'

'Well, this may be a good test of just how valid feng shui is,' put in Captain Malachy. 'If we have a safe journey, it may be a black mark for you, Mr Wong.'

'That means the odds are very much in our favour,' said Sir Nicholas. 'Accidents are thankfully rare. But I do want to make sure you feel comfortable. Is there anything you can do to alleviate the bad luck?' he added, hoping to mollify the feng shui master.

'I try,' said Wong. 'I walk round a bit and take a look.'

❀ ❀ ❀

In the days of the Early Sung, a Prince who was heir to a throne approached a wise man who lived in a cave.

'I want to learn how to be the greatest of kings,' said the Prince. 'Which kings should I visit and what gifts shall I bring them?'

'Visit no kings,' said the wise man. 'Get rid of your rich robes, fine crown and expensive sword. Dress as a poor man and visit each of the Nine Kingdoms carrying only a crust of bread'

So he did.

In each of the kingdoms, he was treated badly, except for the ninth one, where all were treated equally. When he returned

home and took the throne, he declared that the laws be rewritten
so that they protected people who had neither land nor money.

He said: 'When we look after the rights of the least, we look
after the rights of us all.'

Blade of Grass, the only way to protect the rights of a
community is to protect the rights of the individual.

From *Some Gleanings of Oriental Wisdom*
by CF Wong

Joyce was walking along the corridor as fast as she
decorously could when she encountered a familiar face: the
helmet-haired, impeccably dressed Kaitlyn MacKenzie. The
Queen's soon-to-be newest employee gave no indication of
recognising Joyce, but allowed her eyes to drift across her
and move on. This sort of behaviour always annoyed Joyce,
so she made a point of stopping, turning and catching her
attention.

'Hey! Hi, Kaitlyn. Remember me?'

She stared.

'We met, like, yesterday?'

'Oh, yes, hi, uh…'

'Jo. Enjoying the flight?'

'It's all right. I've seen it all before.'

'How's your new job? I haven't seen much of Robbie Manks.
Where's he sitting?'

'He's with me. We're in the Leopard Lounge, on the top
deck. With a young man you'd probably like to meet.'

'And who might that be?'

'Oh, just a member of the royal family. Not that we're
supposed to talk about it.'

Joyce knew this was the moment to make a glib joke but
was struck dumb. A member of the royal family! A young man.
A young *man*. Could it be? Was there the slightest chance that it
could actually be…? There was no choice: she had to ask.

'Is it, er, Prince Will?' Joyce said, her voice instantly sticky
with emotion.

Kaitlyn scoffed. '*Please*. We'd have a zillion extra security guards if it were. Nor is it Prince Harry. If it was, I wouldn't be prowling around down here. It's no one particularly interesting, unless you're totally desperate. Go and check him out if you want.'

'Nah. I'm kind of busy myself, still working on the case. We've made some amazing progress.'

'How very nice for you. I'm going to get a cocktail.'

Ms MacKenzie, looking extra tall in high-heeled shoes, tottered away towards the club bar.

Joyce stood still and pondered. What Kaitlyn had just said stopped her short. This might be the moment when she should find an excuse to visit Robbie Manks and be introduced to a real live royal—a young male one, no less. Young implied unattached, or at least unmarried.

Joyce was no groupie, but she was a young woman. She had been brought up on the same fairytales as other female children have been since the dawn of time. There was no way on earth she could be told that a real, live, unmarried *actual* prince or similar was in the vicinity without at least having a look. And perhaps introducing herself. After all, princes did sometimes date commoners, or even marry them. Look at Prince Charles and Princess Diana—what a fantastic fairytale romance that was! If you discounted the infidelity and lies and misery and death, of course. It was an opportunity that could not be allowed to slip past. And now that Kaitlyn had propelled herself out of the way on her new Jimmy Choos, this was the perfect chance.

Joyce smoothed down her hair, held her hand in front of her mouth to check her breath (which she hoped was chocolatey after the spectacular dessert she'd downed) and nipped up the back steps. She followed the signs to the Leopard Lounge, determined to find her prince.

The first thing she saw was Robbie Manks dozing in a lounge chair amongst a small group of people, most of whom were reading or sleeping. Joyce scanned them, trying to zero in on anyone who might be a prince. There was an empty chair next to Robbie: that must have been where Kaitlyn had been sitting. There were two young men in the group who appeared to be in the all-important twenty to thirty age bracket. One of them was a gaunt, spotty young man in a T-shirt and jeans with a tattoo on his arm: probably not royal material. The other was in an expensive-looking dark suit, watching a movie with a sort of regal disdain. Pay dirt.

'Hi, Robbie. Mind if I join you?' Joyce chirruped, perching on the edge of Kaitlyn's chair.

'Hmm? Sure,' said Manks, his voice thick with sleep. 'Just having a little think here.' He turned his head away from her and immediately returned to his nap.

'Hi!' said Joyce, thrusting her hand out at the young man in the dark suit. 'I'm Joyce. I'm a friend of Robbie's.' She would have preferred to announce herself as 'a professional geomantic investigator on her way to feng shui Buckingham Palace', but she suspected such a line might transgress Manks's endless strictures about discretion.

'Hey,' said the young man in black, failing or choosing not to notice her outstretched hand. He gave her a dispassionate glance that lasted a third of a second and returned his gaze to the television monitor. He appeared disinclined to introduce himself.

Joyce interpreted this haughtiness as confirmation of his elevated status: clearly he was someone grand and impressive who was entitled to treat her as if she was a nobody. She *was* a nobody, comparatively. He must be constantly approached by women. There was no way he could know just what an interesting nobody she was.

But how was she going to find out exactly who he was? There was no other way than to get him talking.

'Cool plane,' she said, immediately regretting it.

The young man did not reply.

'I like it,' yawned the tattooed young man sitting behind her. 'Better than Virgin upper class, even.'

She gave Mr Tattoo a perfunctory nod to acknowledge his comment and refocused on her target. 'I guess the rest of your family aren't on this flight, otherwise there would be zillions more security guards,' she offered.

The young man in black scratched his nose.

Power, Joyce decided, was definitely an aphrodisiac. There was nothing particularly special about the gentleman in front of her. His ears stuck out, there were dark circles under his hooded eyes and he had shaved badly, leaving a patch of stubble under a slightly too-wide nose. Yet she could see past all this. To her, he represented everything contained in the word 'prince': castles and horses and jewels and inter-national fame—in other words, the final paragraph of every fairy story, all the way from Cinderella to the Barbie movies and *Shrek*. At the same time, she felt rather appalled at having these thoughts. She was a feminist; she was independent; she despised ancient patriarchal traditions; and she was generally more anti-monarchist than pro. So why was she so entranced by the young man who was so studiously ignoring her? She guessed the desire to be part of a fairytale must be a primal thing—so deep it swept other things aside, even closely held feminist principles.

But how to get his attention? She decided she needed a different approach. Perhaps she could do something for him. He was probably used to being served. 'I need a drink. I'm heading over to the bar. Can I get you one?'

He shook his head without replying.

She heard Mr Tattoo speak from behind her. 'I'll have one. Apple juice, please.'

'Fine.' Now she was stuck. She had to leave the chair next to His Royal Highness The Prince—she'd decided that his regal manner confirmed he was somewhere very high up in line for the throne, probably straight after Will and Harry—to get a drink for the nonentity behind her. She rose to her feet, gave the T-shirted young man a small, obviously fake smile, and started to walk over to the bar.

'Get me a coffee, please, Joyce. I need to wake up,' Manks mumbled.

'Of course. And how about a glass of rat poison for everyone except the Prince and myself?' she uttered *sotto voce*.

When she reached the bar she found Mr T-shirt Tattoo had followed her.

'I'll help you carry the stuff back,' he said. 'It'll be hard to carry two drinks and a coffee.'

Joyce decided she might as well use this unattractive individual to get clues about the identity of their majestic companion.

'Can you just remind me of that guy's name? I know him but I've forgotten it.'

'Who? Max?'

Ah, yes, that's right. Max. Of course. Max.'

Max? *Max*? Was there any member of the royal family called Max? Any cousin or nephew or half-brother of Prince Will? She could not recall a Max, although she knew the younger generation of royals did have trendy names—there was a Beatrice, wasn't there? And a Zara? But mostly they had boring names such as Andrew and Edward and George, she thought. There was no Max she had ever come across. But these days, there could, in theory, be a Prince Max.

'Royals are strange people,' she mused.

'Tell me about it.'

'Do you hang out with them a lot?'

'Way too much.'

Joyce decided Mr Tattoo must be a schoolfriend of the royal visitor. 'Isn't it kind of fun?'

'Not really. We long to be ordinary. I know that's kind of a cliché, but it's actually true.'

'We? Are you...?'

'A member of The Family? Sort of. I'm afraid so.'

'And Max?

'He's a mate from Gordonstoun.'

'Oh. So. Are you, like, *royal*?'

He smiled. 'That's a funny way to put it. But I suppose I am sort of on that list, so to speak, for better or worse. But don't blame me. It's not my fault.'

'Who exactly are you? Sorry, I *should* know, but...'

'No, there's no reason why you should know. I'm not a famous member of The Family, and hope never to become one. Only a few are famous, thank God.'

'What's your name?'

'Army.'

As in...?'

'Army. Yes. My full name is Edward Peter Andrew Armstrong-Phillips. But everyone calls me—'

'Army. Are you a prince?'

'No.'

'Are you a cousin of Prince Will or anything like that?'

'Pretty much. A cousin once removed. I'm the grandson of Princess Marjorie, who is the Queen's youngest sister. I'm fourteenth in line to the throne, so if the other thirteen pop off, you'd have to call me King. I'd be Edward VIII. Not much chance of that happening, I'm pleased to say.'

'What do I call you now?'

'Anything you like. How about "waiter"? After all, I have offered to carry our drinks to our seats.'

'Forget apple juice. Let's have some Moët,' Joyce said.

She spent the next ten minutes at the bar talking to Army, during which time she discovered he was twenty-four years old but considered himself rather immature. He liked machines and wanted to be a mechanic or an electrical engineer but his family members would not hear of it. He had never had a proper job. His parents wanted him to inherit the directorships of several family companies, but he flatly refused. He complained that he had no idea of the value of money, like most of his royal contemporaries, so it was wrong to put him in charge of looking after the stuff.

In turn, Joyce shared her family history—how her mother had been a career-obsessed television presenter in the United Kingdom and had interviewed an Australian property developer and fallen in love with him. The marriage had been spectacularly stormy—both being prima donnas used to getting their own way. After ten years of shouting, Joyce's mother decided she was not cut out to be a wife, a mother or an Australian and had returned to England to present gossipy midday shows aimed at homemakers. Joyce's father had won uncontested custody of their two daughters. He had expanded his company to various places, including New York and Hong Kong, and had taken the two girls with him every time he moved. Unsettled by the break-up and the peripatetic nature of their lives, the two girls had performed poorly in their studies at various international schools. Joyce's older sister had become increasingly wild and had left home at seventeen, moving to Boston to live with a man whom no one else in the family had ever met. Joyce had reacted in a different way. She had become quiet and indifferent.

Her father had eventually pulled strings with a Singaporean property developer friend and secured Joyce a summer job as an intern in a feng shui consultancy. That summer had changed her life. CF Wong and Associates specialised in doing the feng shui at scenes of crime—studying the harmony or lack of it at places where crimes had occurred and helping police understand what had happened. She'd now been with the consultancy for two and half years. She kept in touch with her sister and her father, but couldn't help but feel abandoned by her mother.

'My parents don't know me at all. Especially my mum. They're a million miles away, literally and in every other way, so I'm happy hanging out in Singapore. I've got a few friends there. My boss is a grumpy old man, but I like the work,' Joyce told Army. 'It's all about helping people and sorting out problems. It kinda mixes business with something a bit more spiritual, which I really like.'

Army absently stroked a pimple on his cheek as he spoke. 'I know what you mean. Like you, I've never been hungry or penniless or on the street. But is that a good thing or a bad thing? Maybe a person needs to be hungry. My main problem is that my ambitions are all screwed up. They have always been tiny—get to level 15 at Game Boy, get a Nintendo Wii, get a nice car, et cetera. But I don't want to run the world, or even a small company. I'm starting to realise there is something desperately wrong with me. I don't want stuff. Everyone else wants stuff, don't they? My mad brood wants me to inherit directorships and estates and all that kind of thing, but who gives a toss? I don't think that sort of thing will make me happy.'

'What would make you happy?'

'That's a hard question. When I was a teenager I had terrible acne and no social skills at all, and cousins and friends were all much handsomer than I was. No one ever looked at me at royal functions. It's the same even now—no one is interested in me, not with Will and Harry around. I'm not saying I don't have friends. I made some good friends at school. I met Max there—he can be a bit of a dork, but he's my best mate. By the way, you haven't told me your name.'

'Oh,' said Joyce. 'Yes, yes, yes.'

She was in love.

❀ ❀ ❀

Dilip Sinha had been pleased to reach Hong Kong in time to get on board Skyparc before it left. He was grateful to Wong and McQuinnie for recommending him to Manks. He had managed to have a good chat with Wong before the feng shui master was summoned to a meeting with Sir Nicholas Handey. Now, the Indian astrologer was trying to enjoy a snooze in one of the leather armchairs on the lower deck—but he couldn't sleep. He had the feeling he was being watched. Half opening one eye, he was curious to note in his peripheral vision a woman with white hair looking intently at him. Unsure of whether to feel insulted or complimented, he turned to catch her eye. 'May I help you, madam?' he said in a neutral tone.

'Sorry to stare,' she said. 'But I was just wondering, are you one of the people travelling with Mr Manks? One of the, er, how shall we say, *mystical* people?'

Sinha was not sure whether he should confirm this or not—having had the same speech about discretion Wong had been given.

'I realise it's supposed to be a secret and all that,' the woman continued, 'but Manks is useless at keeping secrets. He's my cousin. I'm Janet Moore and I'm on the board of Skyparc Airside Enterprises—I'm a non-executive director. It's really through my connections that he got this assignment. Anyway, I know all about the group of mystics that he is importing to clean out all the devils from Buckingham Palace, or whatever it is you do.'

Sinha nodded. 'I see. Well, it is not literally cleaning out devils, but it is certainly to do with removing negative energy and creating the right sort of space for positive energy to settle.'

'So, you are a feng shui master?'

'Not at all. There is a feng shui master on board, a good friend of mine, but I am not he. I am a master of several Indian techniques, including one called vaastu shastra. It is widely seen as the Indian equivalent of feng shui. It is similar in many respects, and there is much overlap in the basic philosophy, and in the final outcomes. But there are many differences, at the same time.'

Vaastu shastra? Never heard of it.'

'Sadly, it is not as famous as feng shui, not having had the marketing that feng shui has had. Yet it is often considered, certainly in India, as being older than feng shui. Indeed, the Indian vaastu associations claim that feng shui is a distorted, bowdlerised version of vaastu.'

'I bet the Chinese don't like that.'

'You bet correctly. They believe the opposite: that feng shui inspired the creation of vaastu.'

'Which do you believe?'

'Generally speaking, creative codes of belief tend to go from India to China, not the other way around. For example, Buddhism quite clearly went from India to China. The Chinese legend of the monkey king, Sun Wukong, is clearly inspired by the much older Indian legend of Hanuman, the mischievous monkey god of Hinduism. Vaastu shastra comes from the early days of the Aryan arrival in India, which is some four millennia old. Feng shui, it is claimed, is also four millennia old—but a few decades younger than its Indian equivalent, I suspect.'

She nodded, but her expression was of a person gathering facts while declining to be impressed by anything. 'So how is it supposed to work? I mean, feng shui, vaastu shastra and all that? It all sounds a bit superstitious to me.'

Dilip turned to face her, swinging his entire seat around— these in-flight swivelable armchairs were a delightful idea, he'd decided. 'Not at all,' he declaimed grandly. 'It is all entirely rational and even scientific to the most rigorous degree.'

She looked sceptical. 'So how would you or a feng shui master change my life? Wouldn't you just move the furniture around and add some trinkets? Hang a solid gold horse from my light bulb or something?'

He shook his head. 'That's the general belief. But in reality, it's nothing like that. Most modern masters of vaastu or feng shui, the good ones anyway, do not come into your house and add things to it. Most homes are overstuffed with items of all sorts. Job number one is to de-clutter the house, to destroy much of the unneeded stuff in it, to clear out the dead energy.'

'Now that makes sense to me,' Moore said. 'My home is full of junk.'

'And, if I may be so bold, the presence of clutter in a person's environment detracts greatly from a person's ability to operate successfully in that environment. Clarity is key—in your physical environment, and in the decisions that you have to make to operate your life successfully. It's really all one- behaviour and environment.'

'It all sounds a bit more psychological than I expected.'

'It is very psychological.'

She leaned forward and placed her chin on her fist. 'So. Can you tell me in a sentence or two how I can fix my life using vaastu shastra techniques?'

He smiled. 'You'll be surprised to hear that I can. These things may be complex on the surface, but they are built on very simple truths.'

He leaned back and joined his fingertips together, looking up and thinking for a few seconds. 'Let me put it like this. Consider your desk, whether it is an office desk, or a table at home where you receive and write letters. What happens at that desk? Answer: every day, a number of letters are received. Or faxes. Or advertisements. These are all items with potential energy implications. They are all bits of paper urging you to react in some way—to buy a product, or respond with a phone call, or change the way you do something. Now what we should do is to react to that potential energy transaction in some way—and thus burn up the energy in it. We should either fulfil it, by doing what it says, or we should make a decision that we are not going to fulfil it, but instead throw the paper away. But, instead, we take that piece of paper and we balance it on our desk, unwilling to make an immediate decision. This happens to a number of pieces of paper every day, and then before we know it, there is a huge pile of pieces of paper on the desk. When it gets too high, we take the pile of paper, and we tuck it into a drawer. When the drawer gets so full it cannot close, we tuck the paper into a cardboard box and stick it under the desk. Soon our desks are jammed with paper—underneath, inside and on top.'

'Good God! You've been spying on me.'

'Alas, it is what most people's desks look like.'

'What's the effect of all these unfulfilled bits of paper? What did you call it—potential energy transactions?'

'I shall tell you. The day comes when you arrive at your desk, and you have lots of work to do, but you can't do it. You feel an incredible amount of inertia. You can't get started. And you have no idea why.'

'You peeping Tom! You've been staring at me through my office window.'

'The reason why you can't get started is that your desk is swamped with frozen energy. It is lying there, waiting to be handled. But the inertia infects everything you do, so that you end up unable to do anything.'

She shook her head. 'It's awful, but it all rings true. What about computers? I use mostly email these days.'

'They're just the same. The only difference is that instead of physical letters arriving at your desk, emails arrive in your inbox. Again, each of them is a potential energy transaction. And again, the right thing to do would be to delete each one, or reply to each one—and then delete it. But that's not what we do, is it?'

'It is not.'

'We leave them there in our inboxes.'

She nodded guiltily.

'And soon there are six hundred emails in our inboxes.'

'Eight hundred.'

'And eventually we select them all and stick them into a file called "archive"—which is simply the computer equivalent of the cardboard box under the desk. And the result is the same. Our email systems become full of frozen energy, and inertia spreads out of it. We find ourselves unable to do any useful work.'

'I've often wondered why I feel like I am walking in treacle. So what should one do about all this?'

Sinha waved a bony index finger at her. 'This is what I recommend. Divide all your paperwork into two piles. One of stuff which is useless and should be thrown away. And one of stuff which you think may be of use one day. Then you throw both piles away.'

'Both piles?'

'Both piles. By that stage, you will have started to feel the benefits that clarity can bring.'

'And I suppose one should delete all one's emails as well.'

'Exactly. Even if you don't, that nice Mr Gates has arranged for the computer to crash every few years, so that all your stuff gets wiped out anyway.'

Janet Moore folded her arms. 'This is surprisingly practical advice. Not what I expected at all.'

'Use the sticky finger technique. Every letter that arrives: pretend it is sticky. Pretend you cannot let it go until you have dealt with it. Only then will the stickiness disappear and you can throw it away.'

Sinha stared into the middle distance as he moved into philosophical mode. 'Business is about activity. It is not about making stuff. It is about *moving* stuff. It is useless to make a million widgets unless you can sell a million widgets. Manufacture is not the key: distribution is. Activity, movement, animation—that's the heart of business. If your desk, your working environment is clear, if your office is clear, if the paths in and out of your hands are clear, then there is movement. Then there is activity. Then there is velocity. Then riches and wealth will grow in the space. There needs to be space for them.'

'You're a genius. Will you come and give a speech at our next AGM?'

'I would be honoured, madam.'

❁ ❁ ❁

Wong had just ordered another portion of Chinese delicacies when he looked up to see Joyce walking towards him in a daze.

'Where did you go?'

'I met someone. Had to talk to him. He is *sooo* amazing. Never mind.' She shook herself and blew out her cheeks to clear her head. 'Listen. I found out something interesting.'

'What?'

'Remember the security guy said there were no cameras on the back stairs? Well, he was trying to get friendly with me just before, and he said there *were* cameras on the back stairs—he said he was spying on me earlier. It doesn't add up.'

'Oh. Interesting. Did you get pictures of crime scene?'

She handed Wong the photographs. He went through them carefully. Most showed Seferis's desk or the wall with the bullet holes in it.

'This all about angles,' said Wong. 'There are few things I notice. One, desk of Seferis is in wrong place. It should be along here a bit.'

'Maybe the guy who did the interior design didn't know about feng shui. I mean, this plane was built in England or France or somewhere, wasn't it?'

'Nothing to do with feng shui,' said Wong. 'Just good design skills. Feng shui and good design skills go together. This desk is in wrong place.'

Joyce stared at the picture. 'Hmm. See what you mean. It's sort of out of balance, isn't it? It should be that way, a metre at least.'

'Yes.'

'Maybe the guy just moved it, so he got more light from the window behind him or something?'

'No. And see the next picture.' In this image the desk leg had been bolted to the floor—and one metre to the left, there was a dent in the carpeting.

'Look. This show the desk was in right position before. But someone move it, and screw it to the floor, so it cannot move back. Mr Seferis was put in that place for reason,' said Wong.

'That may be true, but how do we know that has anything to do with the murder? Perhaps the guy who was in charge of designing the office just wasn't very good at his job and moved things around a few times. Or perhaps the guy at the next desk wanted a bit more space and got Seferis shifted a bit?'

'Maybe so. Look at more pictures.'

Several showed images of holes in the mahogany panelling.

'There were four shots fired,' the feng shui master said. 'Two hit the man, two hit the wall. All four at same angle. They were fired from other side of room, away from the door where they say Paul came in.'

'Well, the guy at the window said Paul and Seferis were arguing for a while, so perhaps they kind of moved around, you know, danced around each other for a bit.'

'Possible. But I think is strange that all bullets were fired at same angle. Seferis was hit by first bullet. Then he started to slump down. If a man was holding gun, the man would have lowered the gun and shot Seferis again, in the chest, many time, to make sure he was dead. But instead, the gun stay at same angle. Exactly same angle. No change. As if fired by blind man.'

'I see what you mean. The first shot goes in his chest. But as he is slumping down, the next goes into the same spot, which is now his shoulder, and he falls further, and the third and fourth go into the wall.'

'Yes. They all go at same angle.'

'You saying he was shot by a blind man?'

'No. Even blind man would have followed sound of the man falling and would have aimed gun down a bit.'

'You saying he wasn't shot by a human? He was shot by some sort of robot that couldn't change angle? That seems weird. Especially since the techies say they saw Paul pull the trigger.'

Wong shook his head. 'The people did not see Paul pull the trigger. Really, they only hear shots being fired. Only one person say he saw what happen.'

'That guy Danny Tang. But he was pretty close. I mean, he was right at the window, or so he said.'

'Only one person need to tell lie to make everyone else misinterpret facts. If Danny Tang did not see what he say he saw, then evidence your friend kill Seferis become much smaller. Evidence only say Paul got on the plane before Seferis died, and got off after someone or something shot Seferis.'

Joyce sighed. 'It makes sense, but it all seems so unlikely. The problem was that there was no one else on the plane at the time. Drexler's heat detector thing proves that. And I hardly think anyone is going to believe a tiny robot sneaked onto the plane, shot the guy, and then sneaked off when no one was looking. It's too science fiction-y.'

'Perhaps. But we must investigate more. I want to see murder scene one more time,' Wong said. 'Need to check something. Angle of firing.'

He scratched at the straggly hairs on his chin and screwed up his lips, deep in thought. 'I need a stick. Can you find one?'

'A stick?'

'Yes. So I can check angle of shooting. A very long, very straight stick.'

Joyce wrinkled her brow. 'We're on a plane. How can I find a stick? There are no forests nearby.'

Wong looked around the room they were in. 'We need long straight piece of something. Anything. Must be something. Fisherman rod?'

She shook her head. 'There are lots of activities on offer on this plane. But fishing? I don't think so.'

The feng shui master looked up at the ceiling. 'I wonder, can we pull off a piece of door frame or something to use as long, straight stick?'

'We're on a plane, CF. Planes don't have sticks lying around. And they don't have doors and things you can pull to pieces without people noticing.'

'What about a broom?'

'I think they probably clean stuff up with a vacuum cleaner.'

The pair lapsed into silence.

Then Joyce's eyes opened wide. 'I've got an idea. Just wait here. I'm going up to the conference room for a minute.'

A few minutes later, she returned. She opened her palm to show a tiny metal device, like a miniature flashlight.

Wong peered at it. 'That is what?'

'It's a laser. People use them as pointers during presentations.'

'Too small.'

'It makes a long, thin, straight line. As long as you like.' She turned it on and a tiny red spot appeared on the wall, seven or eight metres away. And, as it's a laser, it's exactly straight.'

The feng shui master smiled. What a useful tool for a geomancer this was. 'Good. Let's go.'

They went down the lower aisle towards the scene of the crime but quickly met a problem. Police officer Chin Chun-kit was still posted outside.

Wong frowned. 'Problem. How can we get past him?'

'I think I've probably got a better chance of distracting him than you,' Joyce said.

She undid her top button, rolled up her skirt waistband to turn it into a mini, and then strolled, slightly drunkenly, towards the officer. The slouching, bored officer immediately straightened up as she approached. He gazed directly ahead, trying to be formal and unseeing.

'Is this the Chill-Out Room, officer? I really need to lie down.'

'No, that way.'

She swayed unsteadily and he put out his hand to catch her. 'Careful. Chill-Out Room is that way.'

'I'm sure it isn't. I tried that way already.' She leaned against him, grabbing his jacket, and pressing her right breast into his upper arm.

'I think it is that way.'

'Naah. I tried already.'

'Erm. I'll show you. It's just a few steps away.'

He took her arm and guided her towards the back of the plane.

Wong took the opportunity to sneak into Seferis's room. He raced over to the desk and looked at the damaged wall. He tucked the end of the laser pointer into the double bullet hole and switched it on. A red spot appeared on the other side of the room, just under the window frame. The bullet would have crossed the entire room, coming from just below the window from which technician Danny Tang claimed to have seen the whole thing.

The geomancer left the room and headed back to the restaurant where he ordered noodles.

Joyce reappeared a few minutes later. '*Jeez*,' she said. 'My head really is spinning. I don't think I should have had all that Moët.'

Wong slurped his tiny portion of food noisily, and spoke with his mouth full. 'I know where the bullets were fired from. Also I know why they were so small.'

'Tell me, tell me.'

'They were fired from the window—from *outside* the window.'

'But plane windows don't open—that woman Poon told me.'

'No. They do not open. Even on Skyparc.'

'But the guy outside—'

'The guy outside remove outer panel. He was replacing a rivet. He took rivet out, stuck barrel of a narrow gun into hole, and pulled trigger four times. All four shots went at exactly same angle. Rivet hole is narrow and there is only one direction he could fire. Plane body is curved. But he or his partners already made sure Seferis's desk was at correct angle. All carefully set up.'

'If Seferis was sitting at his desk, he would have had his back to the window. How come the bullet went into his chest from the front?'

Wong slurped his second mouthful of noodles and emptied the tiny dish before answering. 'I think man at the window stuck his gun in through the window rivet hole. And then taps at Perspex with his other hand. Seferis stands up and turns around. The man at the window shoots gun. Seferis falls backwards against wall and starts to slide down. The man shoots three more times at same angle, hitting him once in shoulder, and hitting wall twice. The rivet hole is tight and there is no way he can change angle of gun. Still, bullets are small and powerful—even one is enough to kill Seferis. So the man hides the gun and then starts shouting to his comrades that he has seen something shocking: he says he has seen a young man killing Seferis. They have heard the shots. It all seems to fit. So the belief is that engineers in hangar witnessed whole thing: Paul killing Seferis.'

'But Paul was actually upstairs.'

'Yes. Paul was never in the room. Whole claim of murder being widely witnessed actually built around lies of one man only.'

'Danny Tang. But how can we prove Paul never came down?'

The camera tapes for the back stairs. It's not the tapes of Paul going up front stairs that are important. It is the tapes that prove he did not come down back stairs. There is a camera. The images from that camera will show he never came downstairs during time of murder. Silence say more than speech.'

'We need to tell Jackson about this.'

'Yes.'

❀ ❀ ❀

Breathless, Joyce took Wong to the security guard's chamber.

'If we can get the tapes or disks from the camera before someone hides them or destroys them, the lawyers can prove Paul never came downstairs. It kinda shows the whole thing was a frame-up,' Joyce said excitedly.

'Correct. Security man will help us?'

'We gotta try. He seemed friendly. A bit too friendly, actually.'

'How do we get in?' said Wong, looking at the flat panel wall with no door handle.

'We just ask.'

Joyce tapped at the wall and heard Drexler's voice. 'Huh?'

'It's me. Joyce McQuinnie? I changed my mind. I want to try some of your special brew.' She spoke in a flutish, girly voice.

'Heh-heh. I knew you'd be back.'

They heard the door click open.

Drexler's grinning face appeared. 'Hello, darling. We're talking about an irresistible force of nature here. Come to Daddy.' He held out his large hands.

'Uh,' said Joyce, jerking her head to show the guard she was accompanied. 'You know Mr Wong? While we're all here, we wonder if you can do us a little favour.'

Drexler's grin stayed on his face but its sincerity drained away. He lowered his arms. 'Yeah? What do you want?'

'We want the images for the back stairs area at the time of the murder.'

'Why?'

'Because they'll show the intruder never came downstairs at the time of the killing.'

'We don't have tapes showing that.'

'Why not?'

'Uh, there's no camera there.'

'Yes there is. You caught me there earlier today, remember? By the swimwear boutique.'

'Uh, the camera's working now. Wednesday it wasn't. It was broken. It was switched off.'

'Which? Broken or switched off?' asked Wong.

'Hey, what's it to you?'

'Broken and switched off are not the same thing.'

'Are you trying to imply something? I don't need this.'

'Whoa, hold your horses. We're just trying to find out what happened that morning. If Paul Barker didn't come downstairs, then he didn't shoot anyone on the lower level, that's all. It's important to know the truth,' Joyce said.

Drexler spread his palms, as if he was asking her to be reasonable. 'Look. The greenie guy killed the oil guy—we all know what happened. Geez, there were witnesses. All the techies *saw* him do it. Everyone heard the shots.'

'Careful,' said Wong, pointing at Drexler's left hand reaching for the phone. 'He is calling someone.'

Drexler stabbed the redial button on his phone.

Joyce's fist flew to her mouth: it was evident they'd shown their cards to the wrong man. She slammed the door, shutting Drexler in his bunker. Then she started looking around frantically for something to push against the door. Wong had already spotted a drinks trolley, which he swung around and wedged between the security chamber door and the other side of the aisle.

Unfortunately, the door opened inwards—which became apparent when an angry Drexler yanked it open. Wong kicked the trolley so that it tipped into the bunker. Various vessels tumbled off the trolley. They heard a howl of pain behind them as something heavy landed on the man's foot.

They raced off down the corridor—but where could they go? They were in the aisle of an aircraft. There was nowhere to run, nowhere to hide.

Almost immediately, they heard multiple footsteps behind them and angry male voices: 'What's happening?' 'Trouble. That way.'

Joyce stumbled as she raced along the aisle, then she heard Wong fall back and call out to her: 'Here, come here.'

She turned to see him vanish through another small, almost invisible door on the left side of the aisle. She turned and went back to it, jumping through and slamming it shut behind her. It was freezing inside. 'Where are we?'

'Internal emergency door heading to luggage section below.'

Joyce realised the time Wong had spent studying the aircraft plans was paying off—providing them with their best hope of staying hidden.

'He's in on this, right? The security guy.'

Wong nodded. 'Yes. Maybe. Don't know. Is a frame-up. Few people together. Danny Tang, this guy, maybe other people. Don't know. I think some group wants oil company man dead, and get Paul blamed for it. So they arrange a murder.'

'What do we do now? We can't stay here for the whole flight.'

They heard footsteps race past them. They waited until there was silence from outside. Wong gingerly opened the door. There was no one in sight. They crept out.

Joyce chewed her lower lip. 'This is so scary. There are so few directions we can go in. A plane is a rotten place for hide and seek.'

'The best place to hide is plain sight,' Wong said. 'We go back to Gourmet Boulevard. Always many people there. We must tell Jackson.'

As they approached the main dining area, they were intercepted by Robbie Manks. 'There you are. You guys disappeared. I thought you'd decided to parachute off the plane. Come on, there's some jolly interesting people I want you to meet.'

'Mr Manks, we have to tell you something,' said Joyce.

He turned around and started marching the way he came, gesturing for them to follow him. 'What's that? Talk to me as we walk.'

'It's important. We've learned something important about the murder.'

'Really? Excellent. It'll be good to get that whole nasty business cleared up as soon as possible.'

'Paul Baker didn't kill Seferis. We're sure of it.'

'What? But everyone saw him do it. There were loads of witnesses. It's on *video*, for Pete's sake.'

'We need to talk to you somewhere private—explain how we think it was done.'

'Do you really mean this? Bit far-fetched, surely.'

'We know how it was done,' Wong said. 'Mr Paul did not shoot him.'

'Good God.'

Joyce agreed. 'Things aren't what they seem.'

'Often the case,' Manks said. 'Come along. If you want to talk in private, there's a room over here we can use. Step lively.' He raced down the corridor at high speed, and the other two had to almost run to keep up with him.

They approached a door built into a wall which Joyce recognised. 'Why are we here?'

'It's a good place to talk. Nice and quiet. We won't be disturbed. Step inside.'

Wong and Joyce stepped into the room—into the hands of Drexler and the small restraining room he had shown Joyce earlier.

'Now I gotcha,' the security chief said, clamping his big hands on Joyce's arms. 'You should have been more cooperative last time.'

Joyce turned to look at Robbie Manks: 'You're in on this as well, correct?'

The PR officer smiled. 'We've spent a long time and did a great deal of very hard work on this little project for BM Dutch

Petroleum. And we really don't want you guys spoiling it. We need to make sure everything goes forward perfectly smoothly. It's really very important: much more important than you people will ever know. Welcome to Alcatraz.'

Wong and Joyce were roughly manhandled into the restraining chairs, their hands tied to the armrests.

'You can't leave us here for ever,' Joyce said. 'The plane will have to land sometime, and then we'll spill the beans.'

Manks nodded. 'True. But by then, unfortunately, you will be unable to cause us any more trouble. You see, we'll tell everyone that one of the Pals of the Planet, Paul Barker, committed murder. Two other activists, friends of his, equally evil people, came on board the plane to cause even more trouble. We'll tell people you made terrible threats to crash the plane and had to be locked up in the restraining room.'

He turned to the canister affixed to the wall. 'This special gas release system sedates people locked in here. Unfortunately for you, it is going to be accidentally damaged so you get a much larger dose than is safe—sleep, delirium, brain damage, possibly death. That's what's coming your way. If you're alive after a couple of hours in this room, you'll be babbling. What a tragic accident this is going to be. You're heading to dreamland, and you're not coming back. Bon voyage.'

He switched on the device, which gently hissed, then Drexler took a large wrench and smashed the top off it so that gas sprayed out at a higher speed.

'If it's any comfort, this is the nicest way to die,' the security chief said. 'You just go to sleep and that's it. They say the dreams you have are really nice. *Auf Wiedersehen*, suckers.'

Manks and Drexler left the room, sealing the door behind them.

For the next two minutes, Wong and Joyce yelled and shouted and stamped their feet, trying to attract attention. But the room was soundproofed. They could hear no one and no one could hear them. After another sixty seconds, the gas was starting to work on them and they felt drowsy and delirious.

Joyce felt herself going under. Everything was going white. And then she was asleep.

She heard voices. Her mother? Her sister's voice, as a child? She saw the old house in which they had lived. She felt the panic disappearing, replaced by a sense of happy calm.

Then there was another voice, sharper, clearer—a male, calling her name?

'Joyce? Jojo?'

She opened her eyes. It was Army Armstrong-Phillips, a handkerchief held over his nose and mouth.

'Hello, Joyce. I'm afraid I followed you. Hope you don't mind. I saw you racing along with Robbie. Would this be a good time to rescue you?'

'I don't know, what do you think, CF? Would this be a good time to rescue us?'

'What?' Wong asked.

'Get us out of here!' Joyce screamed.

'Okay, okay, I was just asking,' Army said as he unclipped their wrists.

They stumbled out of the restraining room and Army shut the door firmly behind them.

After a few deep breaths of fresh air Wong and Joyce raced along the corridor, leaving Army behind in their wake, and were soon hammering on the staff toilet door.

'Mr Jackson?' the feng shui master called. 'You in your room? Must talk to you. Very urgent.'

The door opened and the loud *slooo* sucking noise of an aircraft toilet flushing could be heard.

J Oscar Jackson Junior zipped up his fly.

'Excuse me. The toilet's not just a secret entrance. It's a working toilet, too. What's the panic?' he said, somewhat indignantly.

'We got news,' Wong said.

Jackson summoned them into his room behind the toilet. 'Uh, just hold your breath as you step through. My stomach's kind of weird these days. Special diet.'

In the envoy's private room, the feng shui master explained that they had worked out how Seferis was killed and how Barker had been framed for it. He explained how Manks and Drexler had tried to silence them.

'Jesus,' Jackson breathed. 'That's nasty. That's really—'

'Army saved our lives.'

'Army?'

'A close friend of mine.'

Joyce said she believed Kaitlyn MacKenzie was in on the scheme too. 'I don't think Paul tricked her into getting him onto the plane. I reckon she approached him. It was all part of the set-up. That's why she's so reluctant to talk about it.'

Jackson tapped his pen on the desk.

'I've got some news for you too. We've been in touch with the authorities in Hong Kong. They've confirmed that someone on the ground in the engineering team was found to be operating under entirely false documentation and has been detained.'

'Danny Tang,' Joyce said.

The police are going to email the details and a photograph to us so we can compare notes.'

'There's email on this plane?' Joyce asked excitedly.

'Kid, this is Skyparc. There's *everything* on this plane.'

'Can I check my gmail?'

'No.'

'What do we do now?' Joyce asked.

'Gather your facts. I'm going to call a meeting—get Sir Nicholas Handey and all the top people in on this. The truth had better come out and be spread as widely as possible before Manks and his people try anything else.'

❀ ❀ ❀

Less than an hour later, the twenty most senior people related to Skyparc Airside Enterprises were in the main upper deck conference room of Skyparc—the room Wong had feng-shuied just one day earlier. There was an air of excitement. Rumours were flying around that there had been an unexpected break-through in the murder investigation.

Sir Nicholas Handey was chairing the meeting.

Robbie Manks and Ryan Drexler were not present—on Jackson's instructions, Sir Nicholas's private bodyguards had detained them and they were under lock and key in the flight attendants' rest quarters.

Jackson was on his feet, explaining the situation into the microphone. 'For many years, people interested in the environment have been aware of increasingly bitter and complex battles between the energy companies and the environmental activists. These have ranged from low-key protests at oil facilities to letter-writing campaigns and to guerilla-type attacks. Fortunately, the vast bulk of the skirmishes have been good-natured. They tended to climax with a pro-environment banner being unfurled at some facility or other. They rarely involved violence or loss of life. The names we associate with such protests include Greenpeace, Friends of the Earth, the Conservation Society, Pals of the Planet, and so on. But there were times when the temperature was raised a little higher, so to speak, with groups like Earth Agents, for example, who did not shun violence.

'The emergence of all these groups, good and bad, resulted in an equal and opposite reaction. The energy groups hired PR companies and spent vast amounts of money advertising themselves as the good guys, people who were just doing an honest day's work and trying to keep your lights switched on so that families could feed their babies and so on. Just as most activists used wit and humour and a light touch, most companies fought back rather gently with advertising campaigns. But just as there were extremists among the environmentalists, so there were factions in the industry who believed that a much tougher reaction was necessary: a reactive group that would share a characteristic with the Earth Agents—a total disdain for the law. I am a worker for a charitable foundation, but I also have a wide brief to keep up to date with developments on both sides of the environmental lobby. My people have been keeping an eye on a secretive group known as Darkheart, set up by renegade elements in the energy industry, to react violently to violent attacks—or to attack first and describe it as "pre-emptive action".

'In recent years, the aviation industry has come under examination because of the amount of carbon damage it does to the environment. So, when this new plane was launched, there was some effort made to portray it as a "green" project, or at least "greener" than other planes: the idea being that if you had to burn carbon, this plane would do less damage than others. Rather lofty claims were made. I am sure people like Sir Nicholas expected criticism of this project. A great many interested parties became involved in the discussion. And this was not just a debate of polarised opposites. There were many people in the middle. I guess the people I represent are among them. I come from a foundation led by one well-connected individual in particular, whom I shall not name. But my employer is at the same time very much part of the establishment. We want Britain and British businesses to thrive—but not at the expense of its environment, or the environment elsewhere on the planet. That's why I am here.

'We expected there to be a not inconsiderable amount of debate about this plane on its maiden world tour. However, we did not expect the shocking events of Wednesday: the murder of Dmitri Seferis. Nor did we expect some other revelations, which have only just become apparent in the past few hours.

'We don't really know the full details of what has been going on, but some very disturbing information has come our way. We are deeply indebted to Mr Wong here, and his assistant Ms McQuinnie, for their work in uncovering some very unexpected information. As you know, Mr Seferis was brutally murdered on this aircraft two days ago. A man, an intruder, was apprehended almost immediately afterwards. He has been charged with murder. But it has emerged that the obvious conclusion was not the correct one in this case. I will hand the floor to Mr Wong at this point.'

'Floor? Not mic?' the feng shui master said.

'Yes. You have the mic. We just call it the floor. It's just…
well…what we say.'

Wong blew into the microphone to check it was working
before he started to speak.

'Someone killed Mr Seferis. That person wanted everyone
to think it was Mr Barker who kill him. But it was not. A small
group of people came up with a plan. This is how we think they
did it. First, one member contact Mr Barker and said she could
arrange for him to get on board Skyparc so that he could cause
some trouble at a particular time. He is a activist and like to
cause trouble. Second, one member of this group moved Mr
Seferis's desk on the plane, so that his back faced the seven-
teenth window. Third, one member of this group switched off
the cameras that would have recorded scenes of the staircase
leading to the lower deck, where Mr Seferis's room was. Fourth,
one member of the group join the engineering team as a window
seal expert, and removes outer covering from window panel,
and takes out one rivet. He places barrel of gun through small
hole. He uses a small-bore pistol to shoot Mr Seferis and kill
him, shooting from outside the plane. He fire four shots. He
then tell everyone he had seen Mr Barker shoot Mr Seferis.'

There was silence at the beginning of Wong's address, but
soon it was punctuated by sharp intakes of breath. Now people
were starting to whisper animatedly to each other.

'Plan very clever,' the feng shui master continued. 'They had
eye-witness evidence that Mr Barker had got into hangar just
before the murder. They had video of him getting onto plane.
They had eyewitness who claims he saw him do the shooting.
They had many people who said they heard the shooting. They
had a video of him leaving plane after the shooting. But really he
had nothing to do with it. He went on to the upper deck of the
plane to cause trouble in a small way. He did not even go downstairs at any time. He heard shooting and decide to leave. What
is clear is that these bad people want him lock up for the rest of
his life and they organise way of achieving that. The mystery is
why they want Mr Seferis dead. He was not a activist, but one of

the people oppose to the activists. He was oil company executive, and had been one for many year.'

Joyce rose to her feet and took Wong's mic. 'The theory I've got is that Mr Seferis had come to realise that all this stuff about global warming was true. He was showing signs of shifting to the other side. Or he was a double agent—a greenie who had penetrated the executive level of a big oil company. Or something like that. We don't really have any evidence for this. But he was listening to *Biscuit Dunked in Death* by The Rogerers just before he died, you know, aha!' The audience looked uncomprehendingly at her.

Wong took the mic back. 'If it is true that Seferis is on greenies' side, the plan very clever. The gang can get rid of two enemy with one shot. They get rid of Mr Seferis by arranging for him to be killed. They get rid of Mr Barker by arranging for him to be blamed for Mr Seferis's death. Mr Jackson mention a group of dirty player called Darkheart. We believe this could be Darkheart project. Now I need to sleep.'

There was stunned silence at this. And then Janet Moore at the back started clapping. And so did Jackson. And so did Sir Nicholas Handey. And so did everyone in the room.

Sir Nicholas rose to his feet. 'Mr Wong, Ms McQuinnie, we'd like to thank you for uncovering this deception. As an initial token of our thanks, we'd like to offer you something. May I give you the keys to the presidential suite? I think you'll find the four-poster beds in that apartment very comfortable indeed. Normally, no one is allowed in there. But in honour of your achievement, I think it behoves us to reward you accordingly.'

❈ ❈ ❈

Ten minutes later, Jackson emerged from the on-board business centre with a photograph in his hand. His brow was knitted. 'Joyce, I got the email with the picture of the fake technician. I'm not sure if…well, here it is. Have a look.'

'Right, thanks.' She took it from his hand but had difficulty focusing on it: her head was still woozy from the gas. 'Hey. This isn't him. This is a woman. The guy I was talking about was younger, a Chinese American called Danny Tang. He did the windows. This is Ms Tammy Poon, the woman who worked with him. She's in charge of wheel mountings or something. I think they got the wrong person.'

'Now that's weird. She's the one with the fake ID.'

'Could there have been two technicians on the team with fake ID?'

'Do you think so?'

'No, actually I don't. Danny kept trying to imply that several people saw the shootings, although when it came down to it, he had to admit it was just him. That woman Poon was more honest. She admitted from the start she wasn't with him and didn't see anything. I don't think they were working together. It's a mystery. I think they got the wrong person.'

'I think we've solved enough mysteries for a while,' said Jackson. 'I need to go get something to eat.'

'Another chicken salad?'

He sighed. 'You noticed?'

'Yeah. You don't have to lose weight. A bit of weight looks good on a big guy.'

'Thanks. You're a pal.'

'And you're a planet.'

He mock-slapped her.

❁ ❁ ❁

Within minutes, CF Wong was snoring loudly in what he liked to think of as 'the Queen's bed', in the largest room of the presidential suite.

Joyce was at the Captain's Bar, eating ice cream and flirting wildly with Army Armstrong-Phillips.

All was at peace with the world.

And then the real trouble started.

Chapter Five

Saturday

In the town of *Cloud Mountain, some brothers organised a competition to construct the scariest ghost.*

The oldest brother stuffed old clothes with straw and made a dead man, which he hung in his doorway.

The second-oldest brother took a piece of wood and carved a fox fairy, which he placed in his window.

The middle brother took a piece of paper and drew a white ghost, which he stuck to his wall.

The second-youngest brother took some sticks and made a forest demon, which he tied to his roof.

The youngest brother did nothing. But he accidentally knocked over his rooftop water tank. He ran off to hide in the forest before his wife came home and discovered what he had done.

The judges looked at each of the ghosts in turn.

When they came to the youngest brother's house, they could see nothing. But the damp floorboards of the empty house creaked and groaned and moaned.

*The judges dropped their writing tablets and fled,
screaming.*

*Blade of Grass, a man finds ultimate comfort in good
friends, good food and good drink. But he finds the ultimate tale
of horror only in his imagination.*

From *Some Gleanings of Oriental Wisdom*
by CF Wong

The bombs went off at midnight. They were tiny packages
of explosives, each smaller than a human fist. Getting a bomb
of any appreciable size onto a plane is supposed to be virtu-
ally impossible these days. When it comes to a VIP plane with
multiple extra layers of security, then it should be impossible.
This particular aircraft had sixteen separate bomb-sensors on
board, designed to detect everything from Semtex-A to liquid-
and gel-based explosive substances. Unfortunately, the bombs
on Skyparc were so small and had been placed so low in the craft
they were not detected by any of the sensors. None of the four
was in the main body of the aircraft.

Three of the bombs contained explosive devices, tiny but
powerful enough to rip steel. Yet it was not the strength of the
devices that was going to cause the trouble, but their locations.
Each of the aircraft's three wheel assemblages had one such
bomb. They were placed on the mechanisms that lowered the
undercarriage. As the devices exploded, the hydraulic systems
were ripped to shreds, blown out of their mountings, or simply
left dangling—all three wheel housings of the plane were left
inoperable. The fourth bomb was slightly different. It was an
incendiary device, designed to release bursts of paraffin and
oxygen, and then ignite a fire. It had been placed in the lower tail
of the aircraft. It went off with a loud *ffft* sound, and the flame
quickly took hold.

The devices all went off in that strange half-night that exists
on planes, a sort of false midnight designed to mark the mid-point
of the journey, and which was, therefore, not actually midnight
according to the body clocks of any of the people on board.

CF Wong, in a coma-like state as deep as the Marianas Trench, slept through it without any reaction.

Joyce McQuinnie was also asleep—but on a sofa in the bar. Army Armstrong-Phillips had placed a blanket over her and loosely tied a safety belt around it.

The pilot, former Royal Air Force Captain Eamonn Turlough Daniel Malachy, was the first person to react. He heard the explosions as a single, rather extended *bang*—and he was immediately concerned.

Things did go wrong on aircraft, rather more often than members of the public were supposed to know. But in ninety-nine point nine nine nine per cent of cases they were predictable things. One system would go down, and a back-up system would spring into place. Everything important in an aircraft was duplicated as there was no room for risks. Such irritations would normally announce themselves through a change in the display in front of him. A light would start flashing. The computers would alert him to a material change they had detected. In rare, serious cases, a little alarm would go off in the pilot's cabin, making sure he did not miss anything.

But a bang? An unexpected, percussive sound? A noise loud enough to be heard over the hums of the one hundred-plus machines in the immediate vicinity of the pilot? That could be seriously bad news. And when you were thirty-nine thousand feet in the air with a load of VIP passengers, any bad news had to trigger an emergency response.

He quickly stabbed a button that alerted the other senior officers, who were resting in their quarters nearby, and told them he needed help. Within a minute, all three were at his side.

'What is it, Captain?' said Enrico Balapit, a half-Filipino, half-American giant of a man with black-brown hair. 'Engine down?'

Malachy shook his head. 'Not an engine. I don't know. There was a bang. A big one. Extended. Maybe more than one—a string of explosions—three, maybe four. Look.'

They stared at the display. Lights had started flashing on all the indicators connected to the undercarriage.

'Jesus. Looks bad,' Balapit said.

'Something. It's...' Malachy was left speechless—unusual for him. 'I don't know. Something bad has happened. Maybe something really bad.'

A *whoop-whoop-whoop* sound erupted in the cabin.

'Hell, there's a fire on board. Where is it? Jesus.'

Balapit slid into his seat and started tapping at buttons on the display. 'It's in the back of the plane. The very back. Seems to be under the tail. Or in the tail.'

'A fire in the tail? Then why are the wheels out of action? None of this adds up. Unless the machines are screwed.'

The displays appeared to show trouble at the extremes of the plane—at the tail, at the wheels almost directly below the pilots, and at the wheel assemblages under the centre of the wings.

'How in heaven's name could four things go wrong at once, at different ends of the damn plane?'

First Officer Ubami Sekoto entered the cabin. 'What is it? Shit.' He stared at the array of flashing warning lights on the pilots' displays. 'Electrical problem in the display?'

'Sadly not. It's bad, soldier. Not sure just how bad, yet, but it ain't good.' Malachy spoke without tearing his eyes away from the blinking lights. 'Go to the back, see if you can find out what's wrong at the tailplane. Get some staff out to the main cabins. Keep everyone calm. Make sure no one is panicking or trying to get out of the doors or doing anything stupid. Don't say anything detailed yet.'

'Yes, Captain.'

It took them several minutes to work out what had happened. All the wheel assemblages had failed simultaneously: main circuits and back-up circuits. The chances of that happening naturally were zero. This was no accident. Someone had blown out the plane's entire undercarriage system. There was no way they could land. But why was there a fire at the back of the aircraft? There were no wheels there. Another explosive device?

Within minutes, Enrico Balapit had contacted ground control at every airport in the vicinity. 'There are airports, but no big ones, and none close to us,' he told Malachy.

'In this particular case, it doesn't matter. We wouldn't be able to land, even if there was. Shit.'

What are we going to do, Captain?'

'Keep in control, soldier. Keep in control.' Malachy glanced at his neighbour. Balapit was visibly shivering. To go from deep sleep to a massive emergency had clearly caused havoc with his nerves and it looked as if he could barely coordinate his hands and eyes accurately enough to operate the equipment.

But he continued to do his job, looking for help from the ground. After a minute, he had a radio link to an air traffic controller from the biggest nearby airport, which was slightly north of them in southwest China. The man spoke understandable English, although with a heavy accent.

'I going to try to find out what's going on,' the man on the ground said. 'I will call local hotel.'

What? A hotel? We're in a burning aircraft thirty-nine thousand feet above your head and you want to book us rooms at a hotel?'

'I want to see if there is any news on CNN or one of those channels about what's happening. This is China. We are not allowed CNN except at hotels where foreigners stay.'

'Understand. Any news at all, I want it immediately.'

'Understand. Over.'

'Jesus.' Malachy shook his head. 'This is crazy. I'm going to concentrate on keeping this bird in the air. Enrico, send a team to the back of the plane with more extinguishers to help Sekoto. Let's hope to God he can locate the fire and put it out. I hope to high heaven it's a false alarm, but if it isn't we'd better piss on it before it spreads.'

Balapit got a signal through to several larger but more distant airports, but then dropped them when the mainland

Chinese ground contact almost directly below them got back in touch. 'Some news has been released to major news channels including CNN about trouble on your plane. There are some reports on it. They started on Reuters and Agence France Presse. Some of the news outlets have pieces on it. I managed to call it up on CNN.com using a proxy server outside China.'

'About us? What's it say?'

'It says a group of activists called Earth Agents have announced that they have bombed Skyparc. It says there is no independent confirmation that anything has happened to the aircraft, which is in mid-flight between Hong Kong and London. I read it to you: "A spokesman for Skyparc initially dismissed the claim, explaining that the aircraft had such high security it would be impossible to get a bomb on board. However, in the past few minutes, the official line from the company changed to 'no comment'. On board Skyparc are a number of top people from Britain, including business leaders and other senior establishment figures".'

'Earth Agents. Those dudes are *bad*,' said Balapit.

Malachy nodded. 'They may be bad dudes, but if they've really blown out the undercarriage and set the plane on fire, we're dead dudes.'

He pressed a button to summon a senior flight attendant to the cockpit. As she entered, he yawned slowly and asked her to bring them a round of coffee. 'Strong coffee. And cookies. I want Mrs Fields. The ones with the chunks of white chocolate and the macadamia nuts. We got some sticky technical problems here and a man needs man-food to fuel the brain.'

In truth, he didn't have the stomach for either the coffee or anything to eat, but it was important to send a message to the rest of the staff that their leader was calm and in full control of the situation. Malachy was fifty-eight years old and had moved on from being a pilot to a senior business executive at Skyparc Airside Enterprises. But he liked to keep his hand in at flying and was the perfect choice as the captain of the cabin crew for the launch of the luxury super-jet. He had offered to command the inaugural flight not just for sentimental reasons, but because he had been one of the team that conceived the project, and he thought of it as his own. Now, he was in the biggest in-flight crisis he had ever encountered: there was nothing in the emergency manuals that offered help for such a situation. They would have to rely on their own ingenuity. Thank God he had a good team with him. He had only flown with Enrico Balapit three times but had found him a steady and reliable partner. They'd spent much of their time teasing each other mercilessly about their Roman Catholic names and upbringings. Malachy, Irish-born, had a string of names, while Manila-born Enrico's middle name was Mary.

By this time, Balapit had got a signal to a contact in London and it was confirmed that Earth Agents had claimed they had placed bombs on board the plane. 'Better keep calm, cool and collected, or I may be tempted to start referring to you as Captain Mary,' Malachy said.

'I may have a silly middle name, but at least people can spell it.'

'You think Turlough is hard to spell? You should see it the Irish way. They spell it T.O.I.R.D.H.E.A.L.B.H.A.C.H. Now there's a challenge for a three-year-old kid at school. All the other boys had names like Bob. I couldn't even spell my own name—I only learned to when I was forty.'

Balapit smiled. 'If I die and you survive, tell my wife I died trying to spell your name.'

'If I die and you survive, contact my cousins and tell them I love them. Their names are Turlough Malachy, Turlough Malachy and Turlough Malachy.'

'All your cousins have the same name?'

'They do. It's a rule in Ireland.'

'I don't believe it.'

'It's true. Your have to name your first son after your father, the second son after your wife's dad, and the third son after yourself. If there's a group of boys, and their fathers are all brothers, and they're named after the same grandfather, they'll have the same name.'

'No wonder they say the Irish are mad.'

'Not mad. I prefer to think of us as lateral thinkers. And I think a bit of lateral thinking is what we need at the moment.'

'What are we going to do?'

'Find a body of water and ditch the plane.'

'I've been looking.'

'Found one?'

The only response to this was a sigh. After thirty seconds, Balapit added: 'I need more time.'

'That's the one thing we don't have, Captain Mary, the one thing we don't have.'

❀ ❀ ❀

The doomed plane was dead calm. The senior staff, with unspoken agreement, had left all the major decisions to Captain Malachy. In the event of approaching disasters, human beings instinctively gravitate towards natural leaders. In this instance, the obvious choice was happily also the one with the most stripes on his sleeves.

Pilots are, of course, provided with detailed instructions about what to say to passengers in the event of any conceivable type of emergency—and inevitable mass death was included in the list of situations with recommended liturgical pronouncements. The underlying principles that guided airline announcements were rather carefully worked out by intelligent and çaring people, although one would never credit it, given the sneering lack of attention frequent fliers gave to airline safety broadcasts. This was the basic shape of it. If the bad thing that had happened was minor, as it was in nine thousand nine hundred and ninety-nine out of ten thousand cases (loss of power in one engine, air-conditioner system on the blink, technical problem in one of the electrical grids), then don't say anything that might remotely cause panic. Instead, say what needs to be said that: (a) fulfils the need to have shown you have kept passengers informed; (b) gives a sanitised-as-possible version of the truth; and (c) is fundamentally a message of reassurance. A tiny chilli hot dog wrapped up in an enormous bun of soft white bread.

However, if the bad thing that had happened was something serious and life-threatening and might not be recovered from (all engines gone, plane with no undercarriage set on fire three and a half kilometres in the air over mountains in China, et cetera), then one had to tell the passengers the plain truth. This was so they could make their final peace with God or Allah or The Divine Cow or whatever they believed in. But, again, it should be done in a way that does not induce panic. It was a matter of overriding importance for decorum and order to be maintained, even if everyone was minutes away from being smashed to smithereens.

Clearly, the authorities who wrote these manuals were British. How does one say, 'We're all gonna die', in a way that does not induce panic? That's the tricky situation that airline staff manuals don't really answer. Instead, they just give general advice. They suggest, sensibly, that the pilot sticks to the facts and sandwiches his comments between softly delivered exhortations to maintain an atmosphere of calm: 'Your tone of voice is as important as the words you choose.'

Malachy had been in the game long enough to know exactly the right tone to take without reading from the manual: 'Ladies and gentlemen, this is your pilot speaking. I have an important announcement to make. I would ask that all passengers listen to this announcement. It is not optional. I am turning off the entertainment system so that you will not be distracted. I will make the announcement in two minutes' time. Please use this time to fully wake up, and to make sure other passengers are awake. If there are older children on board, parents may choose whether or not they wish to wake them. Thank you.'

Leaving a two-minute gap was a calculated risk. What Malachy had done had veered away from the written philosophy of announcements, which emphasised that you deliver the facts cleanly and quickly. But the pilot decided that two minutes was long enough to make it clear to the passengers that this was no normal aircrew chatter of the frequent flier loyalty club/duty free shop/spare change in Unicef envelope/enjoyed having you/fly with us again variety. But it was not such a long period of time that the average passenger would have had time to conjure up nightmare scenarios which could send him screaming up the aisle.

When one hundred and twenty seconds had passed, Malachy was back on the speaker system: 'Ladies and gentlemen, may I have your attention, please? I am sorry to have switched on most of the lights and woken you up, but this is, as I said, an important announcement. A problem has occurred. Let me say, first of all, that there is no need to panic. Problems do occur from time to time on aircraft, and the vast majority of problems are resolved without incident. However, at the same time, I want you to know we are experiencing some technical difficulties. These concern the undercarriage of the aircraft, and we are continuing to work on this, to establish the best way of dealing with the problem. There is also a problem, not fully identified, at the back of the aircraft. Passengers seated there who have not already been asked to move forward, please do so. This area is now off-limits to all passengers. You are free to move about other areas of the aircraft but you may be more comfortable if you are seated with your seatbelts fastened. We are working very hard on resolving both these matters and will keep you informed of our progress. The flight attendants do not have the technical background to answer your questions, but if you have some that you would like to write down and send to my cabin, via the flight attendants, please feel free to do so. I will answer them as I have time. In the meantime, I, or one of my co-pilots, will make an announcement every ten or fifteen minutes to keep you informed of the situation. There is one very, very important thing that I must ask of all of you. We are working hard at solving the problems, but you all also have a job to do in this situation, and your job is every bit as important as ours. Your job is to keep calm, to help others keep calm, to listen carefully to announcements, and to be prepared to do whatever the flight attendants ask you to do. You may wish to use this time to reacquaint yourselves with the information on the flight safety card in front of you and watch the flight safety

video which will be replayed now. After that, we will resume the
flight entertainment system, so that you can relax with music or
a movie if you so wish. Thank you.'

Wong slept through the whole thing.

❀ ❀ ❀

Joyce had woken up for the first announcement but had fallen
asleep again before the second. She was eventually roused by
Army, who had taken to padding around her without straying
far, like a devoted Labrador.

'I think you should wake up now. I think the plane's
crashing or something. We have to get ready for it.'

'Uh,' said Joyce. 'Thanks. Can I get some coffee?' She could
not help staring at the pimple on his chin, which had turned
whitish since she had last seen him. It was not a pretty thing to
see when waking up.

'I guess so. I'll ask the stewardess.'

'Flight attendant.'

'Yes, her.'

'Did I miss any meals? Not that I'm hungry. I need a coffee
though. I'm parched.'

'Okay. By the way, did you hear what I said? I think the
plane's crashing.'

'What?' Joyce looked around. No one seemed to be running
around screaming. Everyone was sitting quietly. The only
surprise was that most people had their entertainment systems
off. 'Crashing? You sure? Doesn't seem like it.'

'Maybe I got it wrong. But the pilot made an announcement, all very low-key and polite—you know how they do
it—but that's what it sounded like to me. He was trying to be
very calm and all that, but I think it was serious. I wonder if we
should do something.'

'Like what?'

'Get in that sort of position, you know, where you put your
head between your knees and say, "Brace, brace".'

'Why would you do that?'

'That's what it says you have to do on the video.'

'I don't think you have to say, "Brace, brace." I think the pilot says "Brace, brace".'

'Maybe everyone says "Brace, brace" together. What does "Brace, brace" mean, anyway?'

'I have no idea. I really need that coffee now, if you don't mind. I'm, like, *dying*.'

'Of course, hang on, I'll get it for you.'

He sped off, leaving Joyce feeling confused and guilty. She was swinging, pendulum-like, in and out of love. Army was skinny and spotty and badly-dressed and a bit of an immature twit, but he was a likeable twit, and might not be bad-looking, if he could be persuaded to have a haircut, a shave, and change his image, his wardrobe, the way he spoke, his mannerisms, his personality, and, well, pretty much everything else. She normally did not like young men who were delicate and winsome and confused, but he was a *real live* royal, and he had saved her life, so it was the least she could do to be nice to him. What on earth was he on about, saying the plane was about to crash? Surely there would be massive panic if that were the case? No one had their heads between their knees saying 'Brace, brace'.

She stood up and looked around again, and was surprised to see a couple in front of her in tears. And then there was a lady to her left with her hands together, feverishly murmuring prayers of some sort. Perhaps something was wrong. She'd better ask Wong—no, he had gone to sleep in the Queen's bed and had given strict orders not to be disturbed. But if the plane was crashing...? She decided she should ask Dilip Sinha, whom she vaguely remembered was sitting in the lounge ahead.

She wandered through the clusters of seats and eventually found him, wide awake, looking at the inflight magazine.

'Hey, Dilip, how's things?'

'Fine, fine,' he said. 'Considering.'

'Considering what?'

'That we're all going to die momentarily.'

'Oh. Army said something about the plane being about to crash. Is it really going to crash? I thought he was just confused.'

'Army?'

'A friend of mine. He's a royal. Possible King of England one of these days, if he plays his cards right.'

'The plane may well crash and we may all die, I'm sad to say. If that is what your friend Army told you, then he is probably right. The pilot made an announcement which has got me rather worried. It was quite difficult to read between the lines, but the gist of it seems to be that the undercarriage has failed. That means we cannot land and there is no sea nearby on which we can make a water landing, so crashing appears to be our only option—and it is not an attractive one.'

'Oh.' Joyce took a minute or so to take this all in. Perhaps she hadn't woken up at all, and this was all part of a dream? It seemed too strange to be real. 'If the plane is going to crash, why are you reading the inflight magazine?'

Sinha turned and pointed to what he was looking at: a map of China. 'Look, I reckon we are about here. I know a fair bit about the geography of this area. I have travelled through much of Asia. I am merely trying to remind myself of the basic facts so that I might be able to go and offer some help to the pilots. I'll see you later,' he said, and headed off to the front of the plane.

'That's good,' said Joyce, who now felt she ought to panic, but simply did not have the energy to do so.

Army arrived with a cup of coffee. 'Apparently they can't do cappuccinos here, because of the pressurised cabin, but they make a pretty decent flat white or double espresso. I got you one of each.'

'That's fine, thanks. I'll take the espresso. And I'm gonna need *loads* of sugar.'

❀ ❀ ❀

Sinha appeared at the pilots' cabin, where a senior flight attendant stood guard.

'I'm afraid you can't speak to the pilots, sir. They're dealing with the undercarriage problems. May I ask you to go back to your seat, sir?'

'I will be most happy to do so. However, I just want to plant an idea in their minds. There is a lake, I think, about five hundred and seventy kilometres from here. It's a reasonably large body of water. It sometimes appears on maps, but often doesn't—it's a poorly mapped area of China, just north of the border with Sikkim. It doesn't appear on this map in the inflight magazine, and may or may not appear on the maps the pilot is using, but I imagine knowledge of bodies of water might help in this situation? Given that the problem, if I heard correctly, is to do with malfunctioning undercarriage?'

The attendant pondered. 'They probably have all the information they need, sir, thank you very much, and I have strict orders not to…Damn it, I'll tell him. Just in case.' She swung the cockpit door open. 'There's an Indian guy here who knows the geography. Says there's a lake to the southeast. Big one.'

Sinha heard one of the pilots bark: 'Get him in here.'

His brow wet with sweat, Captain Malachy stared at Sinha. 'We've got everything in here, conventional maps, radar detectors, satellite maps, a ground link and so on, but I must admit I'm not personally familiar with this area. Tell me about the lake you mention. Is it this one?' He pointed to a C-shaped body of water on the display in front of him.

'No. I know that one—it's a houseboat lake. It's shallow and rather crowded with houses on stilts. It would be difficult and dangerous to land on. Besides, there are rocks sticking out of the middle of it – we call them the summer islands, because they only poke their heads out of the water during dry summers.'

'Where else can we go, then? What's the lake you are thinking of?'

'It's a lake called Nittin Sagra. Quite big and open—not that I have visited it for twenty years.'

On the other side of the cockpit, Enrico Balapit said, 'Let me find it. Southeast, you say?' He tracked the display until he found a small town at the foot of a mountain.

'It's just south of that town,' Sinha said.

The co-pilot brought the computer mouse towards him and located a body of water on the image. 'I'm going to switch it to satellite view,' he said. 'There we go. Damn.'

The exclamation was triggered by the fact that while the lake looked large and open on the map, the satellite view revealed that it had been eaten away at the edges, and a large dam or bridge appeared to have been built across the centre of it.

'Dam is right,' Sinha said. 'Most unfortunate.'

The radio crackled. 'This is ground control A98/11. I'm afraid the news is not good from our end. The nearest suitable bodies of water are quite some distance away.'

While Malachy talked to the control tower, Sinha quietly asked the attendant: 'I thought aircraft were required to fly in routes that kept them within flying distances of water?'

'That's true,' she said. 'This aircraft has a very long range indeed, and we are within the required range of a body of water, the nearest big one being less than two hours' flying time away. But, unfortunately, we have other problems which suggest we may not be able to stay in the air for two hours.'

'Why not?'

'Because, ah, there are other technical difficulties, which, uh...'

'Because the bloody plane's on fire,' Malachy snapped.

'I see,' said Sinha. 'That does put a worrying complexion on things.'

'What are we going to do?' Balapit asked, a nervous tremor in his voice.

'Given that we don't know how long we are going to stay aloft, we've got two choices,' the Captain growled. 'We can fly south to one of the smallish lakes down there. There's water there, but just puddles. We can fly northwest—there's a big body of water there, but it's a long way away. What we can't do is stay on the track we're going. We'll be heading straight into the mountains, and I don't know how long we can stay this high.'

This grim announcement was greeted by silence. Balapit could be heard breathing hard.

Captain Malachy turned and snapped at the senior flight attendant. 'Get everyone sitting down and strapped up tight. I'm turning north. Then I'm going to try some Red Arrow manoeuvres to see if I can get the fire out of the tailplane. It's gonna be a long shot, but long shots are all we have left.'

❀ ❀ ❀

Wong had one of those uncomfortable dreams in which he felt as if he was falling a long distance. The reason for this was that he was in fact falling a long distance.

The pilots had turned several times in a bid to put out the fire—sudden movements, in theory, could blow the flames out and a steep drop could create a temporary vacuum effect, which would deprive the fire of oxygen. But from Wong's point of view, it was an unpleasant experiment. He slept fitfully through the first three such manoeuvres, but the fourth one involved a fall so dramatic that he'd actually left the surface of the bed—not having heard the announcement to fasten his seatbelt.

He opened his eyes, startled to find himself levitating, with the room seeming to fall and his body and the duvet moving upwards off the bed. Was he dreaming? Apparently not. There was a chorus of clattering noises as things on the tables rolled off, some of them flying upwards and hitting the walls or the ceiling.

'Oh. Oh. Oh,' he squealed.

At first he had no idea where he was—his gaze filled with the gently rippling floral-patterned silk that surrounded the four-poster bed. Either he was floating up to it, or it was floating down to him. What was going on? Earthquake? Cataclysm? War? Death? End of the world? All of the above?

When Captain Malachy levelled off, Wong found himself descending equally suddenly onto the super-soft mattress, which was so spongy it seemed to absorb him completely for a second before he emerged and found himself bouncing, jelly-like, on the surface again.

He looked around. Where was he? Some kind of hotel? The notion 'aeroplane' flashed in his mind and everything came back to him. So why was he floating upwards like a weightless astronaut? Was this some function that had been built into the bed—some strange Western sexual perversion, like waterbeds and ceiling mirrors? Was this how Queen Windsor and the Duke of Greece got their kicks? Or was it the pilot misbehaving?

After gravity had returned and been maintained for what seemed like several minutes, Wong decided that it might well be the last of these: the pilot was showing off. This was his privilege, as captain of the plane, but surely he should consider the wishes of his important passengers, especially those in VIP bedding. If the up-and-down movement continued, Wong decided he might take it on himself to complain—not that he had any desire to tell the pilot how to do his work. We all have separate tasks to do. The geomancer saw his own job at the moment as to thoroughly enjoy the fruits of his labours. He loved the huge, soft bed. He would probably sleep a couple more hours, if the pilot could hold the thing steady. But his throat was dry—curse the air-conditioning on airplanes.

There was a *ding* sound and a little light with a picture of a seatbelt stopped shining. The pilot's voice came over the speaker system. 'Thank you for your patience, ladies and gentlemen. This is Captain Malachy again. That little patch of turbulence is over now, and you may use the washrooms again or move about as you wish. However, we would advise that while you are in your seat, please keep your seatbelt fastened. As for the technical challenges I mentioned earlier, I shall keep you informed of any changes in the situation.'

Wong pressed the button to summon a flight attendant, who appeared within a minute, accompanied by Dilip Sinha. The uniformed young woman took his order for a drink, actually three drinks—water, Chinese tea and pomegranate juice—and left to fetch them. Sinha sat down on the edge of the bed and admired the room.

'This is all very *Star Trek*,' he said. 'It's like a hotel room in the sky. Like Bones McCoy's sick bay.'

'This plane very good,' said Wong. 'I think I will use it again.'

'If you can get someone else to pay for the tickets.'

'Of course. Must be *ho gwai*.'

'*Ho ho gwai* indeed, I'm sure.' Sinha composed his features into a look of serious concern. 'Now. On to more serious matters. Have you given any thought to the current predicament? There appears to be a lack of ideas downstairs, which is where we may be of use—you in particular.'

Wong looked at him blankly.

'Oh. Perhaps you have not been listening closely to the announcements?'

'I don't listen to announcements. There should be no announcements when VIPs are trying to sleep.'

'Be that as it may, you should know this aircraft has a problem—a rather serious one. There was a series of bangs, possibly small explosions, and the undercarriage no longer works. We cannot land.'

'What you mean we cannot land? We cannot stay in the sky. Of course we must land.'

'This is true. What goes up...And therein lies the conundrum. The wheels are not working, so we cannot land conventionally. But we cannot stay up here in the sky for very long. Not only will the lack of fuel prevent us from being here indefinitely, but there's a more urgent problem. The plane appears to be on fire.'

'The plane is on fire.'

'Yes. It's not really good news, however one should choose to look at it.'

'*Aiyeeah*. Why not the pilot just stop here in China and we do rest of journey in train? Or better still, stay here in China. Very nice place, very safe.'

'I'm sure the pilot would be delighted to stop in China if he could—but he cannot. There are a number of airports here, but few of them have the facility to land an aircraft of this size and none could cope with a giant aircraft that is missing its wheels. It's a very real problem, I'm afraid, and not an easy one to solve.'

'So what will happen?'

'The tail will eventually be burned off the plane, the fuselage will lose pressure and break up, and all the bits will plummet to the ground and we will all die.'

'Oh.'

'I told you it was hard to make it seem like good news.'

'Any other option?'

'Not really. Well, there is one idea floating around, which I wanted to run by you. It *is* theoretically possible for a plane of this size to make a safe water landing. Difficult, but not impossible. The pilot and I have been discussing bodies of water in the immediate vicinity. There are very few. Now I know that few people have a better grasp of the geography and topology of this part of China than you do, so I wonder if you might feel inclined to come downstairs and join the discussion?'

'Okay. After my tea.'

'Of course. We must get our priorities right.'

❀ ❀ ❀

Many years ago, a King travelled by horse through his kingdom and came to a poor village where he saw something that pleased him. A target was painted on a tree with a single arrow right at its heart.

He rode a few steps further and saw another target, painted on a wall—again, with a single arrow at its centre. All around the village he found such targets—each one pierced just once, with an arrow in the exact middle.

The King said to himself: 'In this town lives the greatest of marksmen. I will ask him to come and train my soldiers.'

The marksman was a boy of just thirteen years old. He moved to the palace and became the greatest leader of the King's bowmen in the history of Old China.

Many years later, the King was on his deathbed. He called the marksman with a question: 'You trained my men to shoot perfectly. But who trained you?'

The marksman said: No one trained me. My arrows were always at the centre of the targets because I painted each target after my arrow landed.'

Blade of Grass, the only thing a man needs to rise to the occasion is to be given an occasion to which he can rise.

From *Some Gleanings of Oriental Wisdom*
by CF Wong

Nine minutes later, Wong was in the cockpit and in a state of extreme horror. 'Cannot! Cannot,' he told Captain Malachy. 'You cannot land plane on top of Tianting West Lake.'

'You're probably right, Mr Wong. I think it is going to be almost impossible to reach the lake, let alone manage a perfect landing on it. But we're going to have to try. It's the only choice we have. If there were other options, I would consider them. But there are none.'

'What's so wrong with Tianting Lake?' Sinha asked. 'It looks big enough on the map.'

Wong explained: 'In Tianting West Lake there are big sea creatures. Dangerous. Large. People will not walk their dogs or children near the edge of the lake. Monsters pull them in.'

Sinha nodded. 'Ah, so that's the place. I've heard of this. There are a few of them in China, aren't there? Lake Kanasi's the one I've been to. Not that I saw a monster there. There's a Tianchi Water up towards Korea that is supposed to have a monster in it, too—human head but buffalo-like body.' The angular Indian mystic looked over to the pilots. 'These are a bit like the Asian equivalents of your Loch Ness Monster. There are supposed to be things in these lakes. Fish as large as cars. Monsters that snatch passing horses from the shore and drag them in. I imagine any Chinese passengers on this plane may feel as uncomfortable as Mr Wong with the idea of ditching the plane in that particular lake.'

The senior pilot sighed. 'Look, I'd love to offer you guys a choice of lakes, so you can choose the most scenic one—perhaps you'd enjoy one with a selection of holiday cabins and a campfire? But this plane is about to fall out of the sky, damn it, and we need somewhere soft to land. Tianting West Lake is our only option. Unless you have other ideas? I thought you told me Mr Wong was an expert on Chinese geography? Does he know of any secret lakes or oceans that just happen to have been left off the map?'

Wong appeared to be pondering something. 'Let me see the map.'

Sinha pointed him to the satellite picture display on Balapit's screen.

'I think we should go that way,' the feng shui master said, pointing to a white blur. 'That would be more safer. We can land there.'

The co-pilot shook his head. 'Er, no, sorry, Mr Wong. That would be a disaster. There's a wall of mountains there. We would slam straight into a pile of rock. It would be a more certain death than landing in a lake of monsters and being gobbled up by a fish as large as a '59 Chevvy.'

There was a crackle and Sekoto's voice came through the intercom. He was shouting. 'Cap'n, it's looking bad. There are loud moans coming from the back.'

'*Moans?* You telling me there's someone in the tailplane, soldier?'

'No, sir. The structure of the plane itself is groaning, not any human being nearby. I think the tail structure is going to fall off. We're going to lose pressure here like mad. It's going to be like being in a giant Hoover.'

'Jesus, Mary and Joseph.'

'Yes, sir. And Muhammad and Allah, too. We need all the help we can get. I'd advise that we don't make any more sudden moves, upwards or downwards. The thing'll fall off for sure.'

'Soldier, we're three miles up in the sky. It's going to be difficult not to make any downward movements. Unless we can park on a cloud.'

'I know, sir. I'm just telling it as I see it. Over.'

'Keep me posted. And Sekoto—thank you. Over.'

❀ ❀ ❀

Wong took a map away with him and sat at a table in the lounge behind the cockpit staring at it. This was a serious problem. But all problems, Wong believed, had a range of possible responses, which went from worst to best. A man's job was not to find the perfect solution, because sometimes such an answer did not exist. No, his job was to conjure up the largest number of options possible and identify the best of them. And the first step in any problem-solving operation was to define the terms of the challenge carefully. Only by going back to basics could one guarantee the possession of a clear picture.

They were over central southwestern China, an area which was hilly to the south and consisted of long flat plains to the north. There were a few lakes, but none was particularly big. The only large ones were hundreds of kilometres to the northwest, towards Xinjiang. But from what the pilots were saying, it was not possible to get that far. They were flying over the edge of Takla Makan desert—the 'land of sand-buried houses'. The area did have water, running in streams from the mountains to the south, but there was no sizeable lake in it. People didn't realise just how vast China was. There were parts of the country—like the one they were flying over now—that were literally two or three thousand kilometres from the sea. It was better to think of China as a planet, not a country. Thinking of it as an orb floating on its own in the solar system gave a better idea of its scale, its grandeur and importance, Wong mused. Pluto, for example, whether it is classified as a planet or a heavenly body, was a mere two thousand three hundred kilometres in diameter. Compare that figure with distances in China: a man travelling from Fuzhou to Urumqi would travel more than four thousand seven hundred and fifty kilometers—more than twice the diameter of Pluto.

In its range of characteristics too, China was a world unto itself. It had its own 'north pole'—the snowy freezing land of Harbin in the northeast, close to Siberia. It had its own Europe—the cool climes of Beijing and Tianjin. It had its own deserts—Takla Makan and Gobi. It had its own Amazon rain forests, on Hainan island; its own Florida, in Kunming, the land of eternal spring; its own Mediterranean coast, in Macau. It was gloriously beautiful and hideously ugly, but mostly the former. Space travellers: welcome to Planet China.

Wong glanced back through the open cockpit door, where he saw the co-pilot doing the same search using a photographic satellite map. The feng shui master turned his eyes back to the table and looked to the south of his map—the Kunlun Shan, one of the biggest mountain ranges in the world, running between the Takla Makan desert and the Tibetan plateau. From this range ran several rivers, including the Karakash, the 'River of Black Jade', and the Yurungkash, the 'River of White Jade'. The rivers joined and fed the Khotan Oasis before crossing the Takla Makan to join the River Tarim.

But no aircraft could land in a river—too shallow, too rocky, too winding. They needed a lake, some sort of large, flat surface. There were many of these in China, literally hundreds. But none was immediately below them. And worse still, the man at the back of the plane had said no sudden downward movements. How could you land without going downwards? They would have to park on a cloud, as the pilot had joked.

Wong put the map to one side and looked out of the window. In the distance, he could see the snowy caps of the southern mountains. How tragic it would be for him to die here, just a few hundred kilometres from the Kunlun Shan, the mountain range where he had spent part of his boyhood and some of his happiest days. Curious that just a few days ago, he had been thinking of the times spent with Uncle Rinchang.

He moved closer to the window and tried to identify the peaks. Which was the one where Uncle had his cabin? One peak, notably higher than the others, must be the Kunlun Goddess, over in the district known as Keriya. There was a slightly lower peak nearer to where they were—Ulugh Murtagh, highest point of the Arka Tagh. Uncle Rinchang's home was on the other side of that peak, a few kilometres to the east.

At that moment, Wong had an idea.

He dashed into the cockpit. 'I know what to do,' he said. 'The aircraft cannot go down to the ground. So the ground must rise up to the aircraft.'

Enrico Balapit scowled. 'Thanks, Mr Wong. We're really busy at the moment. Could you shut the cockpit door on the way out?'

'No, this important. There is a place in the mountains. It very high. A few kilometres high, maybe.'

'We cannot land on a mountain. Now *get out.*' Balapit's voice grew to an angry roar at the end of his sentence.

'Wait,' said Malachy. 'What place?'

'It won't be on the map. I don't know the name. It's a ridge, but shaped like a big flat plain.'

'A plateau?'

'We called it Uncle Rinchang's Walk. Sometimes the locals call it the Fire Dragon's Back.'

Balapit interrupted. 'We need to land on water, not rock, Mr Wong.'

'Uncle Rinchang's Walk is deep snow. Very deep. Very smooth. The snow will hold the plane. Maybe also put out the fire.'

Malachy was thoughtful. 'In theory, I suppose the snow could absorb some of the shock, if it is deep enough, and if there isn't ice under a shallow surface of snow.'

Wong nodded. 'And snow is wet. Usually Uncle Rinchang's Walk is inside a cloud.'

'In a cloud? That's good. It would be wet atmosphere. Dampen the flames.'

Balapit was unconvinced. 'It's a crazy idea. It's never been done before. We have to ditch on water. Come on, Captain, you know the figures. Ninety per cent of crash landings on the ground result in multiple deaths. Ninety per cent of crash landings on water result in most people surviving. Which do you want to be responsible for, Captain?'

Malachy turned to Wong. 'Nice idea, Mr Wong, but my colleague is right. Water landings are a hundred times safer. We're still better off gently lowering ourselves towards a body of water.'

'Then go north,' said the feng shui master. 'In Sichuan you can find a swimming pool maybe.'

He left the cockpit.

❖ ❖ ❖

J Oscar Jackson Junior, charity foundation investigator, private envoy, spy and jailer, had taken his two prisoners into the main conference room, where they sat handcuffed to Herman Miller Aeron chairs. Manks and Drexler were being questioned in case they could add to the store of knowledge about the sabotage to the plane. Several other people had demanded to be allowed into the room, including Joyce, Sinha, Armstrong-Phillips and several staff members from Skyparc Airside Enterprises. Perhaps because of his size and generally authoritative demeanour, Jackson found himself in the situation of chief interrogator.

'Mr Manks, what do you know about the situation on this plane?'

The PR man was beside himself with anger. 'Nothing. Nothing. How could I have anything to do with this? It's ridiculous. I wouldn't plant bombs on a plane and then get on the plane, would I? It would be suicide—literally. This has nothing to do with me.'

'Mr Drexler?'

'Same. Look, just think about it. You can accuse us of all sorts of things, but you cannot accuse us of being raving idiots.

Which is what we would have to be if we put bombs in the aircraft and then climbed on board, knowing that the blasted things would go off halfway through our flight. Be reasonable.'

'Why should we believe a word you say? You have lied and cheated and you were extremely cavalier with the lives of Mr Wong and Ms McQuinnie. They might have died had not Mr Armstrong-Phillips had the presence of mind to follow you and release them.'

'Call us what you like,' Manks said, 'but we know nothing about the bombs, okay? We have no connection to the Earth Agents in any way—they're our sworn enemies, if anything. Can't you see that? I've spent years trying to wipe them out. This may be their revenge against me. Let me go—Her Majesty would not be happy at the way I am being treated.'

Jackson's fists turned white as he squeezed them but he resisted the temptation to use them on the spluttering man.

'We're all going to die, aren't we?' It was a young woman's voice. Everyone turned to see who had spoken. Kaitlyn MacKenzie was standing at the back of the room, her eyes filled with tears. 'Why don't you untie these guys? They may have done something bad, but it's all meaningless now, isn't it? What does it matter if people have done good things or bad things? What does anything matter? We're all going to die together.'

Jackson said, 'Ms MacKenzie, we are talking to these men in the hope of getting information that may help us save this aircraft and our lives.'

'Manks is right—you're behaving like an idiot. I've been in the aviation industry for years, too, you know. We're going to die and we'd better face up to it. The sooner the better.'

'She's right. Let's untie these men. If this is the end, we might as well all end our lives like civilised human beings,' said Army.

Janet Moore, who was standing in the doorway, nodded. 'The best thing to do is to confess our sins and pray for forgiveness. "All have sinned and fallen short of the glory of God".'

Silence flooded into the room. The grim understanding that death was imminent had been under the surface for some minutes; now it had been brought up, a hard, black diamond of horror, dazzling everyone, and making arguments superfluous.

The silence was broken by Drexler: 'Can't they ditch the plane in the sea?'

'We could,' said Sir Nicholas Handey, 'if there was one around here. But there isn't. We're almost three thousand kilometres from the Pacific Ocean, and probably the same distance from the Mediterranean. Even the smaller seas, like the Caspian, are a long way away. The pilots have yet to identify one near us.'

'Jesus.'

'Jesus is right,' said Jackson.

Manks started shaking. 'If...if...if this plane is going to crash, you have to untie us, like the girl says. We'd have no chance of surviving if we're handcuffed inside an aircraft burning on the ground or sinking into a lake. Come on. Please. Show an ounce of humanity for God's sake. Let us die like men.'

Jackson stood up and walked over to the prisoners. 'Maybe Ms MacKenzie is right. At least if we untie you, you can put your hands together and pray. That's the only thing that's going to help us now.'

While he unlocked the shackles, several people in the room burst into tears.

'We should all confess our sins,' advised Ms Moore. 'Is there a priest on board?'

'On an inaugural flight?' Army said. 'This is strictly business, ma'am. Well-connected rich people only.'

'And it would take way more time than we got,' Jackson said.

Manks rubbed his wrists. 'I don't know how we got into this situation,' he said. 'The only thing I have ever done is try to make the world a better place.'

Jackson gave a bitter laugh. 'By cosying up to the royal family and using your connections to secretly do dirty work for the oil giants for big bucks? That's making the world a better place?'

'I know it's fashionable to sneer at the energy companies. But we all use electricity, we all use fossil fuel. I'm doing more to make the world a better place than all your do-goody activists put together.'

Joyce was outraged at this statement. 'Excuse me! We don't all go out of our way to make money at the expense of the world's environment.'

Sinha raised his hand. 'I wonder if I may ask a question or two? If we really do only have a few minutes left before we go to meet our maker, I'm curious to know the answers to a few questions: such as, who placed bombs on this plane and who is ultimately responsible for our deaths? Although whether that question needs one answer or two answers, I can't say.'

'I reckon BM Dutch Petroleum is responsible for our deaths,' said Joyce. All that fake stuff about green fuels and so on—no wonder it made the activist groups furious. It's no wonder the crazy people at Earth Agents decided to blow up the plane.'

'That's a fair argument,' said Jackson. 'The production of this plane and its accompanying fuel did raise the ante on the whole debate about fossil fuels and depletion of carbon. It made it a focus for the arguments.'

Sir Nicholas Handey raised a long, elegant finger. 'If I may just defend my little project, here? We do, very genuinely, see this plane as an improvement on previous aircraft when it comes to the effect on the environment. There are numerous environmental improvements on this plane—we have a whole booklet on that topic alone.'

Army raised his hand. 'Yeah, Sir Nicholas, I read that booklet. It's all very nice, but it's rearranging the deckchairs on the *Titanic*, isn't it? So this plane is not quite as bad in destroying the environment compared to rival planes. So what? On the big scale of things, there's hardly any difference. It farts out one smidgen less pollution than the previous ones—big deal.'

'But that's how change happens, Mr Armstrong-Phillips. In incremental stages. We haven't yet developed a plane that does no harm whatsoever to the environment, but if we do, this plane will be seen as having taken a major step in that direction.'

Several people started to speak at once, but Jackson raised his arm and bellowed: 'Enough.' The room became silent again. The big American let his gaze travel from face to face. 'Somehow, I don't feel that a debate on carbon emissions is the best way to spend our last minutes. I'm going to go away and write a letter. I suggest other people do the same.'

Several people nodded and picked up the note pads.

'I'm going to write to my mother,' said Army.

'Of course, we don't know if our letters will survive or not. If anyone in this room survives this, please tell anyone who asks that J Oscar Jackson Junior spent his last minutes thinking about two little girls—Martha and Marianne.'

This unexpectedly personal note from Jackson caused the weepers in the room to wail even more.

Robbie Manks pointed an angry finger at Jackson. 'Before this meeting ends, one thing I would like to say is that I am not responsible for our deaths in any way. I have spent my life fighting against lunatic activists and I have not had the help and support I have deserved. I am a man of principle and honour and decency. The reason we are going to die is that some lunatic activists have bombed this plane. If people had helped me fight these people, get them locked up, instead of placing stumbling blocks in my path, we'd have rid the world of extremist greenies years ago.'

Kaitlyn MacKenzie pointed her finger at him in return. 'Shut up, Robbie. You disgust me. How can you talk about having principles and being honourable? What a load of crap. You hired me to seduce Paul Barker and get him onto the plane on Wednesday. So you could frame him for a murder. You used hard cash and a promise of a fancy job in London to get me to do your bidding. You used me to frame a guy who really does devote himself to trying to stop the suits flushing the world down the toilet. Decency, my arse. And talking of my arse, you can't keep your bloody hands off it, which totally disgusts me.'

This outburst left Manks speechless with fury. 'That is pure slander,' he said. 'You cannot prove a word of it.'

'Sue me.'

'I am not responsible for the bombs on this plane, in any way, shape or form,' growled Manks.

Joyce said: 'How about you telling us what you are responsible for, creep?'

Manks breathed slowly and deeply, like a wounded bull. 'You will no doubt see me as being responsible for the death of Mr Seferis, but the fact is, he was a turncoat. He was responsible for his own death. The energy firms had given him huge responsibility and he had become a traitor to the cause. He allied himself with the sort of people who want to stop common, decent people from having electricity for their schools and hospitals, fuel for their ambulances, power for their nurseries, for their maternity wards. I'm proud to be a member of Darkheart. We were set up to combat turncoats like Seferis and terrorists like the Earth Agents—people who have put bombs on this plane and are directly responsible for our deaths.'

Jackson sat on the table. 'So tell us, Manks, how did you kill Seferis? Was Mr Wong's theory right?'

'I'm not owning up to anything,' he responded. Then he sighed, and his eyes dropped. 'When the leaders of Darkheart wanted "something done" about Seferis, I argued against having him, er, taken out completely. I suggested he just be sacked, so he could run off and join the sickly do-gooders, where he belonged. But I was overruled by others. They wanted a, er, cleaner solution. They wanted to kill two birds with one stone—him and Pals of the Planet.'

Joyce said angrily: 'So you framed Paul Barker.'

The PR man gave her a cold smile. 'It was not my idea.'

'Whose was it?'

'I'm not saying.'

Kaitlyn MacKenzie rose to her feet. 'If these are the last minutes of our lives, I'm not going to spend them talking. There are much better things I can think of doing.'

She turned and pointed to Max. 'You,' she snapped. 'Come with me. See the rest of you later. Or not, as the case may be.'

The sultry, black-suited young man looked shellshocked, but he obediently rose and followed her. Many of the men in the room watched Kaitlyn's lithe hips as she strode powerfully out of the room, the young man following childlike in her wake.

Joyce turned to Army and murmured, 'You know, for once, I think Kaitlyn has the right idea. Come on.' She grabbed his hand.

Army Armstrong-Phillips turned a bright shade of crimson as Joyce dragged him out of the conference room.

Jackson sighed. 'What it is to be young and carefree,' he said.

'Who needs to be young?' said Ms Moore, giving him a strange, leering smile.

'I gotta go see the pilots,' Jackson said hurriedly. 'See where we're up to. They may need my help.'

❊ ❊ ❊

Oscar Jackson found a quiet space in the lounge and started writing on a page in his notebook. He wanted to leave a letter for his children, who lived in New York with his estranged wife.

'Dear Martha and Marianne,' he wrote. 'This is just a little note to say that your Daddy loves you. Perhaps you two will be the only thing I have successfully achieved in my life. If that's so, that's fine: it will all have been worth it.

'Your Daddy has learned that the purpose of a person's life is to learn what it is to love someone, and learn what it is to be loved in return. You helped me learn those things, so I'm thankful to you. I love you both as much as a person can love another person. There's no greater achievement a person can hope to achieve than that. Maybe you won't really understand this letter until you are much older, but that doesn't matter either. I just wrote it to say thank you. And to say I love you. And to say remember me, just occasionally, as you grow up and learn about love and life. That's all I ask. Your loving Daddy. PS. Look after your mom. She's a great lady.'

He looked at the letter and wondered what to add to it. But he found his vision becoming blurry. Once he'd blinked his eyes clear enough to reread what he had written, he realised there wasn't anything else to add.

❀ ❀ ❀

Battling against mounting odds in the back of the plane, First Officer Ubami Sekoto radioed through to Captain Malachy. 'Captain? We haven't got the fire out completely, but we seem to have got it cornered for the moment, at least. As far as I can see, which is not very far at all, the bulk of the blaze has been extinguished. But there's a lot of smouldering going on, and we can see little licks of flame in various corners. The trouble is—it might explode at any moment.'

'Can you swamp the thing in foam?'

'We're trying. The main area we can access is flooded, but the fire is probably still burning behind the panelling. The stews' lower cabin went up like a fireball. We've got that under control—well, semi—but no promises. The thing is still groaning and creaking. The structural damage is really bad. And there's another thing that's got me worried: the ground under my feet is getting hot.'

'Shit.'

'I don't know what to do. If we fill it with more foam, it may just get so heavy it will snap off.'

'There's smoke coming out of that luggage rack above your head,' yelled a flight attendant.

'Jesus—open it gently.'

A ball of flame erupted from the luggage rack. They stepped back hurriedly. At the same time, the carpet below their feet started steaming.

Sekoto closed his eyes. 'Shit. It's in the luggage hold. That's it.' He grabbed his walkie-talkie and shouted into it. 'The fire is eating into the luggage below us. It'll go up like an Australian bush fire. We're finished, Cap'n Malachy. This is the end game.

We've no more than a few minutes left. If you are going to land, it's now or never.'

The burning plane screamed onwards, still hundreds of kilometres from the nearest lake.

❀ ❀ ❀

Just fifty metres further up the body of the aircraft, peace and contemplation were the order of the day. 'Impotence is a strange thing,' Sinha mused, sitting in a purple spotted chair in the Leopard Lounge, gazing idly out of the windows.

'Do I want to be listening to this conversation?' asked Ms Moore. 'Is this not what is meant by the phrase "too much information"?'

Sinha turned to her with a smile. 'Let me assure you, I am not talking about sexual dysfunction, madam, but about something quite different—the horror of being in a state of total futility when immediate action is essential for the continuation of life.'

'Oh. I see.' Her eyes dropped to her hands, which were idly clasped in her lap. 'But do we really just have to sit here? Isn't there anything we can do?'

Sinha raised his index finger. 'Indeed, there are several options from which to choose. I've made my choice.'

'Which is?'

'I'm going to have another cup of tea.'

'Good idea. I'll join you.'

❀ ❀ ❀

'Jesus,' Malachy said, Sekoto's words echoing in his ears. 'We're out of time. We're landing. I don't know where or how, but this big bird is coming down.'

The feng shui master returned to the door of the cockpit, holding his map and his feng shui compass in the other. 'South,' he said.

'Don't say it, Mr Wong.'

'Is better than landing in Tianting West Lake.'

'We are not going to land in Tianting West Lake.'

'We are not?'

'It's too far away. We're losing the tailplane. The plane's about to break up.'

'So what are we going to do?'

'I don't know…I don't know. For the first time in my whole, bloody, brilliant, heroic, self-righteous life, this Hero Captain Pilot doesn't know what to do.'

Wong made to leave the room.

'Wait.'

He turned around.

'Come here. Sit there. Tell me again about your Uncle Rinchang's favourite walk.'

Wong unrolled his map.

Seconds later, the plane yawed steeply to the left.

❀ ❀ ❀

The scene was white, cold, hard, unyielding, rocky and massive in scale. The mountains were not of the earth. Nor were they of the sky. They seemed to stand between the two. The Chinese legends of the mountains as the pillars between heaven and earth made perfect sense—indeed, it was difficult to see this area as anything other than a region of transition between the land of the humans and the vault of the stars: the land of the gods.

The peaks cut through the clouds, reaching for the moon. Below them, no ground was visible; only layers of shifting mists, like wraiths. Captain Malachy sensed that here Skyparc, 'your office in the sky', had turned into something tiny and delicate: a butterfly in the Grand Canyon, a daisy in a hurricane, a flying ant threading its way between skyscrapers. They headed directly towards a mountain.

Co-pilot Enrico Balapit was apoplectic. 'This is madness. We have no chance. *No* chance. We are going to be blown to bits. This plan is suicidal.'

'Yes. As were all the others.'

'Captain Malachy?' There was ice in Balapit's voice. He stood up, his eyes blazing, nostrils flaring and teeth grinding together.

'Yes, Captain Balapit?'

'If you do not come to your senses, I will have no option but to relieve you of command.'

'Come *on*. Sometimes you have to put the rule book away, Enrico, and just go with your gut.'

'Oh, that's what this is, is it? Feel the force, Luke? I want to live.'

'You think you're the only one?' Malachy spoke with quiet dignity 'We're not going to crash into a mountain. We're looking for a flat, snowy plain—the Fire Dragon's Back. Stop whining and help me find it.'

Balapit spat his words between his teeth: 'Do you realise, if there is one rock sticking up from that ridge, one boulder, one bloody stone, we're going to flip over and fall upside down into the nearest gully?'

'There are no stones,' Wong said. 'Wind has polish the plain for a long time. A million years or more. Then there is thick layer of ice on top. Then thick snow on top of that.'

Malachy said: 'Balapit, the one thing that will do most to make sure we don't flip over and fall upside down off a mountain is if you sit down and do your bloody job.'

The co-pilot stood immobile for several seconds. Then he slid back into his seat.

'Atta boy.' Malachy turned to Wong: 'This plateau, how long, exactly, is it?'

'It is two-three *li*, maybe, about three kilometre.'

'Long enough—just.'

Wong crossed his fingers behind his back. It had been a long time since he had been twelve years old.

❀ ❀ ❀

'Ladies and gentlemen, there's an old Irish saying which says: "May the road rise up to meet you." Apparently, that's also a Chinese saying, too, which makes me feel better.'

He paused and took a deep breath, anxious to sound as calm as possible. 'I'm pleased to inform you that we've found a spot, with the help of a passenger, where the road actually does rise up to meet us. On the mountain range in front of us there is a flat area, a road of a sort. Who knows why someone would build a road in the air like that? I can't answer that. You could ask Mr CF Wong, a passenger whose uncle was one of the people who built that road, or discovered it, at any rate. Perhaps it was designed for this moment. I don't know. Only divine providence knows. Anyway, I am deeply grateful to whoever decided to put it there, because we are going to test it out. Nevertheless, this is almost definitely going to be a bumpy landing, so you will need to get into brace position.'

In the Presidential Suite, Army Armstrong-Phillips and Joyce McQuinnie emerged from under the duvet, where they had been energetically doing what she liked to call 'making out'.

'Brace, brace,' they yelled at each other.

And then they dived back under the bedclothes.

❊ ❊ ❊

The plateau was covered in thick cloud. The plane would have to land blind. Captain Malachy used radar and sonar devices to detect the hard surface of the ground and create coordinates on which the flight computers could lock. He controlled the descent by hand, with Enrico Balapit working beside him. They threaded through cliffs of grey and white, glimpsed through breaks in the cloud, passing the Arka Tagh on their way to Uncle Rinchang's Walk.

'One hundred and fifty metres,' breathed Malachy.

And then their windows were filled with nothing but blind white cloud.

'Brace, brace,' Balapit barked into the microphone. The passengers shrieked.

Skyparc hit the ground. There was a loud *whump* noise as it made contact with the snow and sent several tons of it into the air. The plane shuddered, bounced ten metres upwards, and then descended again, hitting the snow at a less steep angle the second time. This time it stayed on the surface.

The plane skidded forwards on its belly. The metal screamed. The passengers screamed. The pilots screamed.

The overhead compartments were shaken open, showering bags, coats and spare blankets onto the heads of passengers. A food trolley that had been accidentally left unlatched shot out of its hatch, flew into the air and bounced off the galley ceiling. One of the toilets exploded from the pressure beneath it.

The massive aircraft hurtled forwards, much too fast, completely out of control, for a full kilometre. And then it veered to one side, looking as if it was going to career to the left and fall off the ridge—but it somehow righted itself and ended up moving forwards on the centre of the plateau once more.

Malachy and Balapit yanked furiously at their controls, but they seemed to have no effect.

Skyparc continued to move forwards at high speed without slowing. In front of them was an unforgiving, grey, rocky peak—which the plane was approaching steadily.

'Slow it down, slow it down,' Balapit shrieked.

Malachy was trying to use the retro jets to slow the plane's momentum, but there was a problem: 'They're full of snow,' he shouted over the thunderous noise of the plane's belly tearing up against the frozen ground. 'There's no response.' Tons of ice crystals thrown up by the initial touchdown had been gulped up by the front vents of the engines.

As Skyparc closed in on the far end of the Fire Dragon's Back, the top of the tailplane finally cracked and the structure started to break away. It stuck into the ground and acted as a brake, cutting right through the snow layer, etching a line into the hard ice below.

The plane slowed, twisted, and finally came to a halt at a forty-five degree angle to the ridge, anchored by the trailing tailplane.

There was sudden, complete, wonderful silence.

And then it vanished in a chorus of screams, cheers and yells that echoed off the sides of the Kunlun Shan.

Joyce grinned up at Army. 'Free, 1978,' she said.

'What?'

'"All Right Now". Yeah, baby, we're *all right now*.'

Chapter Six

Tuesday

A PLANE TOUCHED DOWN at Heathrow Airport. Not a Skyparc. Not a giant plane of any sort. Just an ordinary Airbus 340. On it were some tired but happy travellers: a group of thrilled-to-have-arrived passengers who had expected to be on a memorable, history-making flight—but had not anticipated just how memorable and history-making it was destined to be.

They had been quickly rescued from Uncle Rinchang's Walk by an airborne division of China's People's Liberation Army, bringing in blankets and hot tea, and escorting them in small groups to a lower plateau where they filed into a series of waiting helicopters. There were a few broken limbs, and many bruises and abrasions. But no lives had been lost.

The choppers shuttled them to a Chinese town called Shache for cursory medical check-ups. They were then sent to the nearest big city, which was Islamabad, just over the Pakistan border, where they were placed in the hands of representatives of their nearest embassies for repatriation. After a day's rest and

215

a good night's sleep at the five-star Serena Hotel in the shadow of the Margalla Hills, part of the Himalayan mountain range, Airbus Industrie of Europe chartered an A340 to pick them up and fly them to their original destination six thousand kilometres away: London. They arrived nine hours later.

❊ ❊ ❊

Joyce stopped on the top step, taken aback. '*Jeez*. Who are all these people?'

'Well-wishers, I guess. We must have been on the news and stuff.' Army gave a wave to the crowd. 'We're celebrities.'

'Yikes.'

Captain Malachy was standing behind them. 'A tarmac meet 'n' greet. How nice. How rare,' he added. 'You should feel honoured, kids. The airport authorities in London very rarely let family and friends onto the air side—just on very special occasions. A delightful custom. They should revive it more often.'

The passengers walked down the metal aircraft steps, gazing at the large crowd waiting to greet them and waving to family members they recognised. Although there were several hundred people present, they were kept in order by a barrier of velvet ropes, like a crowd waiting by the red carpet at a movie premiere. There were also several soldiers present, some dark-windowed cars, and clusters of people in front of the barriers: more VIPs.

'Good grief,' said Army Armstrong-Phillips. 'My great-aunt's here.'

'Your aunt? Not your parents?'

Then it occurred to Joyce who he was talking about. 'Your *great-aunt*? You mean, like *her*?' Her hand covered her mouth.

Army said: 'And lookie here. She's brought her grandsons with her.'

This time it took less than two seconds for Joyce to work out the family connections and guess to whom he was referring. Her eyes grew wide and she dropped the bag she was holding.

'You mean? *You mean?* Where? *Where?*' This last word was uttered in a state of feverish excitement. She dropped his hand and abandoned him, pushing her way down the rest of the staircase and racing towards the crowd.

Army turned to the pilot. 'When Prince Will appears, everything else is forgotten. It's the story of my life.'

Behind them, passengers streamed off the aircraft, breaking into happy yelps as they spotted friends and relatives and started running.

❀ ❀ ❀

Wong and Sinha stood to one side, watching the emotional reunions with a very Asian disdain for public shows of affection.

'Welcome to London. It's not so bad, is it?' Sinha said, looking around the cluster of airport buildings and filling his chest with iced air. 'The West is really just like the East. A little chillier, perhaps, but not really any different.'

The feng shui master looked unimpressed. 'Just wait,' he said. 'Too much drama in the West. Even getting here, too much excitement. Bombs, violence. Very Western. Hope we can go home soon.'

'Surely you can't wait to see Buckingham Palace?'

'Can't wait to see my home,' the geomancer said.

'Why so sour?'

'Not been paid yet. And person who promise to pay—he is locked up. Jailbird now. Who is going to pay me?'

Sinha made a sympathetic cooing sound. 'I see the problem. Jackson may still pay you—although you may have to wait until all the court cases have gone through. It has all become a bit complicated. Probably take months to work it all out.'

'Months?'

'Oh, yes. Maybe years. It will all be bogged down in a morass of legal claims, I expect. Could go on for a decade. Remember Jarndyce v. Jarndyce?'

Wong scowled, thinking of Arun Asif Iqbal Daswani and his knife-wielding friends, waiting for him back in Singapore. Expecting to be paid in a few days.

Aiyeeah. Why did the gods hate him so?

❀ ❀ ❀

The sky, grey and dark, began to open up. Mischievous gusts of wind appeared from nowhere and knocked hats off the heads of people in the crowd. Headscarfs were pulled out of shape and scarves whipped away.

Then, just minutes later, the wind dropped and it began to snow. Large, fat flakes descended slowly, meandering in the air as they found their way to shoulders and the tops of shoes.

'Pretty,' said Janet Moore to Dilip Sinha, as her hair became whiter.

❀ ❀ ❀

Army gave his great-aunt a hug and then wandered around, looking for Joyce. She appeared squealing, banshee-like, out of the crowd and grabbed his hand, sucking him into the throng of people.

'Come,' she said. 'There are some people I want you to meet.'

He followed obediently. 'If it's my cousins once removed, I've already met them.'

But it was two young people, a European girl with short, dark hair, and a stocky Eurasian man.

'This is Nina and Jason,' Joyce said. 'They're my friends from Hong Kong. It's so weird—they saw me off in Hong Kong. And now they're here.'

Nina shook Army's hand and explained: 'When we heard your plane crashed, but everyone survived and would be flown on to London, we got money from our folks to fly over to London and greet you guys. We thought it would be nice if there was someone waiting for Joyce, her folks not being very good at remembering she's alive and all that sort of thing. I hope you don't mind me saying that, Joyce?'

'No.'

Nina whispered to Joyce. 'Should I curtsy to him or something?'

'Nah. I hope you don't mind. I told them you were a royal.'

'I don't mind,' Army said generously.

'I also told them you were totally ordinary.'

'I am. *Totally* ordinary. And proud of it.'

Jason grabbed Joyce's shoulder. 'Kid, did you hear the news about Paul?'

'No?'

'Abel went to see him several times. Kept him in the loop about what was happening with you. Then, as soon as all that stuff came out on the news about new evidence being discovered in his case, Abel started proceedings to get Paul out of jail. He should be out on bail soon, if not already.'

'That's brilliant. I feel…I feel…ooh, Eric Clapton, 1977.'

'"Wonderful Tonight",' said Jason.

'Let's go out and have some fun, the four of us,' said Nina. 'If you guys are not too tired.'

'Well, we have had a fair bit of excitement the last couple of days,' said Army, catching Joyce's eye.

Joyce entwined her fingers with his. 'Bachman Turner Overdrive, 1974,' she said to him.

The young man wrinkled up his face in thought as he tried to play the game. 'Got it,' he said. '"You Ain't Seen Nothin' Yet".'

Joyce touched his lips with her finger.

❊ ❊ ❊

Enrico Balapit and Ubami Sekoto stood on the top of the aircraft steps, looking down at the scene below them.

'I can't quite believe it, can you?' the co-pilot said.

The first officer shook his head. 'Crashing the world's most expensive plane—that was not fun.'

His companion nodded.

'But surviving the crash? That was pretty cool.'

'You want to grab a drink?'

'No…I want to grab a case of drinks.'

Balapit brushed the snow off his colleague's shoulders. 'It's settling. Going to be a white Christmas.'

'Leave it. I like the snow.'

'I guess you don't get a lot of snow in Tanzania.'

'Only on top of Kilimanjaro.'

'Let's not talk about mountains. I've had enough mountains to last me a lifetime.'

'Agreed. One exception: they do this thing called Nacho Mountain in the canteen.'

'I'm there.'

❀ ❀ ❀

'Mr Wong! Mr Wong.'

The feng shui master turned to see who was calling his name. He was astonished to see the tall, swaying figure of Cecily-Mary Crumley of OffBox tottering up to him in extra-high heels. 'Oh. Miss Crumley. How are you?'

'Mr Wong, I heard you were on the plane that crashed, and the passengers were on their way to London, so I thought I might as well come and greet you.' She gave him a warm smile—not at all the reception he would have expected from a prospective business partner in a deal which had fallen so spectacularly apart.

Maybe she was just a very forgiving person? He started to apologise. 'So sorry about—'

'Did you hear the news from Cindy?' she asked.

'Cindy?'

'Cindy. Daswani.'

'Oh, him. What news?'

'About the pens?'

'The pens.'

'The highlighters.'

'Yes. No.' He did not want to be reminded of their existence.

But Ms Crumley clapped her hands together in delight. 'Before I left Singapore I made some enquiries—just on a sort of million-to-one off-chance that anyone might want highlighters with black ink. I found one of the wholesalers who did stationery supplies to Asian governments. It was amazing. Civil servants all over east Asia were looking for exactly this sort of product.'

'They were?'

'They *all* wanted the pens. Perfect for censorship, you see—they're always worrying about what they call "sensitive" news. Our little black pens were perfect. A quick flick of your wrist and the information is gone. They have ranks of people doing that sort of thing.'

'Ah. I see.'

'My wholesaler got orders for all one hundred and eighty thousand pens in twenty-four hours. It looks like it will be an annual order from several of the governments in Asia. It's going to be one of our biggest lines.'

'You sell them?'

'Every last one. It's huge. I want you and Mr Daswani to make more of them. Just the same. Black ink only. I'll send you details.'

Wong was speechless. He eventually managed to breathe one word: 'Good.'

'One last thing.'

'Yes.'

'Here's your cheque.' She pulled open her handbag and pulled out a file containing an envelope with the name Harmoney on it. 'Sorry about the delay.'

The feng shui master took it in his hand and bowed. He tried to say the words 'Thank you' but he was having trouble breathing.

❀ ❀ ❀

As the crowd started to thin into a handful of small, scattered clusters and head for the buses taking them to the main terminal building, Joyce heard someone call her name.

'Jojo! My *darling.*'

The young woman spun on her heel and her jaw dropped. The shaven-headed woman racing towards her looked familiar but alien at the same time. 'Mum?'

Joyce's mother had had her trademark Big Hair removed, and was now sporting an ultra-short style that showed the shape of her head and made her look like a post-punk female rock star. She had an earring in the top of her right ear and was wearing trousers.

'My darling sweet baby—I was *so* worried.' She swept Joyce up in her arms and tried to swing her round, but then decided she was too heavy. So she just hugged her tightly and scattered air kisses near her cheeks, being careful not to smudge her make-up. 'My sweetheart. You're safe.'

'Yes, Mum. I...I didn't expect to see you here.'

'I haven't been able to eat or sleep since I heard you were on that plane. Oh, my darling. Let me hold you. Let me look at you.'

She put her hands on both sides of Joyce's face, squeezing mercilessly. Then she gave a theatrical sniff and pulled out a handkerchief conveniently sticking out of the top of her handbag and started dabbing her eyes.

'It's nice to see you, Mum,' said Joyce, lowering her head onto her mother's left shoulder.

'This side,' whispered the older woman, transferring Joyce's head to her right shoulder.

Joyce nestled into the fabric—something that was denim-ish and designer-ish at the same time—then realised what was going on. 'Are you filming this?'

'Keep your head down, baby girl,' her mother said, applying force to Joyce's neck.

Joyce jerked her head upright and looked around. Five metres away, a film crew with a hand-held camera were circling them.

'Mum, you're filming this.'

'Yes, dear.'

'You look different. But you haven't changed, have you?'

'No, dear.'

❊ ❊ ❊

J Oscar Jackson Junior grabbed Wong's arm and tugged him to one side. The feng shui master groaned. There seemed to be no end of people who wanted to physically drag him places this week.

'The boss wants to meet you,' Jackson whispered.

'The boss?'

'Her Majesty. As you approach, you bow from the neck down. Then you address her as "Your Majesty" the first time you speak to her, and "Ma'am" from then on.'

'Mum?'

'Ma'am.'

Wong was propelled in the direction of a white-haired lady wearing a raincoat, headscarf and dark glasses. She was elderly but stood very straight, reminding him of Sir Nicholas.

'That her?'

'That's her.'

'No crown?'

'It's in her handbag.'

Jackson stopped and bowed. 'Your Majesty. I am pleased to introduce Mr CF Wong, the feng shui master.'

Wong bowed from the head down, more of a nod, really, and said: 'Hullo, Mum.'

Jackson stepped back to allow the two of them to have a private discussion.

She smiled, tilted her head and inclined it slightly. 'You're the gentleman who guided the plane to the frozen lake in the mountains where it could land safely, I understand, Mr Wong.'

'Yes, Mum.' He bowed again. It seemed the right thing to do.

The Queen smiled and her eyebrows rose an eighth of an inch. 'I'm not really used to people calling me "Mum",' she said. 'Except my children, of course.'

Wong nodded again. That fool Jackson had given him the wrong information. Caused him to make a serious error of protocol. Of course one shouldn't call the Queen 'Mum'. He racked his brain—what was her name? Robbie Manks had told him that day driving around Chek Lap Kok airport—Elizabeth something. Elizabeth, Elizabeth, Elizabeth...?

'Happy to meet you, Mrs Vagina.'

The Queen smiled again and her eyebrows rose a further eighth of an inch. 'Never mind. Names and titles are such a bore. I just wanted to thank you for what you did. It was important for the country. Skyparc may be based on a European plane, but it is basically a British project. And I'm not just thanking you on behalf of my country. One of my own family members was on board, young Armstrong-Phillips, so I have a personal debt to you.'

This was shaping up into the sort of conversation the geomancer liked. One of the richest people in the world was acknowledging a personal debt to him. Well, she could clear the debt very easily by simply giving him a small country she no longer wanted. Or even a medium or large one. He quite fancied Australia. It was well away from the violent West, and could easily be made into an outpost of Asia. It was also said to have the best Chinese food outside China. This line of thought reminded Wong that the Queen was a property mogul of significant stature. He decided this might be the safest discussion topic for them. They could use their shared interest in that area to get to know each other better. But he didn't want to scare her. Perhaps he should start by suggesting some small, foot-in-the-door investments.

'Your main business is real estate, yes, Mrs Vagina?'

She thought about this. 'In a manner of speaking, I suppose it is.'

'I wonder, have you consider investing in Shenzhen? Is a place in Guangdong province, China. High-rise apartments quite cheap. Two-bed, five hundred square feet, less than half a million Hong Kong dollar.'

'You'd recommend it as an investment, would you?'

'Oh yes. I think perfect for you.'

'I don't think I've been to that part of China.'

'You can buy one flat, leave it empty, use it as holiday home for yourself and Mr Vagina. Price will go up, up, up. Guarantee.'

'Sounds very interesting. Perhaps we can talk about it later, when you visit my present home.'

'My pleasure, Mrs Vagina.'

Jackson, approaching, caught the end of this conversation. 'That's Regina,' he whispered sharply at Wong. Then he turned to the Queen. 'I apologise, Your Majesty. I should have briefed Mr Wong better.'

'I enjoyed talking to Mr Wong. And I have told him we will continue the discussion later, at the palace.'

'Of course.'

Wong could not help rubbing his hands together.

She nodded once more and left them, a smile playing on her lips.

❀ ❀ ❀

Prince Charles's private envoy delivered Wong back to his friend Sinha and then marched straight past everyone, head down. Jackson was sure there'd be no one there to greet him: after all, he was a single man these days, focused on nothing but his career. But he felt as if he was a changed man. These last days, he'd learned a lot about life, and about love, and about himself, and about what was important and what was not. He'd decided to go home, get some sleep, and then call the boss. Ask him for a couple of weeks off—maybe a month even, so he could go and get some rest, think about things, find out what he needed to do with his life.

But then he stopped short, his jaw dropping.

Among the squeals from the crowd were calls of 'Daddy, Daddy,' from tiny voices he thought he knew. It couldn't be, could it?

'Martha? Marianne?'

He saw his ex-wife standing waiting for him as everyone else melted away, one of their daughters in front of her, the other perched on her shoulders. 'Vanessa. Hi.'

His steps speeded up, as did his heartbeat. 'Hello, my darlings.' He ran over as fast as he could, and kissed all three of them, in tears for the first time in years.

❁ ❁ ❁

In the beginning of creation, the Red God and the Blue God were choosing their elements. Two gifts lay on the altar for them. A bottle of water and a burning candle.

The Red God was more kindly than the Blue God, and allowed him to choose first.

The Blue God said: 'I choose water. It cannot harm me.'

The Red God was left with fire. He picked it up carefully and held it at a distance.

As the gods' party started, the Blue God shared his water with everyone else. But every time he filled a glass, he noticed his vessel becoming emptier.

The Red God lit everyone's candle. But the more he shared his fire, the more fire there was.

Blade of Grass, many folktales tell stories of bottomless jars. Such things really exist, and are there to be found.

From *Some Gleanings of Oriental Wisdom*
by CF Wong